PRAISE FOR CINDY SAMPLE

"Cindy Sample dishes up another 5 star mystery romp featuring
Laurel McKay, her zany entourage, ;
hunky detective Tom Hunter. In *Dyii*
celebration adds Wild West Antics
amateur sleuth rides herd on ;
—*Linda Lovely, Author of th*

"Cindy Sample's *Dying for a Dude* is fabulous from the get-go.
It's a perfect blend of intrigue, mystery and romance—what else
could a reader ask for? Don't miss the Laurel McKay books. Like
me, you'll be 'dying' for the next one."
—*Brenda Novak, USA Today Bestselling Author*

"Fast paced, suspenseful, poignant yet funny, *Dying for a Dude*
is a top-of-the-line 5 star murder mystery that offers everything
to mystery buffs."
—*Heather Haven, Award-Winning Author*

"Quirky narrative peppered with quips. An intoxicating recipe for
fun... *Dying for a Daiquiri* is a must read for the romantic mystery
reader and contemporary romance reader!"
—*Once upon a Romance Reviews*

"Cindy Sample has created a heroine all gals can identify with and
admire as she keeps going with wit and determination, even in the
face of a homicide arrest. Sample's *Dying for a Daiquiri* combines
humor, romance and mystery, a recipe that yields a great book.
Kick back with a tall, cool drink and enjoy this 5 star read!"
—*Mary Beth Magee, National Reviewer, Examiner.com*

"Cindy Sample's writing is positively fun, imaginative
and all around tantalizing."
—*Romance Junkies*

"Cindy Sample knows how to weave a story that satisfies and excites. Time literally flew by as I turned the pages...simultaneously harrowing, exciting, tender, and uplifting, a true who-done-it combined with a romance that will warm the heart and sheets."

—*Long and Short Reviews*

"Sample's sleuth is an endearing character readers will adore."

—*RT Book Reviews*

"Cindy Sample has mastered the art of REAL dialogue. The characters are wacky and believable. Any woman who constantly finds herself in awkward situations will love this book. This is a story that will make you wonder "who did it" and make you laugh out loud. Of course, the romance simply is divine!"

—*BookReviewsRus*

"All of the elements of an excellent cozy mystery. Interesting characters, plot and setting. Fast paced writing. I struggled to figure out what it was that stood out that made me really enjoy the book and I decided it was the tone. *Dying for a Dance* is a feel-good book, it makes you smile."

—*Examiner.com*

"I have rarely been more cheered up by spending time with a book. *Dying for a Dance* is the perfect antidote to a bout of the winter blues."

—*Kings River Life Magazine*

"*Dying for a Date* is packed with zany characters, humorous situations, and laugh-out-loud narrative. Consider reading this book in one sitting, because once you start, you will be reluctant to put it aside."

–*Midwest Book Review*

Other Books in the Laurel McKay series

DYING FOR A DUDE

A LAUREL McKAY MYSTERY

Cindy Sample

CINDY SAMPLE

DYING FOR A DUDE
By Cindy Sample

Visit us at http://www.cindysamplebooks.com

ISBN: 1502844052
ISBN 13: 978-1502844057

DEDICATION

This book is dedicated to my first reader and mother, Harriet Bergstrand, the most supportive mother a daughter could ask for, and my wonderful children, Dawn and Jeff, who are incredible adults. How lucky and proud I am of both of you.

CHAPTER ONE

Inch by inch the vise tightened until I cried out, "Stop, stop, you're killing me."

My nemesis pulled even tighter. "I'm going to finish this if it kills *me*."

"But," I said, gasping for air, "I can't breathe."

"Oh, suck it up, Laurel," said Liz, my best friend. "If women in the nineteenth century managed to wear this apparel, certainly a resilient twenty-first-century woman like you can handle it."

With a final yank, she finished tying the laces and stepped back to look at her handiwork. I pressed my hands against my ribcage and glared at her.

Liz shoved me in front of her full-length bedroom mirror and beamed her approval at me. "You'll knock those cowpokes dead."

I stared at my reflection. The bright red feather tucked into my copper-colored curls, fluttered whenever I moved my head. The feather matched my crimson lipstick and the satin skirt that swished against my fishnet-covered legs. Unfortunately, the black bustier she'd purchased from Hangtown Hannah's consignment shop barely covered my ample chest. This outfit was a wardrobe malfunction just waiting to happen.

"Now I know why historical romances always refer to heaving bosoms." I winced as one of the stays pricked my tender skin. "I'm about to heave my breakfast."

"Well, luv, you're the one who is always complaining you need to lose weight," Liz said. "This could be the answer to your dieting prayers."

I groaned in response. A week living on cabbage soup, the latest Hollywood diet fad, would be preferable to another minute in this getup.

"Wait until Tom gets a glimpse of this outfit." Liz's hazel eyes sparkled brighter than her diamond stud earrings.

As I pictured my six-foot-three boyfriend, I sensed my cheeks turning the same color as my skirt. I shook my curls and the scarlet feather floated down to the floor. "I'm not sure how Tom will feel about me flaunting my, um, assets in public."

"Oh, bother. He can't bloody complain if it's for a worthy cause." My British friend's accent always intensified when she grew excited. She bent down, retrieved my feather and shoved it back into my hair. "The Sassy Saloon Gals raise a wagonload of money for the annual Wagon Train event in June. It's too late for me to find another replacement. Think of it as your public duty."

That worked for me. But would it work for Detective Tom Hunter, the head of homicide for the El Dorado County Sheriff's Office? He served the public by solving murders. I sensed his definition of community spirit might not include me exposing a substantial amount of my soft tissue to the residents of Placerville, our small town located in the California Gold Country between Sacramento and Lake Tahoe.

"So how are things going with you two lovebirds?" Liz asked. "Is it a match made in heaven?"

I shrugged because I wasn't certain how to answer my friend's question. Technically, our relationship was a *match made in homicide*, since the detective and I had met the previous fall when I became a suspect in a double murder investigation. Once he'd solved that case, we'd begun dating. But between Tom's burdensome profession and the responsibility we each had of raising our children, our date nights were limited.

I smiled in anticipation of our impending date this evening, envisioning a night of mutual community spirit, an event that occurred far less frequently than we desired.

My fingers fumbled with the long laces of the corset. "Would you help me get this contraption off?"

Liz began the tedious job of untying the garment. She had only loosened a portion of the strings when the singing of my cell phone drew my attention.

"Hold on. It's my grandmother's ringtone." I ran to my oversized canvas tote, which perched on her nightstand, successfully discovered my phone beneath the clutter and hit the answer button.

"Laurel, it's your Gran," said a quavering voice.

"Is everything okay?" I asked.

"No, it's not. You need to come here. Now."

"What's the matter?" My heart and mind raced as I worried what new calamity had beset the eighty-eight-year-old woman on the other end of the line.

"Your mother's disappeared," she said.

"What?" I shrieked.

"I was watching her and then she vanished." The sound of fingers snapping demonstrated her point. "Just like that."

And just like that the dial tone buzzed in my ear. Gran had disappeared as well.

I tried calling her back but only got a busy signal. My grandmother doesn't believe in newfangled things like Caller ID or Call Waiting. She's also the proud owner of what is probably the last rotary wall phone in the county, and possibly the country. After five frustrating attempts to call her back, each busy signal increasing my anxiety, I finally gave up.

"Sorry, Liz," I apologized as I threw my cell into my purse and hooked it over my shoulder. "Gotta go. Gran needs me."

I raced out of Liz's bedroom and flew down the stairs. It took me less than a minute to back down the driveway of her Mediterranean style home and head toward the freeway.

Liz and her husband, Brian, reside in Serrano, an affluent El Dorado Hills community located thirty miles east of Sacramento, close to her plush Golden Hills Spa. Since my grandmother lives in the former gold rush town of Placerville, I had a twenty-minute drive "up the hill" as we locals refer to it. As you drive east from Sacramento, the hills increase in size until they eventually become the Sierra Nevada mountain range. As my car sped up Highway 50, the fresh late snow on the distant mountains reminded me of dollops of whipped cream.

Halfway to Gran's house, I realized I'd been so concerned about her and Mother that I'd neglected to change out of my saloon girl outfit. At least, I could breathe with ease since Liz had loosened the laces.

I arrived at my grandmother's pale blue clapboard Victorian in nineteen minutes flat. A fire engine and a rescue vehicle parked on the pine-tree-lined street did nothing to relieve my anxiety.

I pulled my twelve-year-old hybrid behind my mother's new SUV. No bird would dare relieve itself on her gleaming white vehicle, although winged creatures love to decorate my periwinkle Prius.

I zipped down the sidewalk, wondering why Gran thought Mother had disappeared since her car was parked in the driveway. I stood on the front porch and stabbed at the doorbell repeatedly. The peal of chimes echoing through the house while no one appeared at the door only ramped up my concern. I finally pushed on the heavy oak door, and it squeaked open.

I sniffed. No smoke that I could discern, which was a huge relief. My heels clicked and clacked on the scuffed wooden planks as I zipped through the rooms calling out to my grandmother. Although my eyes and ears didn't detect anyone inside the house, my nose discovered treasure in the kitchen.

A fresh-baked peach pie rested on the royal-blue-tiled countertop next to two empty cups and saucers. One cup bore an imprint that had left many a rose-colored lipstick stain on my own china, confirming that Mother and Gran had chatted over coffee. But where was Mother now? And why was the fire department here?

I shoved open the screen door leading to my grandmother's back forty. Technically, her property comprised only ten acres, but it was still a large parcel of land, especially this close to the Placerville city limits. Rows of fragrant pink, peach and red roses lined the graveled paths throughout her garden. Unfortunately, this was not the time to stop and smell the roses.

I shaded my eyes from the afternoon rays and eventually spotted some figures clad in navy-blue uniforms standing near the back property line, at least two hundred yards away. I darted through the star thistle and headed in their direction.

Ouch. The destructive yellow weeds ripped through my fragile stockings, leaving untidy black strings hanging down my calves, but my concern for my mother's well-being took precedence over any damage to my costume.

Breathing heavily from my trek, I finally reached the group of people standing in a semi-circle around a large hole partially covered with worn wooden planks. I exhaled a sigh of relief when I spied my petite grandmother alongside the men. Gran and I used to be the same height and weight, but lately she seemed to be shrinking and now stood a few inches shorter than my five foot four and a quarter. Gran's natural hair color remains a mystery, even to me, since the woman is addicted to wearing wigs in every color and style. She could be Cher, Dolly Parton or Lauren Bacall on any given day of the week.

Today her carrot-colored curls resembled a cross between Lucille Ball and Bozo the Clown. I tapped her on her shoulder. Gran jumped and whirled around. Her faded blue eyes, under orange-penciled brows, widened when she recognized me.

"Gran," I said, "what happened?"

"Laurel, thank goodness you're here." She introduced me to the men who shifted their gaze from the gaping hole in the ground to me. Their four pairs of eyes zeroed in on my loosened bustier, which now exposed letters A through C of my double D's.

I hitched up the garment and scowled at the men. My grandmother stared at me.

"What on earth are you wearing? You look like a hussy." She cocked her head. "Or a Kardashian."

"It's a costume. I'll explain later. Where is Mother, and why is the fire department here?"

"Is that you, Laurel?" A disembodied voice drifted out of nowhere.

I swiveled my head to the left then to the right. I looked up toward the cloudless blue sky. Nothing. Only one direction remained. I inched closer to the opening in the ground and peered down. Way down into coal-black darkness where a pair of eyes gazed back at me. Did a wild creature fall into the hole?

My breath caught as my brain finally caught on.

I leaned forward and cried out, "Mom?"

CHAPTER TWO

"Are you okay?" I hollered.

"I twisted my knee," Mother yelled in return. "How soon can they get me out of here?"

The four men shook their heads rendering a negative answer to her question.

"Hang in there," I shouted back at her. "They're working on it."

"So what is this hole thingy?" I asked the stocky, balding firefighter next to me. "And how are you planning on bringing her up?"

"We think it's a shaft from one of the abandoned gold mines," he said. "It looks like someone boarded it up a long time ago. The planks warped over the years, and your mother fell right through. There's over a hundred gold mines located around Placerville, so it's not the first time something like this has happened. Especially this close to the Gold Bug Mine. A few years ago, a tractor just dropped through the earth and landed in an old shaft."

My mouth opened almost as wide as the hole we viewed. "Gran, were you aware of this particular mineshaft?" I asked.

She shook her curly orange head. "I didn't suspect there were any shafts not properly closed off."

"Why was Mother walking so far from the house?"

Gran rubbed the toe of one ratty gray slipper in the dirt. She looked as guilty as a kid caught sneaking a piece of pie. My stomach gurgled at the thought of the peach pie waiting back at the house.

Maybe if I waved it under the men's noses, it would incent them to come up with a solution.

"You know your mother. She's such a know-it-all." The tiny spider veins around my grandmother's nose darkened as she scowled. "I warned her not to traipse around up here, but she insisted on walking the property line, searching for some darn easement."

Gran crossed her arms over her thin rose-pink cardigan. "It's not my idea to sell this property."

"You're too old to live alone," echoed my mother's voice from the cavern below.

"And you're too annoying to—" Gran stepped forward, but I stopped her before she tumbled down to join Mother in the mineshaft.

One of the men finished a conversation on his cell. "We're getting someone specially trained for this type of extraction," he said.

I sent Gran back to the house and asked her to brew fresh coffee for the men. And to call my stepfather. It would be easier to bolster my mother's spirits if she and her own mother weren't butting heads. I tried to keep Mother occupied while they collected the necessary equipment and people.

"Did you find any gold down there?" I asked her.

Mother hesitated a few seconds before responding. "I landed on something hard. Maybe I will find a nugget or two." Her voice brightened with the thought that her tumble could result in a financial windfall. Given the current price of gold, even a pebble-sized nugget would be worth a designer purse or two.

Fifteen minutes later, two new members of the fire department joined our group. One of them was almost my height but half my girth and possibly half my age. She introduced herself as Tina and quickly donned some equipment, including a long emergency safety line, which the men tied around one of the massive cedar pines. Then she carefully rappelled her way down the shaft. I held my breath, worried that Tina might knock some rocks loose creating an even more hazardous situation for my mother.

The murmur of voices soon echoed up to us. I hoped my mother's injury was not severe. Her career as a real estate broker keeps her busy especially during the summer months. Mother would not be happy if this accident affected her mobility.

Suddenly a bright light flashed from the bottom of the mineshaft followed by a high-pitched scream. Then a second scream. I dropped to the ground, crawled to the edge of the hole and peered down.

"Are you okay?" I called out.

Mother and the rescue worker huddled together. The firefighter's Maglite pointed in the direction of a pile of narrow white sticks.

Whoa! The sticks were attached to a pelvis. And above the pelvis, a bone-white skull glowered at us through empty eye sockets as if we were personally responsible for disturbing its slumber.

CHAPTER THREE

Less than thirty minutes after the discovery of "Mr. Bones," the rescue team successfully hoisted Mother up the shaft using a harness and some sort of pulley system they referred to as a ladder gin. Mother probably would have preferred a gin martini.

Earlier, one of the men had snatched a couple of chairs from Gran's patio. Mother dropped into the cushioned chair with relief. They urged her to let them take her to the hospital to get checked out and have her knee examined. She refused, insisting it wasn't anything serious. She finally acquiesced to letting one of the men wrap her knee for support.

Mother assigned me the job of picking dirt and other icky stuff from her formerly perfect coiffure and from the back of her ivory linen blazer. Her black pants could probably be dry-cleaned, but her jacket was torn in several places and beyond repair.

I plucked a tiny white object from the fine blond strands of her short hair.

"Oh, ick." I dropped the item faster than a hot coal.

My mother flinched. "What was that?"

"Oh, nothing. Only a piece of..." my voice trailed off. No need to mention she'd sported a chip off the old skeleton.

I decided to switch Mother's focus to something more cheerful—her new husband. "Bradford should be here soon," I said. His arrival was certain to cheer her up. It had only been a few months since my mother, Barbara Bingham, a widow for thirty years, had married retired detective Robert Bradford. They initially met when Bradford and his then partner, my new honey, Detective Tom Hunter, were investigating a primary murder suspect—me!

At first, I doubted Bradford's intentions, positive that the tall bald detective was wooing Mother solely with the purpose of finding enough evidence to place me behind bars. Several months later when I became embroiled in another deadly affair, Bradford rescued me from a frigid death in the depths of Lake Tahoe. I immediately became one of his biggest fans.

Mother had flourished as well as mellowed since she met the detective. I love my mother, but she is a perfectionist who expects perfection from everyone else. As far as I was concerned, anyone who could loosen up my uptight mother was okay in my book.

Speaking of uptight, I desperately needed to change my clothes into something far less revealing. Gran had tightened the strings of the corset for me. According to her, I still looked like a hussy, but at least I was keeping my goods to myself and away from the gaze of the over-appreciative firemen.

Before they took off, the firefighters stretched yellow and black "caution" tape around the hole. Due to Gran's property being outside the Placerville city limits, the crew contacted the El Dorado County Sheriff's Office about the discovery. Tina and her partner said they would remain until the police arrived.

I whispered to my mother. "Do we have any missing relatives that you know of?"

She recoiled at my suggestion. "Don't be silly. Whoever that is has most likely been lying there for decades, maybe a century or more."

Despite the May temperature being in the mid-seventies today, a chill enveloped me from my feathered head to my polished red toes. Approaching voices distracted me from my somber thoughts. Gran hopped through the weeds, trying to keep up with the long strides of the tall man next to her. His tousled chestnut head bent low as he listened to her chatter.

My heart ricocheted from one end of my bustier to the other as I greeted the newcomer.

"Hi, Tom." I smiled at the detective. "Guess you heard what Mother stumbled across."

"Not exactly how I imagined we'd be spending the evening together, Laurel." Tom moved closer and lowered his voice.

"Although that outfit is definitely an incentive to get my job done faster."

Gran must have set the volume on her hearing aid to high. "Keep your eyes topside, sonny," she chastised him. "You've got work to do."

Mother morphed into broker mode. "Those remains need to be removed at once. The listing for this property went live on the MLS today, and I'm supposed to hold an open house here tomorrow afternoon."

"Barbara, let's make sure this is nothing out of the ordinary," Tom said in his soothing baritone. "It's likely someone who fell down the shaft a long time ago. Even if there's evidence of foul play and it's under our jurisdiction, it would be considered a cold case. Obviously, timing is no longer critical."

Gran scowled at him. "Don't you need to do some detectin' before we open my property to the populace? Once people hear what's been discovered, those crime-scene looky-loos are gonna be all over this place. I don't need a bunch of nosy folks tromping all over my clean floors, rummaging through my closets and such. I got enough skeletons to worry about."

Mother lifted her perfectly plucked eyebrows at me, and I raised my need-to-be-tweezed brows back. What was Gran muttering about skeletons?

A large burly man loped through the backyard, crushing the weeds attempting to impede his progress. He reached my mother's chair and crouched down next to her.

"Barbara, are you okay?" asked Robert Bradford, her concerned husband. "Your mother called and told me you fell down a mineshaft. You could have been killed."

She patted his bear paw-sized hand. "I'm fine, dear."

His expression brightened and the relief on his craggy face was evident as he stood. "You were very lucky."

"That's what the fire crew said, but I just twisted my knee a little." Mother rose from her chair. "See, I can walk by my ..." She took two steps, winced then fell back into the chair. "Well, I'm sure I'll be fine by tomorrow. I don't have a choice. There are signs to put up, cookies to bake, flyers to send out, and..."

"Laurel and I can help with that," he replied. The stern look my stepfather directed at me indicated my assistance was not an option.

Tom and I sighed in unison. Our plans for a long-awaited night alone were quickly going down the drain, or, in our case, down the mineshaft.

Tom and Bradford went to chat with the two firefighters who'd stayed behind. Even though Bradford had retired from the force almost six months earlier, the two men had forged a strong partnership and friendship. Tom frequently sought advice from the older man.

Tina, the firefighter who assisted in Mother's rescue, gestured in a frenzied manner. Tom fiddled with his right ear lobe as he listened to her. That was one of his tells, indicating something about the conversation bothered him.

Tom walked over to me. He removed his keys, wallet and cell phone from his pockets and plopped them into my hands.

"Going somewhere?" I asked.

"I want to check the remains myself. Make sure nothing critical is missed. I'd hate to haul the crime scene guys all the way out here tonight if it's not imperative."

Tom borrowed a hard hat and secured the harness. Then the firefighters slowly lowered him into the gaping hole. I joined the others who watched his descent. Bradford and Tina both held huge flashlights aimed to light the way for him. My tall broad-shouldered boyfriend jostled against the rock walls, encountering a tougher time squeezing down the narrow shaft than my slender mother and the petite firefighter had.

The shaft, which appeared twenty-five feet deep, widened near the bottom providing Tom room to maneuver. He squatted and examined Mr. Bones' remains. For several minutes, the only sounds we heard were a few muttered expletives reverberating up the shaft. As the sun's rays plummeted behind Gran's house, Tom requested they bring him back up.

It took a few minutes to haul him to the top. Once he unhooked the safety equipment, Tom brushed dirt off the front of his jeans. I lent a hand and wiped some smudges from his posterior. From the dark look on his face, my swipes were as close to a caress as either of us would receive tonight.

"Did you discover something?" I asked, not certain I wanted to hear his answer.

"Some remains of old clothing chewed up by rats most likely," he said. Mother and I both shuddered, envisioning the critters she briefly cohabited with down in the shaft.

"Plus this." Tom pulled his gloved hand from his front pocket. "I'm not an expert on its age, so the medical examiner will have to complete tests on the body, or what's left of it."

We leaned forward to peek at Tom's discovery. Although the object was smaller than today's modern cartridges, there was no doubt in my mind what Tom had discovered—a bullet.

"So what does this mean?" Tina asked.

I had the answer to that question. It meant that the only person getting any action from my detective tonight was an old sack of bones.

CHAPTER FOUR

Tom called in to headquarters and requested some crime scene techs. Although the corpse had obviously been dead a decade or two, or fifteen, the detective still needed to follow official protocol. Bradford seemed torn between helping his injured wife and assisting at the crime scene. I imagined it must be difficult to stop detecting after spending forty years on the force.

Since whoever killed the victim was long gone, my family didn't need to remain at the site. Bradford and I supported Mother as she hobbled back to Gran's house. Oddly enough, my grandmother seemed more excited than disturbed by the commotion.

She rubbed her liver-spotted hands together. "This is like watching *CSI* only better. I wonder if I should call the Red Hats to come over."

"This is no cause for celebration," Mother admonished Gran. "We need to get your property sold while the market is hot. I don't think a dead body will be considered a property improvement."

"Well, that dead body sure improved my disposition." Gran chortled to herself. She scurried around her kitchen, making coffee and setting out homemade cookies for the men.

I swiped one of her chocolate and toffee chip cookies off the etched glass tray. Yum. When I bent over to grab another cookie, my corset protested loudly. I couldn't wait to change out of this ridiculous costume and into a pair of shorts and a tee shirt.

DYING FOR A DUDE

"Are you ready to go home?" Mother asked me, her face pale and drawn. I could see she was in pain even though she would be the last person to admit weakness.

"Sure. Is it safe to leave Gran alone with all of these forensic people wandering around?"

"The better question," Bradford chimed in, "is whether the crime techs will be safe with your grandmother and her friends."

Two members of Gran's Red Hat group had already arrived, dressed to kill with red boas wound around their necks and hats the size of turkey platters perched on their heads. The women directed the crime scene personnel where to go. The technicians didn't seem to mind their elderly groupies since the women plied them with cookies.

Mother limped over to Gran's side. "Please keep out of their way, Ma. We need to get this issue resolved as soon as possible so you can move to Golden Hills Manor."

"There's no rush to lock me up at the Manor," Gran muttered, "I'm still in my prime, you know."

Tom entered the kitchen through the back door. He shoved his hand through the hair tickling his shirt collar. "You might as well go home," he said to me. "This could turn into an all-nighter. There are strict rules when exhuming a body this old."

"Is it okay for Gran to be here?" I asked as I reached up and flicked some dust off his formerly white polo shirt.

He nodded. "She'll be fine. Her friends can keep her company."

"Will you still be able to attend the Cornbread and Cowpokes event with me tomorrow night?"

His chocolate-brown eyes lit up as he glanced down. "Will you be wearing that outfit?"

"Nope. I have to save it for the Wagon Train Parade."

"Too bad," he said with a rueful smile. "I've always been partial to black lace and red satin."

My toes and every other nerve ending began to tingle as his gaze roved up and down my costumed body.

Ever the businessperson, Mother joined us and interrupted my fantasizing. "Tom, do you think I can hold the open house tomorrow?"

He shook his head. "You'd better cancel it. You're more likely to have crime show addicts and historians than bona fide purchasers." Tom took the baggie with the bullet out of his pocket and showed it to his former partner. "Do you know anyone who's a specialist in old guns and ammunition?"

It didn't surprise me that Bradford nodded. He'd been a member of the El Dorado County Sheriff's Department since he graduated from the police academy. Tom, a widower with one young daughter, had relocated from San Francisco to Placerville only fifteen months ago.

"Deputy Fletcher is into old weaponry. He's a member of the historical society, too, so if he can't identify it, one of the other members should be able to."

Tom thanked him then left to complete his thankless exhumation. I walked over to my grandmother and hugged her goodbye.

"Be a good granny, okay?" I said. "Don't give Tom or his crew any trouble."

She threw me a wide-eyed "Who me?" look and went back to grilling the crime techs.

I grabbed one more cookie then followed my mother and stepfather out the door. I figured if I couldn't devour Tom tonight, I'd settle for second best—devouring Gran's homemade cookies.

CHAPTER FIVE

The phone trilled on my nightstand the next morning. I knocked the receiver over then jumped out of bed to retrieve it before the caller hung up. My contact lenses rested in their pink plastic case on my bathroom counter, so I squinted at the name on the display.

"Morning, Liz," I mumbled.

"What happened to you yesterday?" she asked. "I worried all night about your mother and your granny. Or were you and Tom too busy playing Sheriff and Saloon girl to call me?" Her husky laugh carried over the phone line. "Aren't you happy I provided a little fantasy for the two of you?"

"What you provided was a corset torture chamber. It took me an hour to extricate myself from that thing." I directed a baleful glance at the garments piled on my blue plaid wing chair.

"Didn't you and Tom have a hot date last night?" she asked.

I plopped back on top of my covers and shared the skeletal discovery with my friend.

"Ooch. I wonder who the dead guy is," Liz said. "Do you think one of your relatives killed him?"

"Don't be ridiculous," I muttered, not mentioning that her question had also occurred to me.

"You never know if there's a black sheep or two grazing under your family tree," she said. "I have to run. Let's catch up at Cornbread and Cowpokes tonight. I'll see you and Tom there, right?"

"Maybe. He might not make it if he's still working on this case."

"That's too bad. Although this case sounds like it's cold enough to have freezer burn."

On that note, we signed off. I entered my bathroom and began my morning routine. I popped in my left contact then heard my kids yelling my name downstairs. I glanced at the clock. Nine a.m. They weren't supposed to be home until noon. With only one lens in place, I cautiously trod down the stairs to find out why they'd returned so early.

Jenna, my sixteen-year-old, and her recently turned eight-year-old brother, Ben, had spent the night with their father. My ex-husband is a builder, and the previous year he'd relocated to Southern California for a few months to complete a historical renovation. Hank finished that job in February. His current project involved restoring a former gold rush hotel in downtown Placerville.

The kids were overjoyed about their father's return to town. Joy wasn't the word I would use to describe my state of emotions now that Hank was a continual presence in our lives. Annoyed would be a more apt description. Since I was in a relationship for the first time since our divorce three years earlier, Dr. Phil would probably tell me I should no longer be upset that my former husband left me for another woman.

But Hank's infidelity still stung. Instead of nailing roof shingles, he'd been nailing his client.

Ben rushed up and threw his arms around me. I ruffled the thirty-odd cowlicks in his shaggy brown hair. "What are you kids doing back so early?" I asked.

My tall, whippet-thin daughter wheeled her navy overnight bag over the threshold. "Dad got a phone call, and he has to meet with the owner of that building he's working on."

The man in question walked through the front door. "Hi, hon. Did we wake you?"

I bristled at the endearment but decided to ignore it. "You have to work on a Sunday?"

Hank's dark expression almost matched the black San Francisco Giants baseball cap he wore to hide his receding hairline.

"Spencer wants to review some overruns in the budget. I told him whenever you restore a historical building you have to follow the code. He's gonna try cutting corners, but I'm not letting him do it."

I nodded in agreement, a rare occurrence. "Good for you. The Hangtown Hotel is an important project, and the renovation needs to be properly completed. That building will be the showcase of Main Street once it's finished."

"That's what I keep saying." Hank sighed. "I don't know what the deal is with him."

"Maybe he's running out of money. His campaign for District Six Supervisor must be costing a fortune. I don't think there's an intersection where Spencer's face isn't smirking at me."

"Oh, he definitely hasn't let me forget about the election. That's part of the problem. Spencer is already counting on winning the seat and holding his acceptance speech in the building. I told him I couldn't guarantee it would be done by then."

Hank shuffled his feet. "I better get going. Are you going to the fundraiser at Mountain High Winery tonight? I'd love to have you be my date." His voice softened and he moved closer. "You're looking real good lately. Have you lost weight?"

My son, who possesses bionic hearing only when he chooses, piped in. "Mommy's taking Bimbo classes."

Hank looked confused, and I corrected Ben. "Zumba classes," I said. "Dance and cardio combined."

Hank smiled. "Bimbo, Zumba, whatever it is, you look great. So about that date?"

Since I'd rather rope a bull than accompany my ex to a social event, I declined. "Sorry, Tom and I are going together." Ever the optimist, I hoped the detective would be cavorting with me tonight and not with a skeleton.

A wistful look crossed Hank's face. "Okay, guess I'll see you there." He moved forward to hug me, but I stepped back and said goodbye. My cell rang as I closed the door behind him.

"Hi, Tom. I'm glad you called. How's it going?"

"Not well," he replied. I could sense the frustration in his voice. "We not only have to treat this as a cold case homicide, but we need to ensure the site isn't compromised from a historical standpoint."

I clucked sympathetically, and we chatted a few minutes more before he signed off, apologizing for not being able to attend tonight's event. In the past six months, the two of us had spent far more time without each other than together. A few months ago when Tom cancelled a trip to Hawaii for Liz and Brian's wedding, I had questioned if it was possible to have a successful relationship with a homicide detective. Then he arrived on the Big Island and swept me off my feet.

Into his arms.

Nine hours later, I strolled along the scenic grounds of Mountain High Winery, arm in arm with the other main squeeze in my life, the man who was always there for me, Stan Winters, my GBFF, gay best friend forever. My friend, who idolized Carson Kressley of *Queer Eye for a Straight Guy* fame, never missed an opportunity to create a fashion statement. Tonight's attire included a cream satin shirt detailed with red-beaded swirls and a mile of matching fringe across the front and back. Tight-fitting designer jeans and a taupe cowboy hat almost as large as the state of Texas completed his outfit.

I turned and the brim of his Stetson just missed colliding with my forehead. "Geez, Stan, you are one dangerous dude. Can't we park your ten gallon headgear someplace other than on your head?"

"Sorry," Stan apologized. "But I need the hat to complete my ensemble. I really want to fit in with the guys riding in the Wagon Train."

Considering that ninety percent of the colored glass beads sold in Placerville adorned his shirt, Stan's outfit seemed better suited for a Las Vegas showroom. We joined other partygoers waiting in line at the outside wine bar. Two bartenders dressed in burgundy polo shirts embossed with the Mountain High logo kept busy pouring wine for the insatiable crowd.

I recognized Chad Langdon, one of the owners of the Camino winery and a long time customer of Hangtown Bank where Stan and I both work. We finally reached the front of the line. "Hi, Chad," I said. "This is a lovely event."

Chad frowned, and I visualized him sorting through his mental rolodex trying to remember my name.

"Oh, hey, Laurel," he said. "Good to see you again. What can I get for you?"

I ordered a pinot noir, and Stan decided to try their old vine zinfandel.

"This is a nice coincidence," Chad said. "I have a loan question I've wanted to ask someone. Maybe I can bend your ear later on when it's not so crowded."

I peeked over my shoulder at the restless and thirsty throng behind us. A tall cowboy, dressed in faded jeans and a faded black hat, glowered at me.

"Sure," I said to Chad. "We'll be around. Thanks for the wine."

The excellent pinot noir required a hearty dinner, so Stan and I stood in another lengthy line. Once our paper plates were loaded with pulled pork, beef ribs, multiple starchy salads and cornbread, we looked for a place to sit and spotted Liz and her husband, Brian, at a picnic table under a large cedar pine. Brian was chatting with a handsome urban cowboy who sat across from him.

When Stan and I appeared, the dark-haired stranger who looked to be in his thirties, rose and sauntered off.

"Did we interrupt something?" I asked.

"Not at all," said Liz. "You saved me from being bored to death from dreary legal chit chat."

Brian, an El Dorado County Deputy District Attorney, jerked his thumb in the direction of the man who'd vacated the seat. "Since I lost a case against one of Rex's clients, I'm more than happy to say goodbye to that hotshot."

The four of us ate in silence, enjoying country rock tunes played by a local band. My feet kept rhythm with the contagious beat of the music. As twilight set in, the constellations glimmered in the velvety night sky. I sipped my wine and watched a few couples strut their stuff on the temporary dance floor set up for the fund-raising event.

Liz and Brian eventually joined the dancers. Her husband might be a successful prosecutor, but he would never survive on *Dancing With the Stars*. But when you're in love, who cares if your partner is waltzing to a two-step?

A perfect evening for romance yet here I sat next to my gay friend. Stan shared a wistful smile with me, probably thinking similar thoughts.

I sniffed the air. The fragrance of cedar pines and barbeque combined with a familiar scent from my past. As my nasal memory bank shifted into overdrive, I sensed the whisper of beer breath tickling my ear lobe.

"May I have this dance?" murmured a low voice.

"Tom?" I jumped out of my seat, elated at his presence. The man standing next to me wrapped his arms snugly around my waist.

I turned and realized this man stood several inches shorter than my six-foot-three boyfriend.

I frowned and pulled away from Hank's embrace.

The welcoming smile on his face disappeared, but that didn't stop him from offering his calloused palm to me. His eyes pleaded with me to take it.

"C'mon, Laurel," he said. "One dance for old time's sake?"

I shook my head then sighed as the band began playing one of my favorite songs by Rascal Flatts. My sandaled feet automatically tapped to the beat of "Life is a Highway."

Hank beamed what looked to be an alcohol-enhanced smile. "Only one dance and I promise not to bother you anymore."

I threw a plaintive look at Stan who ignored it and shoved me into Hank's arms. "If you don't dance with Hank," he said. "I'll be forced to two-step with you."

Some choice—the rhinestone cowboy or my ex-husband. I reluctantly let Hank lead me onto the dance floor. Once we began moving, I gave myself over to the music. Even the realization that I danced with Hank didn't remove the grin from my face.

The song ended, and the dancers clapped and hooted. The musicians switched gears and slowed down the tempo. Couples moved closer together, and Hank attempted to do the same with me. I pushed him away and stomped off the floor. I'd had enough bonding for the night.

Hank followed me, hot on my irritated heels. He grabbed my hand and pulled me to an abrupt stop.

"Laurel, aren't you ever going to forgive me for leaving you?" he pleaded.

I stared at him for a few seconds before replying. "I have forgiven you, Hank, but I've moved on. You need to do the same."

Three years ago, Nadine Wells hired my husband to replace the shake shingles on her roof. It only took a few days before *she* replaced me. Then nine months ago, she replaced Hank with a prominent plastic surgeon in the area.

Hank must have spent considerable time in personal reflection while he worked in southern California. Since his return, he'd seemed determined the four of us would become a family again. While I was pleased our kids could spend time with their father,

I couldn't seem to get across to him that I was no longer part of the equation.

The shrill sound of a microphone penetrated my eardrums. The musicians departed and on the stage, Chad Langdon introduced Darius Spencer. The District Six Supervisor candidate wore a plaid shirt, pressed jeans and a cowboy hat so shiny it probably still bore the price tag—suitable attire for a politician in vote-getting mode. The small crowd applauded enthusiastically as he began a prepared speech. Hank's attention zoomed to the stage, and I was grateful for the distraction.

Spencer wasn't the worst politico I'd ever heard, but he wasn't particularly riveting. In the crowd, I spied three familiar faces—the attorney who'd been conversing with Brian earlier, Doug Blake, the owner of my favorite bookstore and Abe Cartwell of Antiques Galore. I hadn't realized the two Main Street proprietors were fans of the candidate's no-growth platform, but they appeared to be listening intently. I wondered if Spencer's pro-growth opponent, Tricia Taylor, would also address the gathering.

Growing bored, I prepared to depart when Doug asked Spencer about the Hangtown Hotel renovation. His inquiry piqued my curiosity, so I decided to stick around. My ex surprised me by interrupting with his own comment.

"Yeah, Spencer," said Hank, "how about telling these folks about your cost cutting measures on the hotel?"

The candidate's face turned the same color as the calico bandanna tied around his neck. "Hank, this is not an appropriate forum for that discussion."

People turned their heads to stare at Hank. Embarrassed, I sidled a few steps away.

"What forum would you suggest I use to tell your constituents their candidate is willing to sacrifice their safety to help his campaign bottom line?"

Spencer struggled to contain his anger as the crowd increased in size. I moved back to Hank's side, grabbed his hand and tried to pull him away, but he dug in his scuffed boot heels. His stubborn nature hadn't diminished since we'd split up.

"Cat got your tongue?" Hank snickered. A few of the bystanders tittered at his comment. Spencer thrust back his shoulders and

23

marched in our direction, people moving aside to let him through. His next remark, punctuated with repeated pokes to Hank's chest, demonstrated there were no fluffy kitties interfering with his vocal prowess.

"Hank McKay," Darius Spencer yelled, "you're fired!"

CHAPTER SIX

During our fifteen years of marriage, I'd frequently criticized my ex for acting first and thinking second. Hank stared at Spencer for a few seconds before he raised his right fist and punched his about-to-be former employer's pudgy jaw.

Spencer's beady black eyes widened. He stepped back, and then he dropped. To the ground. Landing at my feet, in fact, right on my polished toes. Although on the short side, Spencer's entire weight pressing on my bare toes caused me to shriek.

Spencer's wife, Janet, whom I knew from our weekly Zumba classes together, joined in the chaos. Her screams rose to an operatic level as she rushed to her husband's aid. Within seconds, two El Dorado County Sheriff's deputies formed uniformed bookends on both sides of Hank. He stood silent, chest heaving, rubbing his red swollen fist.

One of the officers assisted the candidate to his feet.

Spencer pointed a shaking finger at Hank and sputtered, "Arrest that man."

"Hey, hold on there," said Stan, rushing to our aid. With his supersized cowboy hat, he looked as fierce as Yosemite Sam.

Two more deputies appeared, both of whom I knew since we'd all graduated from El Dorado High School. Fortunately for Hank, the star quarterback of our high school team, the men had all played football together.

Hank directed a woozy smile at the taller, sandy-haired deputy. "Hiya, Fletch."

Fletch shook his head at my ex. "Hey, pal, I think you've had one beer too many." Chuck Kramer, the other officer, turned to Darius Spencer. "Are you all right, sir?"

Some Good Samaritan had filled Spencer's bandanna with ice cubes and he pressed the frozen compress against his reddening jaw. The glare Spencer sent Hank looked even icier than the compress.

I elbowed Hank and whispered in his ear. "You better apologize before they arrest you for assault."

"Yeah," Stan said in agreement, "and throw in a free night's lodging for you at the county jail."

Chuck ushered Spencer and his wife over to a picnic table so they could converse in private, while Fletch remained with Hank and me. I hoped Janet wouldn't hold Hank's punching her husband against me. She seemed like a nice woman although somewhat on the quiet side. Even though future fisticuffs were unlikely, I wondered how she felt about her husband running for office. It couldn't be easy assuming the public role of a candidate's spouse.

The rest of the spectators drifted off, many of them to the dance floor where the band rollicked once again.

"What were you thinking?" I asked my ex.

"I guess I wasn't, thinking that is." Hank shrugged his shoulders. "Must have been a gut reaction to him firing me. Geez. What a mess."

"If you don't want the kids to see your face plastered over the front page of the *Mountain Democrat*, you'll suck it up and apologize to Spencer."

Hank exchanged glances with Deputy Fletcher, his former teammate. Fletch nodded in agreement. The two of them walked over to the table where Spencer held court. I followed, prepared to latch on to Hank's fists should he feel compelled to slug his boss again.

"I'm sorry. I was totally out of line," Hank said to the candidate. "Guess I had a few too many beers. Please accept my apologies."

Spencer narrowed his eyes. I could almost visualize the inner workings of a politician's brain as he tried to determine whether forgiveness would be beneficial to his campaign. He finally stood and put out his hand to Hank. My ex shook it heartily.

"So I'm back on the job?"

Spencer's forehead creased then he nodded.

"Looks like you don't need us here anymore," said Fletch. He turned to Hank. "Obviously you're in no condition to drive. Do you have a ride home?"

Hank gazed at me with a worried expression on his face. What's an ex-wife to do but agree to pilot her former spouse to his house?

"I'll get him home," I told Fletch. "Thanks for your help."

"Not a problem. Hank never could hold his drink." Fletch clapped Hank on the back. "Besides you have enough trouble on your hands."

I reared back, startled. "What are you talking about?"

The deputy shifted nervously. "Didn't Tom tell you about our discovery this afternoon?"

My face must have relayed my confusion, so he clarified his comment. "I'm kind of a history buff, so Tom asked me to look at the bullet he found in the mine shaft your mother fell into."

I couldn't decide if my one glass of wine had completely muddled my mind, or if Fletch was speaking in riddles. "What about that bullet? Will it help discover who the victim is?"

"That particular bullet narrows the time period down within a few decades, but there were other items the crime scene techs discovered in the shaft that will also help."

"That's great news," I said, my smile wide. "Anything that will help identify the body?"

Fletch nodded. "We're not positive, but the victim might be George Henry Clarkson."

I knew the Clarkson family had settled in this area shortly after James Marshall discovered gold at his Coloma sawmill in 1848. Almost a decade later, my great-great-grandfather moved from Kentucky to Placerville.

"That's amazing," Stan said. "How could you identify someone from that far back?"

"We found a brass buckle in the shaft that was severely tarnished but with the initials GHC engraved on it."

"How can you be sure it belonged to George Clarkson merely from the initials on the buckle?" I asked.

"Unless you're related to a Clarkson, like one of the guys in our department," Fletch replied, "you probably wouldn't know that he disappeared sometime in the eighteen sixties, leaving his wife and young son behind. No one ever heard from him again."

Stan rubbed his hands together in excitement. "Terrific detecting, Deputy."

Hank shared his enthusiasm by belching in agreement.

I scowled at my ex and turned my attention back to Fletch. "Do you have any idea who could have killed him?" I hoped the discovery meant Tom wouldn't need to put in long hours tracking down a 150-year-old villain.

"Unfortunately, yes." Fletch said.

Hank, Stan and I exchanged puzzled looks.

"But that's good news, isn't it?" I said. "To identify the murderer so quickly?"

"We not only found the belt buckle," Fletch replied, "but we unearthed another item of jewelry identified by the granddaughter of the presumed killer."

"This is like *CSI* meets the History Channel," Stan exclaimed. "So you already determined whodunit?"

"I bet my granny was delighted with your discovery." I smiled at the thought of my mystery-addict grandmother. "She's a total crime buff."

"She didn't appear all that excited when we asked her to identify the watch we found." The deputy's clear blue eyes seemed concerned. "That watch belonged to Harold Titus, your great-great-grandfather, which makes him the prime suspect for having pulled the trigger."

I stared at Fletch's serious countenance. I vaguely recalled him pulling my braids in the fourth grade. Was the deputy now intent on pulling my leg?

"You're kidding, aren't you?"

Fletch shook his head. "Even though this is a cold case, I probably shouldn't have mentioned any of this to you."

"Well, I'm glad you did. My granny must be beside herself. She's always been so proud of the history of our family, not to mention being a member of the DAR."

Fletch chuckled. "Your grandmother is one tough old bird." When I narrowed my eyes at him, he rephrased his comment. "I mean she's one sharp senior citizen. She told the detective that you and she would get to the bottom of this crime. That her grandfather didn't murder anyone."

"Well, I'm no historian, but we certainly will. There's no way anyone in our family murdered a Clarkson or anyone else."

"Hunter said the minute you found out about the evidence you'd morph into Jessica Fletcher."

"Excuse me?" I growled, affronted that my boyfriend compared me to the elderly female detective Angela Lansbury played on *Murder She Wrote*. I thought of myself more as the West Coast's version of *Castle's* sexy Nikki Heat. Except for my height and weight, that is.

"Bet your mother isn't too happy with your boyfriend now." Hank snorted then belched again.

I sighed. It was time to get my ex-husband to his apartment and then learn more about this potential nineteenth-century scandal enveloping my family.

Stan offered to drive Hank home, but I figured I could handle being his chauffeur for one night. I delivered my ex to his doorstep where he demonstrated his appreciation by trying to plant a slobbery kiss on my lips. I managed to avoid his misguided urge and led him to his sofa where he dropped into instant slumber. His snores serrated my eardrums as I closed the front door behind me.

An hour later, comfortable in my plaid wingback chair, I chatted on the phone with my mother. "How's your knee?" I asked.

"It's much better," she said. "If only I could get rid of this new headache."

"You mean the discovery of my great-great-grandfather's watch? How do you think it landed in the shaft next to the skeleton?"

"I have no idea. Your Gran thought they were partners in a mine at one time. She was only five when Harold died at the ripe old age of ninety, so she doesn't remember much about him."

"I hope Tom can determine the real murderer."

"Robert says if a cold case like this appears cut and dried, they'll write it up the way they see the evidence. Which means your great-great-grandfather will go down in history as a murderer. We absolutely cannot let that happen. Can you imagine the impact that news would have on the price of Gran's house?"

Only a real estate broker could discover that her great-grandfather was a murderous villain and reduce its impact down to dollars and cents. Sometimes I admired my mother's analytical mind. Other times she frightened the heck out of me.

"I hope your boyfriend realizes how important this situation is to our family," she said.

"I'm sure Tom will do whatever it takes," I responded, not entirely certain my affirmation could be backed up.

"We'll see." She sniffed. "If he doesn't pursue it, we'll have to find the real culprit ourselves. At least we won't have to worry about a killer coming after us, since whoever did it is long dead."

Depending on how much research we'd need to do through dusty tomes in the historical museum, I thought it far more likely we'd die of boredom.

CHAPTER SEVEN

The next morning I pushed open the glass double doors of the two-story brick edifice that housed my employer, Hangtown Bank. Sherry, the receptionist, waved at me while she spoke into her headset. I patted the six-foot-tall burled wood bear that Gordon Chandler, the bank's President, had purchased for his large Victorian home a few years ago. Since Dana Chandler possessed far superior decorating taste to that of her husband, she evicted the bear within minutes of its arrival and had it delivered to the bank's lobby. Employees and customers alike had taken to greeting the bear when they entered the bank.

In honor of the upcoming Wagon Train festivities, the bear sported an enormous dove gray cowboy hat that Stan would undoubtedly attempt to filch. Someone had tied a blue bandanna the size of a tablecloth around the bear's twenty-two inch neck and attached a handlebar moustache above his ferocious carved snarl.

Smokey the Bear with a dash of Tom Selleck.

Over the years, I'd held several different positions at the 150-year-old local bank. By the time Ben turned two, Hank was bringing in enough income as a contractor that I could quit my position of branch manager and become a stay-at-home mom. After our divorce, which coincided with the decline in the construction industry, which led to the decline in my child support, I had been lucky to return to the bank's Main Street headquarters in a mortgage underwriter capacity. I enjoyed underwriting loans, but after three years, I wanted a change. When a position in the business development department of the bank opened up two months ago, I'd applied for it.

Although my marketing expertise is on a par with my culinary abilities, in the past I'd managed to impress Mr. Chandler with my sleuthing skills. He figured anyone with as fertile an imagination as I possessed should excel in promoting the bank.

He might not have realized the extent of my creative brain. No one informed me there is a fine art to promoting a conservative bank. Sponsoring non-profit fundraisers and local athletic teams are examples of appropriate promotions.

My ad displaying the infamous "Hanging Man" of Placerville with advertising copy that read, *Hangtown Bank wants to rope in your account,* evidently was not a model example.

Bruce Boxer, my boss, had slashed the flyer with a red marker and placed it in the middle of my desk with a sticky note on top. His illegible scrawl practically shouted his displeasure with me.

NEW COPY BY NOON. DON'T SCREW UP!

I stared across the room wondering if my career move had been a mistake. What would happen if I "screwed up" again? Would the bank allow me to transfer back to the mortgage department, or would they throw me into the street, forced to live off day-old baguettes from Hangtown Bakery?

A hand waving in front of my face disturbed my gluten-filled reverie. Stan plopped into the one and only visitor's chair I'd squeezed into the office, crossed his khaki-covered legs and leaned forward. "You look like you're a gazillion miles away. Did you figure out the mine shaft mystery?"

"I'm more concerned with figuring out how to save my job." I handed Stan the glossy flyer with the photo of the Hanging Man dummy.

My former assistant cringed. "How much wine had you drunk when you came up with that slogan?"

"None. Maybe that's the problem. I thought the ad would get people's attention."

Stan sniggered. "You succeeded at that."

"Mrs. Needham, one of our oldest and richest depositors, thought the ad 'too tacky' for words. Luckily only a few flyers were given out." I eyed my failed endeavor. "I love the history of this town and think we should use it to promote the bank. The gold rush era produced some great stories. The fact that Placerville was named Hangtown after the townsfolk hung some murdering thieving bandits from an old oak tree is fascinating stuff."

"Speaking of Hangtown scandals, did you speak with your detective about your own family mystery?"

"Tom's coming over for dinner this evening so we can discuss it then."

Stan winked at me. "Do you two have a passionate rendezvous planned?"

"No. We have a passionate game of Yahtzee planned," I replied. "All three kids will be at the house."

"No wonder your creative juices dried up. You need to stimulate your endorphins."

"You are absolutely right." I shoved back my chair and marched down to the break room. Within minutes, my creativity, fueled by a Snickers bar, produced a new flyer perched on my boss's shiny mahogany desk.

If he didn't like this one, he could shove it up his pompous ... pompadour!

A few hours later, I stood in front of the stove, a frilly apron tied around my waist, stirring a large pan of fettuccine Alfredo sauce. My daughter ambled into the kitchen and burst out laughing.

"Mom, I almost didn't recognize you in those duds," Jenna said, her auburn ponytail swinging back and forth as she shook her head in amazement. "I thought Martha Stewart dropped by for a visit. Are you hoping to convince Tom you're a domestic diva?"

"Don't be silly," I said.

She was right, of course. I also hoped my detective would not detect the empty jars stuffed deep in the garbage that bore the label of the sauce I planned to serve for dinner.

The doorbell rang and Jenna offered to greet our guests. I slid a tray of fresh made garlic bread—okay, frozen garlic bread—into the oven, closed the door and jumped when two hands wrapped around my waist. I whirled around so I could properly greet Tom with a welcoming kiss.

My face fell at our surprise visitor. "Oh, it's you," I said to Hank. "I wish you'd stop grabbing me."

"Nice way to greet the father of your children," he said.

If I wasn't the mature mother of his children, I would have rolled my eyes.

"What are you doing here?" I asked.

"I wanted to thank you for driving me home last night. I guess I had a little too much to drink."

"You think?" I set the timer on the oven then turned to him. "So are you and Spencer back on good terms?"

Hank shoved a hand through his thinning dark blond hair. "I hope so. Another issue came up today. We need to replace the copper plumbing throughout the building. It's only forty years old, but it hasn't held up. Spencer is gonna have a fit when he finds out."

"You haven't told him yet?"

"We're meeting at five tomorrow morning."

"Ouch. Early."

"Contractors don't get to sleep in like bankers. Anyway, Spencer is giving a speech to a Sacramento Rotary club at seven a.m. so he said he'd meet me at the building first. I can't order the materials without a check, and he still hasn't paid me my last installment per our contract."

Hank reached for a pink cardboard box he'd set on my tiled counter.

"What's that?" I asked, my salivary glands perking up. Pavlov would have a field day with my visceral reaction to the square pink box.

Hank grinned and untied the string. He popped open the cover, and I peeked inside the box. Yum. Chocolate frosted double fudge brownies from the Hangtown Bakery.

I couldn't help but be touched by his thoughtfulness. "You remembered how much I love their brownies."

Hank's voice grew soft and his green eyes twinkled as he moved closer. "I remember everything about you, honey, your likes, your dislikes, your…"

"Boyfriend? Remember him?" A deep baritone interrupted Hank's recitation. Although my heart rate had ratcheted up once I discovered the brownies, it was nothing compared to the palpitations Tom's presence generated.

Tom strode across the room, wrapped his arms around my waist and kissed me as if I hadn't been kissed in days. He delivered more heat in that kiss than in the Alfredo sauce erupting over the top of the pot and bubbling on to the stove.

Whoops. I reluctantly released myself from Tom's embrace and turned off the burner. I grabbed a sponge, wet it and proceeded to clean the hot white mess dripping down my stove, my dinner somehow managing to imitate my life.

"I didn't hear you arrive," I said to Tom.

"Ben must have been watching for us because he opened the door before we could knock. He and Kristy are up in his room." Tom glanced at Hank. "Are you joining us for dinner?"

Hank smiled. "Sure, thanks for the invitation."

"Hey, wait a minute," I sputtered. I started to push Hank out the back door when Jenna entered the kitchen. She zeroed in on the pink box and popped it open.

"Thanks, Dad. You remembered how much Mom and I love those brownies."

"Nothing but the best for my girls." Hank put his arm around Jenna. She leaned in and granted her father a big smile.

"So what's for dinner, Laurel?" Hank sniffed looking puzzled. "Burnt toast?"

Crap! I snatched a kitchen mitt and flung open the oven door. What happened to my timer? The garlic bread had transformed from frozen to a Cajun blackened version. I yanked the nasty smelling pan out of the oven and set it on a trivet. I glared at the controls before realizing I'd reset the clock instead of setting the timer.

Between the Alfredo spill and the murdered garlic bread, I felt like throwing my apron away and calling it a night.

Tom dumped the bread into my stainless garbage can and asked what he could do to help.

"I've been craving some of Mountain Matt's pizza," said Hank. "How about I order a couple extra-large for dinner? I know you love their veggie special." He dialed a number on his cell and left the room to hopefully phone in an urgent pizza order.

Our fifteen years of marriage had not been a total loss if my ex still remembered my food preferences. I contemplated my boyfriend, wondering how long it would take before he and I had that kind of relationship.

Tom walked over and put his arms around me. I leaned in and rested my head against his burly chest.

"I'm sorry about dinner," I mumbled, on the verge of tears.

"Not a problem," he said. "I like pizza."

"How about Hank?" I asked.

"Him, I don't like so much, but I can survive his company for one night."

In the eight months since Tom and I first met, we'd spent some odd evenings together. A few of them even included face time with a killer. Eating dinner squeezed in between my ex and my boyfriend ranked right at the top of the list.

The first few minutes consisted of complete quiet accompanied by the sound of three adults, one teenager and two eight-year-olds chomping on their pizza slices. Pumpkin, our homely black and orange kitten, sat under the table, waiting for a stray veggie to come her way, courtesy of my son. I wished Ben loved his greens as much as our weird cat did.

Hank finally broke the silence.

"Thanks again for bringing me home last night." He grinned at me. "You're always there for me, hon."

Ben stopped chewing and looked up, a smudge of tomato sauce decorating his small pointed chin. "How come Mom drove you home, Dad?"

Hank and I exchanged looks. "Um, there was a problem with my car last night," he finally said.

I almost snorted mozzarella up my nose at Hank's response. I supposed an incapacitated driver could be considered an automotive issue. But I saw no need to share Hank's alcoholic excess with our kids.

"I heard Deputy Fletcher also came to your rescue at the fundraiser," Tom said. "Lucky for you."

Hank smirked at Tom. "There's nothing like the relationship between a quarterback and his tight end. Fletch and I took the team to the state championship our senior year at El Dorado High."

Ben reached for another piece of pizza. He bit off half the slice and attempted to talk at the same time. "I'm gonna be a quarterback, too. I got your arm, don't I, Dad?"

"You sure do, son. Maybe when you grow up, you can join my construction company. Wouldn't it be fun to work together?"

Ben shook his head. "Nope, I'm gonna be a detective. Like Tom." He smiled first at Kristy and then at her dad.

Tom grinned at Ben, but I could tell my son's innocent comment upset his father. Hank didn't respond, in itself a sign that Ben's remark perturbed him. This seemed like the perfect opportunity to quiz Tom on his new cold case.

"We can use a detective in this family, Ben. We have a family mystery to solve."

My son's ears perked up. His green eyes widened, and he actually dropped the rest of his pizza back on to his plate. I'd finally learned how to get his full attention.

"We do? How many dead bodies do we got?"

"Do we have," I said, automatically correcting his grammar.

Ben looked confused. "How many dead bodies do we got to have?"

Tom's shoulders heaved as he tried not to laugh at Ben. Or his mother.

I narrowed my eyes at him. "So, Tom, how many dead bodies do we got to have before you figure out my great-great-grandfather didn't murder George Clarkson?"

Jenna's mouth opened and closed before she managed to squeak out a question. "Someone in our family killed a Clarkson? Is he related to Rich Clarkson?"

"There's a Clarkson on every corner in this town, Jenna. I suppose Rich must be related to George in some fashion."

"I hope my great-great-great-grandfather didn't kill any of Rich's relatives," Jenna said. "He's totally awesome."

"I'm sure your great-great—" I hesitated because I was having a difficult time keeping track of the greats dangling from the branches of our family tree. "Anyway, I doubt Harold Titus had anything to do with George Clarkson's death. Just because they discovered Harold's watch in the mineshaft does not make him a killer. Maybe George stole the watch and happened to be wearing it when he died."

"Hey, that's a good possibility," Hank chimed in.

It was good, wasn't it? I patted myself on the back for coming up with a reason to remove Harold as a suspect.

"We haven't finalized anything yet," Tom said. "There will be a lot more investigating before we close the case. I promise."

"You better continue to look for another suspect," I said. "Otherwise you'll have to contend with three generations of the Titus women digging up our own clues."

"Make that four." Jenna raised her glass of milk, and we clinked to our female solidarity and the pursuit of truth, happiness and frosted chocolate brownies.

CHAPTER EIGHT

I woke in the middle of the night with my bladder screaming at me. Once awake, I couldn't go back to sleep. I thought back to our dinner the previous evening. It ended amicably enough although Hank refused to get the hint his presence wasn't needed or wanted by his ex-wife. He seemed determined to deprive me of my boyfriend's company. And his kisses. Tom and I only managed to exchange one chaste goodnight kiss before he and Kristy drove home.

Hank and I needed to sit down and discuss my personal situation. Just because he was currently single and seemingly intent on spending time with me did not mean the feeling was reciprocal. We had both grown up and moved on.

At least, I had. It was time for him to start a new life as well.

It took forever before I fell back to sleep only to be awakened a short time later when the phone rang. Outside my bedroom window, the sky resembled a Turner painting in swirling shades of pink and blue.

I switched on my nightstand lamp and mumbled "Hello" into the phone.

"I need your help," the caller whispered.

"Who is this?"

"It's your husband."

"What?"

"It's Hank."

"Oh, why didn't you say so in the first place? And stop referring to yourself as my husband. That spec home sailed a long time ago. You're not my—"

Hank interrupted before I could throw any more confusing metaphors into the mix.

"Laurel, listen to me. I'm in trouble and I need your help."

Geez. What now? I grabbed the clock and brought it so close to my myopic eyes that my eyelashes dusted it clean. A few minutes before six. What kind of trouble could Hank be in before the sun rose?

"I thought you were meeting Spencer at five," I muttered into the phone. "Did he show?"

Hank paused for a few seconds before he replied. "Kind of."

"What?"

"Spencer is here. In a sense."

I sighed. "Hank, I need to jump in the shower and get ready for work. Can you speak in plain English?"

"I'll try," he said with a catch in his voice. "I overslept this morning. When I arrived, Spencer wasn't waiting for me, so I figured he left to get to his Rotary meeting."

"He was probably ticked off at you for being late. Did you try calling him?"

"Yeah, that's when I heard his cell ringing upstairs."

"Maybe he left his phone behind when he drove off."

"Spencer didn't drive off," Hank shouted into the phone causing me to shrink back.

"Listen, Hank, if you're going to yell at me I'm hanging up."

"Don't do that," he said, the fear in his voice unmistakable. "Please."

In the background, I heard sirens, the shrill sound gradually increasing in volume.

"Where are you?" I asked.

"Upstairs in the attic of the Hangtown Hotel."

"And you have no idea where Spencer could be?"

"I didn't say that," he muttered. "You know the dummy that hangs over the Hangman's Tree building a few doors down from the hotel?"

"Of course. I used the Hanging Man dummy in one of the bank's ad campaigns recently." Or attempted to until my boss shot me down.

"Well, now there's two of them."

I leaned back against my pillow. "Did vandals string up another dummy? Don't worry. It's not your concern."

Hank's loud sigh boomed over the phone. "It's my concern when the new hanging man isn't a dummy."

I was about to chastise Hank for being a dummy himself when he finally elaborated.

"Spencer is hanging from the scaffolding of the Hangtown Hotel!"

CHAPTER NINE

The phone slipped and banged against my front teeth. "What do you mean Spencer is hanging from the scaffolding? Is he dead?"

"Well, I haven't examined his body," Hank said, "but he's looking kind of limp and, um, dead-ish."

"Did you call the police?"

"No, I called you first." My ego was impressed Hank called me first. My brain decided he was an idiot.

"I heard sirens in the background a few minutes ago," I said. "Are the police there now?"

"Someone must have realized he wasn't a dummy and called the cops. Two police cars parked on the street in front of the building. What should I do?"

I rested the phone on my shoulder, which left my fingernails free for chewing. Certainly gnawing my nails down to their nubs would help me come up with a solution.

"I don't think you have anything to worry about," I said. "Just because you and Spencer scheduled a meeting this morning doesn't signify anything. But why would someone kill him and string his body up?"

"Crazy, huh? Should I go talk to the officers?" Hank's voice shook. He must feel awful after such a grisly discovery. I was feeling nauseous myself thinking about it.

"You can't hide up there forever. The detectives will want to examine every inch of the building before long. Why did you go inside? Didn't you notice Spencer hanging out front?"

"I always park my truck in the Center Street garage and enter through the rear door. Spencer has a reserved spot in another lot. Since the door wasn't locked, I assumed he'd already arrived. When I didn't see him, I figured he must have left. I called his cell and heard it ring up above me so I climbed the stairs to the second floor." Hank gulped before he continued. "At first I thought someone had moved the dummy again. You know like the time he went missing and ended up sitting in a chair at the Liar's Bench bar. I almost had a heart attack when I realized it was Spencer."

I tried my best to reassure him. "You have nothing to worry about. The two of you merely have, I mean had, a business arrangement. Go downstairs and explain your situation to the officers. It's far better if you tell the cops now than if they find out later you were on the premises. I'm sure the police will understand."

Silly me.

Ninety minutes later, I stood on the sidewalk alongside a throng of spectators across the street from the old Hangtown Hotel. Yellow crime scene tape formed a barricade around the brick and clapboard building Hank was in the middle of renovating. Crime scene tape also covered the scaffolding. A few early birds displayed photos taken with their smart phones before the police took down Darius Spencer's body.

I shivered, either from the early morning temperature or from the ghastly sight of Spencer's limp frame that the woman next to me insisted on sharing via her iPad. The high definition version. Whoever hung Spencer intended to make a statement. No attempt had been made to disguise the death as an accident.

My heart went out to Janet, the victim's wife, and their children. Losing a spouse was tragedy enough, but to have him killed in such a horrific manner would be even more devastating.

I'd expected Hank to be in the crowd, but I had yet to see him around. He might still be talking to the police or he could have gone home. Main Street had been cordoned off to vehicular traffic, but that hadn't stopped people from parking a few blocks away and scurrying along the sidewalk to check out the crime scene behind the tape.

Jake Russell, the owner of Hangtown Bakery, true to character, chose to profit from the crime by setting up his portable kiosk next to the barricade perimeter. The curious spectators could sip a cup of java and nosh on a jelly-filled doughnut while watching the Hangtown version of *Law and Order*. While I applauded Jake's ingenuity, profiting from a murder lacked good taste.

Although Jake's incredible pastries lacked for nothing.

A car bearing the insignia of the El Dorado County Sheriff's Office stopped in front of the barricade. The driver rolled down his window and spoke to the city cop who then let the vehicle through. I recalled that the Placerville Police Department normally utilized detectives from the county for homicide investigations. The driver pulled behind a fire engine parked in the loading zone in front of Antiques Galore. The passenger door opened, and a dark-haired man unfurled his large frame out of the car.

I grinned. My homicide hotline had arrived on the scene. Once the detective entered the building, he would be off limits.

I called out his name. Tom halted, his internal "Laurel" GPS zeroing in on my location. He must have told the deputy accompanying him to go ahead because the younger man walked inside while Tom headed toward me.

"Excuse me," Tom said. The crowd parted as if he'd majestically commanded the Red Sea to divide in half. He grabbed my hand, and we weaved in and out of the spectators until we reached the corner of Main and Sacramento Streets.

"What are you doing here?" Tom asked. "Shouldn't you be at the bank?"

I glanced at my watch. "I still have ten minutes to spare. Hank called early this morning to tell me about finding Spencer, so I thought I'd see him here."

Tom's chiseled features hardened causing him to resemble a Bernini sculpture. "What do you mean Hank called you about Spencer? You're not saying he had anything to do with the murder, are you?"

"You're calling it a murder already? Normally you officials say a death is under investigation until you're positive it's a homicide."

"Someone hung the guy from the scaffolding. He doesn't appear to have done it on his own, so it's not an accident nor a suicide."

I frowned at Tom. "Do you know if the city police talked to Hank?"

He shook his head, looking even more confused than I felt. "I have no idea what you're talking about. What's the deal with your ex?"

"Hank and Spencer scheduled a meeting for five, but Hank overslept and didn't enter the building until close to six. He claims he didn't notice anything unusual until he called Spencer's cell. When he heard the phone ringing, he went up to the second floor and discovered the body hanging from the scaffolding. Then he called me. And I told him to talk to the police."

"Hank called you?" Tom asked. "Not 911?"

I shrugged. "I didn't say Hank was smart. But he's not a killer."

Tom's eyes softened. "I realize the man's an idiot. He let you go, didn't he?"

Aw. After that compliment, I could have thrown my arms around him, but two men dressed in suits crossed the intersection and stopped to speak to us.

Tom nodded at the men. "Mayor Briggs, Supervisor Winkler. What can I do for you?"

"What's the situation here, Lieutenant?" asked the mayor, his face flushed and his navy and yellow print tie somewhat askew. Then his gaze shifted to me. "Are you assisting Detective Hunter?"

I could think of a dozen ways I'd like to assist my detective, but I doubted Mayor Briggs had any of my R-rated scenarios in mind. Tom shot me a look indicating it was time for this civilian to trot down to her office while the police and politicos attended to business.

Fine with me. I winked him a goodbye and headed down the street.

I entered the lobby of the bank, which bustled with customers. Although crime scene tape blocked the sidewalk a few doors down, it had not impeded foot traffic. I returned to my supply closet turned office. I shoved my well-worn black Coach purse, a present from my mother, into my desk drawer and turned on my computer. Seconds later, Stan landed in my visitor chair.

"Can you believe what happened?" he asked.

I shook my head as I typed my password into my computer. "I saw photos of Spencer's body hanging from the scaffolding, but I still can't come to grips with it. Such a tragedy."

"And a pretty ballsy thing for the killer to do," Stan said before adding, "volleyball-sized balls."

I nodded my agreement. "Was it someone with a huge ego, or someone who hated Spencer so much he wanted to make a grand statement?"

Stan rested his chin on his palms. "Could one man have done it alone?"

I pondered his question half wishing I'd seen the victim myself, half relieved I had not. "I'll have to ask Hank if he thinks one person could have strung him up."

"Have you talked to him today?"

"He called me this morning. Right after he found the body."

Stan's mouth opened wide enough to swallow a mouse. The one resting next to my keyboard. "OMG. Your husband killed Spencer?"

"Hank is not my husband and don't be ridiculous. He wouldn't kill a fly."

Well, my ex had eliminated a few hundred flies in his lifetime, and I'd personally witnessed him use a shovel to slice off the head of a rattlesnake. But we were talking about a man here, not a snake.

So I thought.

"Did you forget Hank punched Spencer at the Cornbread & Cowpokes soiree?" Stan reminded me.

"He merely imbibed a little too much that evening. Remember, Spencer had just fired him. Well, temporarily, until Hank apologized for his idiocy. Besides that's not a sufficient reason to kill someone."

"You never know what makes people snap." Stan stood, smoothed his pressed trousers and snapped his own manicured fingers. "Let's hope the police agree with you."

CHAPTER TEN

Stan departed my office, but his final remark lingered on. I'd expected Hank to call me back after he met with the police, and his lengthy silence began to unnerve me. I dialed his cell and was almost ready to hang up when he picked up and whispered a soft hello.

"What's going on?" I asked. "I'm worried about you."

"Thanks, hon. I appreciate that."

"Did you experience any problems explaining your situation to the cops?"

Hank cleared his throat. "I decided they were busy enough without me interfering, so I left."

"You left the crime scene?" I could hear my voice growing shrill. "Without explaining you were there?"

"After you and I hung up, I walked downstairs and went out the back door to drop off my tool box in the truck. Then I decided to drive home. I figured the cops would call me if they had any questions. You think I screwed up by not hanging around?" He chuckled. "Hey, that's funny."

No, it wasn't funny at all.

"There's not much you can do about it now," I grumbled, "except wait until the gendarmes come banging on your door."

"The who? Oh, you really think they'll want to talk to me? I'm only the contractor."

I ticked off all the reasons the police would want to interview him, beginning with his fingerprints covering every wall of the building, him punching Spencer Sunday night and concluding with his presence at the scene of the crime.

"Laurel, I punched Spencer out of frustration combined with one too many beers. After I apologized to him, everything was cool with us. Certainly there are far more people who had a reason to kill him."

At least one person must have a reason. His killer.

"You've spent a lot of time with Spencer lately," I said to Hank. "Why don't you come up with a list of possible suspects? Whoever is investigating this case might appreciate the help."

"Great idea. You always were smarter than me." Hank paused, waiting for me to disagree with him. It would be a very long wait.

"I'll stop by the house tonight, and we can put our heads together," he said. I started to protest, but he clicked off.

Seconds later, my cell rang. Mother. I debated between answering the call and doing what I should be doing at nine in the morning—my job. I was still annoyed with my boss so Mother won this round.

"Did you hear about Spencer?" I asked her.

"What? Oh, yes, terrible thing. Although he was an annoying rodent of a man."

I stared at my cell phone to confirm it was my normally classy mother on the line. "Did you refer to Darius Spencer as a rodent?"

"I once called him a rat-faced liar to his face, so that would be an affirmative, dear."

"You didn't happen to ask your husband to hang Spencer from a pole, did you?"

"Of course not," Mother replied. "If I were to murder someone, it would be far more subtle."

"Good to know," I said. "But why are you so down on Spencer?"

"No reason other than he foreclosed on one of my clients. He not only cheated me out of a commission, he stole their home right from under them."

"You never mentioned anything about that to me."

"It occurred a few years ago when you were still dealing with your post-divorce issues. The Beckers held plenty of equity in their house, but they had both lost their jobs and couldn't keep up with their loan payments. Spencer acquired the Becker mortgage from the original construction lender and promised to work with them. I found a purchaser for their home, but we needed some time to work out the financing details. The next thing I knew, he'd foreclosed and the sheriff was knocking on their door to evict them."

"That's horrible," I said. My mother put her heart and soul into helping buyers and sellers of homes. For Spencer to go and unnecessarily evict them seemed wrong.

"When I ran into Spencer at a chamber meeting, I told him exactly how I felt about him shoving that poor family out their front door. He laughed and told me to suck eggs."

"Do you think he made a practice of cheating people? It's hard to believe a politician would lie for his own benefit."

And what fantasy world did I live in?

After Mother stopped laughing at my absurd comment, she informed me about the real reason for her phone call. "Your Gran is driving me crazy."

I felt like saying, "So what else is new," but restrained myself. "What do you want me to do?"

"She's refusing to let me list her house until we prove her grandfather didn't murder George Clarkson. She claims the Hangtown Historical Society is threatening to kick her off the board. And to rescind her nomination for the Distinguished Historian Award that will be given at the county fair. The award and that organization mean a great deal to her."

"I doubt Tom has closed the file yet, so I'll discuss it with him. He's going to have his hands full with Spencer's murder investigation now."

I could practically hear the wheels of my mother's active brain grinding through the phone line. "If Tom is distracted by the new murder, Mr. Bones may not be a priority. That will give you time to research and determine who did it."

I sighed. "You are aware I have a full-time job."

"Yes, but you're good at solving puzzles. If you don't agree to figure it out, your grandmother will try. We can't have her running around town grilling the descendants of those early settlers in search of a killer from the last century."

I giggled at the image of my grandmother dressed in a pastel blue trench coat and matching fedora gumshoeing it down Main Street. An octogenarian Nancy Drew on the loose.

"Okay, tomorrow I'll plan on spending my lunch hour at the historical museum," I said. "Maybe I can come up with a list of ancient suspects."

I hung up just as my boss arrived at my office door, bearing an armload of files and a frown that appeared sand blasted on his face.

CHAPTER ELEVEN

My boss, Bruce Boxer, resembled the dog of the same name, but was not nearly as attractive. I couldn't tell if his bark was worse than his bite, but I preferred not to find out. As Vice President of Business Development, his job description included luring local merchants and large depositors to our bank, using print advertising and online social media. Another important responsibility included attending every social, political and non-profit function in town.

When I initially applied for this position, I visualized spending many hours outside of the office as compared to hunkering at my desk all day underwriting loan files. I looked forward to mingling with members of the local Chambers of Commerce, participating on fundraising committees and attending a variety of social events and mixers.

So far, my duties had left me desk bound with nary a swizzle stick or Swedish meatball slotted on my professional calendar.

I greeted Mr. Boxer with a less-than-hopeful smile and a question mark in my eyes.

He threw a slick piece of paper on my desk. The same flyer he'd rejected the day before. Only someone had modified it. The artist had drawn a face on the hanging man that resembled the victim. In case there was any doubt, the unknown person included some verbiage—Slimebag Spencer gets what he deserves!

"Where did you find this?" My hand trembled as I gripped the flyer. This couldn't be good. For the bank or for me.

"Someone taped it to the bulletin board next to the bank." Mr. Boxer loomed over me, his left eye twitching erratically like a broken turn signal. "One of our customers brought it in. I thought I ordered you to get rid of those flyers."

"I did, but we'd already handed a few of them out before we pulled them from the advertising kiosk. I dumped the remainder in the recycle bin."

My boss looked as if he wanted to stuff *me* in the recycle bin.

"I am really sorry," I apologized. "Is there anything I can do?"

He fell into the empty chair in front of my desk. "Not at this point. I hope none of our customers associates the bank with this horrendous crime."

"It could be a kid pulling a prank." That option appealed to me.

"I hope the police agree," he said, his eye still twitching but at a slower rate.

"Shoot." I dropped the flyer faster than if I'd picked up a hot tamale. "Our fingerprints are all over it."

Mr. Boxer's face paled. "I never thought of that. Should I call the police?"

"That's okay, I can handle it." I grabbed my cell out of my purse and hit speed dial. "I have my own personal hotline."

My homicide hotline must have been engrossed in his investigation because he didn't return my call. I tucked the modified flyer into a large baggie in case Tom wanted to look at it. I never leave home without them. Although my preference is to use them to transport meals that I can't finish, as opposed to crime scene evidence.

Hank also didn't respond to the two messages I left on his voicemail wondering whether he still intended to come to the house that evening. I decided dinner would be a bountiful repast of hot dogs and leftover pizza accompanied by a huge salad.

Ben, Jenna and I were sitting at the table, almost finished eating when Hank strolled into my cheerful yellow kitchen.

"How did you get in?" I asked. We live in a safe rural community, but I always lock the doors at night.

He dangled an array of keys before he shoved them into his jeans pocket. "I still have the key to your house." He lifted his ball cap off his head, placed it over his chest and winked at me. "And to your heart, I hope."

Jenna chuckled. I could feel my eyeballs wanting to roll in their sockets, but I forced them to stay put. I added another item to my "to do" list. Change the locks.

Hank opened an oak cabinet and grabbed a plate from the bottom shelf. He pulled out the cutlery drawer, which jammed before finally sliding free. "It would make more sense," he said, "if you rearranged your steak knives and flatware like this." He shifted the utensils around. "Then the knives wouldn't get stuck."

I felt like rearranging one of the serrated knives in Hank's chest. Just because he built our house, Hank thought it gave him permission to advise me how to organize it.

Rather than get into yet another argument, I switched subjects. "Did you contact the police?" I asked.

Hank slid into the spindle-backed chair across from mine. He grabbed a slice of pizza and chewed for a few seconds before answering. "I talked to the dispatcher this afternoon. Told her I'm the contractor for the renovation, and they could call me if they had any questions about the remodel."

"Why'd you need to call the police, Dad?" asked Ben, taking one more slice before his pizza-loving father demolished the remainder.

"Darius Spencer, the man who owns the building I've been working on, died today."

Ben chewed on that comment while he chewed on his pizza. "So do you still got a job?"

"Have a job," I muttered.

Both McKay males looked at me, the unofficial grammar police, then at each other. Hank shrugged his shoulders. "I guess I should talk to his wife. I didn't even think about who I'd be reporting to now."

"Is Darius Spencer that creepy looking guy on all the billboards who's running for Supervisor of the Sixth District?" Jenna said.

Hank and I nodded in unison.

"Did he have a heart attack?" she asked. "That picture makes him look like he has a permanent case of indigestion."

"The police haven't determined the exact cause of his death," I said. "Although it looks as if someone murdered him."

Jenna blinked startled blue eyes at me. "Do you think someone plans on killing all the candidates?"

"No, I don't think there's a politician-offing serial killer out there," I responded. "I'm sure the police will resolve it quickly."

"Is Tom working on the case?" Ben asked. My son reached into his shorts pocket and pulled out the shiny gold badge Bradford had given him when he retired from the Sheriff's Office. Ben treasured the badge as well as his new grandfather. "Maybe Tom could use my help," he said.

The doorbell rang and my heart jumpstarted. Perhaps my favorite detective decided to return my phone call with a personal visit. I rose from my seat and darted through the family room, barely avoiding stomping on Ben's Game Boy that as usual, he'd tossed on the floor.

I flung open the front door and greeted my boyfriend who stood next to an El Dorado County Deputy Sheriff.

Hmm. Why did I have the feeling this wasn't a social call?

CHAPTER TWELVE

I resisted the urge to leap into Tom's arms since a uniformed officer stood by his side. I recognized Deputy Mengelkoch from a previous visit when I was the subject of a murder investigation. I blushed, remembering the officers rummaging through my lingerie drawer in search of the murder weapon. I hoped that vision wasn't burned in Mengelkoch's memory like it was in mine.

"We're looking for Hank," Tom said. "He's not at his apartment, so I thought I'd try your place. He seems to spend a lot of time here lately." Tom pointed to the ten-year-old black Ford F-150 decorating my concrete driveway with fresh oil stains. "That's Hank's truck, right?"

I nodded and both officers stepped into my wood-plank entry. "We're finishing our supper..."

Hank joined us in the foyer. "Can I help you, Tom?" Hank's words were polite, but his tone of voice truculent. Was my ex reluctant to help the Sheriff's Department? Or was it my detective boyfriend who needled him?

"We have a few questions for you," Tom said, "about your relationship with Darius Spencer."

"You already know I'm renovating that old hotel of his," Hank said.

"Yes, I'm aware of that. It would help our investigation if you could answer some questions that have arisen."

I'm not sure what Dear Abby would advise when your boyfriend, the head of homicide, tells your ex-husband he'd like to chat. I tried to remain calm and invited Tom and the deputy to join us in the kitchen.

Tom shook his head, declining my suggestion. "We need Hank to accompany us to the station. It's a more appropriate venue."

"You're not arresting me, are you?" Hank yelled. His eyes, which he described as jade green and which I referred to as swamp green, bulged like oversized marbles as they bounced from Tom to Deputy Mengelkoch and back to Tom again. "I've done nothing wrong."

I moved between the two men, resting a palm on Hank's chest, worried he might feel the urge to punch Tom. My ex didn't need assault against a police officer added to his other problems.

Hank's raised voice must have carried into the kitchen. Ben skidded into the entry, followed by his sister.

"Are you having dinner with us?" Ben asked the men, his face puzzled.

Tom's cheeks reddened. "Not tonight, but thanks for the offer."

Jenna, a straight A student, is no slouch in the analytical department. She stared at the four adults, giving an extra long glance at Deputy Mengelkoch. The young deputy was cute, a shaggy-haired, freckle-faced preppie all suited up in his official khaki shirt and forest green slacks.

"So why are you here?" Jenna asked Tom.

"They want to talk to your father," I said, worried Tom would extract a pair of handcuffs at any minute.

"About Spencer's murder?" she asked.

Ben's eyes grew wide. "Dad, are you going to help Tom solve the case?"

It was Hank's turn to flush. "Well, uh..."

Ben reached into his pocket and pulled out Bradford's old badge. He plopped it into his father's hand. "See, you can be an official detective, too!"

Hank's eyes watered as he gazed at the badge. "Thanks, son." He turned to Tom. "Do you want me to go down to the station?"

"Yes, it will be easier for us to, um..." Tom glanced at Ben, "solve the case if we're all together at the Sheriff's Office."

I felt my mascara pooling on my cheekbones as my eyes filled with tears. A mixture of emotions assailed me: fear and concern for my ex-husband combined with pride and love for my son. As for my boyfriend, despite my not being thrilled about him taking my children's father back to the station, I was grateful for his tactful handling of this awkward situation.

Hank left with Tom and the deputy. At first, I worried they would require him to ride in the backseat of the squad car, but they informed Hank he could follow them to the sheriff's office.

My chest flooded with relief at that statement. I reassured the kids the detectives merely wanted their father's assistance, and my remarks seemed to satisfy both of them. After repeating my mantra to my children, I decided the statement most likely was true. After working with Spencer for several months, Hank might have personal insight into who would have wanted the man dead.

The home phone rang while I stacked the dirty dishes in the dishwasher.

"Hi, Gran." I rested the receiver on my shoulder while I rinsed off the rest of the plates.

"Did you solve this case yet?" she squawked.

"Case? You mean Darius Spencer's murder?" I asked.

"No, not that Spencer twit. Good riddance to political rubbish."

"Good grief, Gran. What did you have against him?"

"Oh, he comes from a long line of political nitwits. His father, Ned Spencer, was a classmate of mine. If Ned's father hadn't acquired so much land around here during the depression, I don't know how those fellows would have made a living. Ned served on the Board of Supervisors for eight years which was about seven years and 364 days too long."

I'm not the most politically astute person in town, but I vaguely remembered Spencer's father had been a county supervisor twenty plus years ago. Back when I was more interested in the high school quarterback than local politics.

"Anyway, child, you need to concentrate your investigatin' on our case," Gran said. "We gotta get Harold off the hook. And fast."

"Harold died more than eighty years ago. I don't think he's in that big of a hurry to get his reputation cleared."

"It's not his name I'm worried about. It's mine."

"Settle down, Gran, you don't want your blood pressure to jump." The last thing we needed was for her to get overexcited and drop dead worrying about this long dead case. Putting Hank's situation out of my mind for the moment, I asked, "Are you taking your meds?"

"I had a ginger ale and whiskey. That will medicate me for now. So what's our plan?"

"Meet me at the county historical museum tomorrow at noon. We'll delve through the books together and try to come up with a list of suspects."

"That's my girl. I'll bring some supplies to help with our detecting."

I envisioned my grandmother draped in a cape and deerstalker hat. "You mean magnifying glasses for reading those handwritten journals from the nineteenth century?"

She snorted. "That's not a bad idea. I'll throw one in with a dozen of my oatmeal raisin cookies."

If there's one thing my grandmother has learned over the years, it's how to bribe her family to get her way.

CHAPTER THIRTEEN

The phone rang early the next morning while I assembled our lunches, trying to avoid stepping on Pumpkin, who could smell tuna from a mile away. By brown bagging my own meal today, I could devote my entire lunch break to visiting the museum with my grandmother.

I glanced at Caller ID and grabbed the phone.

"Hank, are you okay?" I'd tossed and turned all night worrying about his interview with the Sheriff's Department.

"I'm fine," he said. "I didn't return home until after midnight and didn't want to call you that late."

"How did it go?"

"Okay, I guess. I thought Tom would interview me, but I waited over an hour for two other detectives to show up."

Curious. I would have felt better with Tom in charge of the investigation, but maybe he was too busy with other cases.

"What did they ask?"

"Nothing out of the ordinary. I discussed the remodel and some of the issues that came up recently. They wondered how someone could have gotten into the building, but I didn't know how many keys Spencer gave out."

"Did they mention any potential suspects?" I opened the refrigerator door and grabbed a container of sliced fruit while I waited for Hank's answer.

"Nah, they questioned me but wouldn't answer any of mine."

"What did they say about your assault on Spencer?"

"It wasn't an assault, Laurel, merely an altercation."

"An altercation that involved your fist and his face," I clarified.

"Yeah, well, I explained to the detectives I had too much to drink that night. And that we shook hands afterward, so no harm, no foul."

That might be true in Hank's case, but someone definitely caused Spencer to foul out—permanently.

"What are you going to do about finishing the renovation?"

"I can't do anything while it's a crime scene, although they said they'd be done late today. I should give Spencer's wife my condolences and find out if she wants me to continue. It would be a shame to leave the building in its current shape. The Hangtown Hotel would have been the pride of Main Street when we finished."

And the pride of Hank McKay. I had to hand it to my ex-husband. The man knew how to renovate a building.

His tone brightened. "As long as the building construction is in limbo, I'll have lots of free time. I can spend it with you and the kids."

I glanced at my rooster clock hanging over the sink. I could almost visualize the cocky bird crowing at me to get my tush in gear. I told Hank that since summer break began the next day, the kids would enjoy hanging out with him. In the meantime, their mother had better things to do, like driving the kids to their last day of school and herself to work.

Promptly at noon, I pulled my Prius into a parking space next to a fire-engine-red Mustang convertible I lusted after. Sporty convertibles, unfortunately, are not practical modes of transportation for soccer moms. They are also not a sensible choice for eighty-eight-year-old drivers who can barely see over the leather-wrapped steering wheel, but that didn't stop my grandmother from purchasing her muscle car.

Gran claimed it was a deal she couldn't pass up. I'm sure the car salesman felt the same about his elderly customer—a sucker he couldn't pass up.

The museum was located in one of the many buildings comprising the El Dorado County fairgrounds and staffed by volunteers from the historical society, of which Gran held a long-time membership. I pulled open the heavy door and followed the scent of oatmeal cookies to the small research library where Gran chatted with several of the volunteers.

Gran grabbed my wrist with a strong grip and dragged me over to meet her friends. "Here's my granddaughter, our own little Nancy Drew."

She introduced me to the three white-haired women, all of whom bore a strong resemblance to Agatha Christie's elderly sleuth, Miss Marple. One of the women went behind a desk and reached into her large handbag. I half expected her to yank out a set of knitting needles, but instead she slid a pair of heavy-duty reading glasses out of a Vera Bradley blue paisley case.

"So, Virginia," asked the petite woman, her pale blue eyes magnified a hundredfold behind the glasses, "I understand they found old George Clarkson in your backyard."

Gran nodded, the platinum curls of her Marilyn Monroe wig bobbing up and down. "That's what Laurel's honey said."

Three fluffy white heads spun around to gawk at me. "What Gran, that is Virginia, means is that my detective, well, he's not actually mine, he belongs to the Sheriff's Office, I mean..." I babbled on and their faces became even more confused. "Anyway, after the crime scene techs examined the mine shaft, they concluded the skeleton was likely to be George Clarkson. They ordered a DNA test, but it's not a high priority."

The tallest of the women squinted at me. "Why do the cops think Virginia's grandfather killed Clarkson?"

Gran answered before I could. "They found a watch with my granpappy's name engraved on it down in the mineshaft, Betty, and that's all it took for them to decide he's a murderer."

"That's all they have?" Betty folded skinny arms over her flat chest. "Lazy asses. My great-aunt, Lulu Cook, the first female deputy sheriff of El Dorado County, wouldn't put up with such nonsense. Trust me, with us researching it, I bet we can shred their so-called evidence into mincemeat."

The other women nodded vigorously and I smiled watching them. My very own *History Detective* team. At first, I worried the excitement might be too much for the women, but as the octogenarians zipped up and down the aisles pulling out books and manuscripts, I realized having a mystery to solve could be a gift.

The women no longer seemed to care that Placerville's version of Nancy Drew was onsite. Since my presence didn't seem necessary, I decided to check out the displays. It had been ages since I'd visited the museum, and I'd forgotten some of the local stories I'd learned in grammar school.

I chuckled at the sketch of Charley Parkhurst, one of my favorite characters. He was a Wells Fargo stagecoach driver by day, but he had a reputation as the toughest, most alcohol-swilling gambler at night. Old Charley set all the stagecoach speed records back in the 1860s and even foiled a stagecoach robbery. Not until a doctor showed up at his deathbed did people learn Charley was a woman.

Way to go, Charley!

Gran and her friends seemed exhilarated by the opportunity to research the 150-year-old murder, so I kissed her soft wrinkled cheek and drove back into town. A few blocks from Main Street, the traffic on Highway 50 came to a sudden halt. I slammed on my brakes and barely missed smashing into the oversized Tahoe in front of me that blocked my view. To avoid the vehicle backup, I turned right on Pacific Avenue and parked along the street in a residential area. Parking in Placerville can be a hassle during certain events like Third Saturday Art Walk and Girls Night Out, but a traffic jam in the middle of the week seemed odd.

By now, a line of cars and trucks were bumper to bumper on California Highway 49, the primary north and south thoroughfare through Placerville and the gold country. I scurried down the sidewalk, curious to know what event had attracted this lunchtime crowd.

As I drew near the Hangtown Hotel, two men shepherding huge video cameras stepped in front of me. I scooted around them wondering how I would enter the bank with such a large crowd obstructing the entrance. Not until I laid eyes on the KNBA logo embellished on a white van did it click. The media had arrived.

My boyfriend, dressed in his official uniform of khaki shirt and forest green trousers, conversed with a female newscaster against a backdrop of bright yellow tape. Tom frowned and ran a hand through his thick chestnut hair as the short-skirted, stiletto-heeled reporter prattled nonstop.

Vehicles crawled down Main Street as their distracted drivers and passengers used their camera phones to take pictures of the partially reconstructed hotel covered with crime scene tape. I had a feeling this would not be a case of any publicity is good publicity. The City of Placerville and the County Chamber of Commerce take a great deal of pride in their community. A tremendous amount of time and labor went into planning the annual Wagon Train festivities. It would be a crime if this crime eclipsed the historic event.

I sidled closer, curious if Tom or the detectives he'd assigned to the case were announcing an arrest. Leila Hansen, a reporter for KNBA, placed the mike inches from her plump collagen-filled lips. She gazed into the cameras, her sultry expression more appropriate to the bedroom than the sidewalk.

"I'm here in Placerville with Lieutenant Hunter of the El Dorado County Sheriff's Department," she greeted her television audience. She swiveled her left hip to the side and addressed Tom. "Detective Hunter, what progress have you made on the grisly murder that occurred at this site yesterday?"

Tom leaned over and spoke firmly into the microphone. "I'm afraid it's still far too soon in the investigation, but we're examining all evidence from the crime scene as well as interviewing different sources."

"Is there any way this murder could be connected to the victim's political campaign?"

"I can't comment on that," he said.

"Darius Spencer was a respected leader in the Placerville business community," she said. "How much of a priority is this murder for your department?"

A flicker of annoyance crossed Tom's tanned face, but he maintained a neutral expression. "Homicide is always a priority for our department. We are using all of our resources to solve this crime as quickly as possible. If you'll excuse me, I have nothing further to say."

Tom attempted to bypass Leila, but she wasn't about to miss an opportunity to out scoop the other evening broadcasters. She stuck one slim leg in front of Tom to halt his departure.

"Do you think someone is crazy enough to reenact those hangings of more than a century ago?" Leila's voice switched from husky to horror-filled.

A man in a red plaid shirt yelled out, "Maybe an unfriendly spirit got him. This old hotel is rumored to be haunted."

Leila's thick-lashed violet eyes widened at this unexpected and *National Enquirer* worthy comment.

Tom's face froze. I doubted he'd considered the possibility that Spencer's death could be the first of many. Even worse was the thought of a vengeful ghost unhappy the owner was tearing up his home sweet home. Many of the historic Main Street buildings were known for their spirited spirits. Had Hank noticed any signs of paranormal activity in the building?

I shivered and wondered if a ghostly spirit had passed through me. I spun around and sighed with relief when I realized the door to the air-conditioned drug store had opened behind me.

Tom grabbed the microphone and addressed the camera. "This murder was committed by a person, not a ghost, and I would appreciate it if you didn't sensationalize it any more than necessary. Thank you. The Sheriff's Office will keep the media apprised of our progress."

Tom thrust the mike to Leila who handed it off to another woman. The newscaster latched onto Tom's arm and continued to question him. I figured Tom could use an interruption from the nosy newsy, so I wormed my way through the onlookers who began to disperse once the broadcast ended.

I approached Tom and waited for him to register my presence. When that didn't happen, I leaned forward trying to catch Leila's next question. She licked her lips and with a rapt look in her eye, laid her palm on his forearm. "I'm sure our viewers would also like to know if the detective in charge of this case is single."

Tom took a surprised step back, allowing me the opportunity to answer Leila's question.

"No, he's not." I pulled myself up to all five feet four and a quarter inches and thrust out my assets. "Are we done here?"

Leila eyed my chest, which I hoped was not covered with crumbs from the oatmeal raisin cookie I'd snagged from Gran. It's hard to be impressive when you're wearing your lunch.

She smiled and extended her hand. "Leila Hansen. Are you assisting in the investigation, Miss—?"

"No, she is not," Tom answered for me. "Thank you, Ms. Hansen. We'll contact you with any updates." He placed his hand on the small of my back and propelled me along the sidewalk, away from the news crew but in the opposite direction of the bank.

Tom opened the door to Hangtown Bakery. He surveyed the room, but it appeared safe from media intruders. He led the way to an unoccupied table, pulled out my chair for me then practically fell into the opposite seat.

"Tough day?" I reached across the table and took his large hand in mine. Our fingers remained intertwined for a few heavenly minutes.

"I need to get back to the office," he said. "But I had to escape that woman first."

I released his hand. "Where did that guy come up with the idea of a homicidal haunt?"

Tom tipped his wooden chair so far back I thought he would fall over, but years of practice had refined his tipping to perfection. "Who knows? It's bad enough to have a public spectacle like Spencer's murder, but for the media to add a paranormal element is sheer idiocy. All I need are a bunch of loonies running around with electro-magnetometers trying to mess up the crime scene."

"So you don't think an annoyed ghost knocked off Spencer?" I giggled, thinking that any self-respecting spirit would have taken it out on the contractor.

Tom shook his head. "No, this was plain and intentional murder."

I moved closer, curious if he would share any details with me. "Nothing has been mentioned about *how* Spencer was murdered. I assume he was killed before he was strung up?"

Tom nodded. "We found something that could be the murder weapon," he said. "But we won't know for sure until after the autopsy. So his death could have been unplanned, a crime of passion of sorts. If so, then why the public hanging? What did the killer intend?"

"What do you think?" I asked.

Tom's brown eyes darkened until they matched the filling in the bakery's midnight chocolate cupcakes. I shook my head at my fantasizing, wondering whether I was hungry or horny.

"What I think is none of your business, as you very well know," Tom said. "So how come you're not at work?"

I glanced at my watch. Oops. I hoped Mr. Boxer was taking a long lunch himself.

"Gran and I met at the museum during my lunch break. She and some of her friends from the historical society are currently combing through the museum looking for George Clarkson's murderer. It's one way of keeping Gran out of your hair."

He threw his palms up. "As far as I'm concerned they can research old journals and books to their heart's content. My primary goal is to solve Spencer's murder before those clues go cold. Tell your Gran she's officially deputized."

I laughed. "Throw in a badge for her, and you'll get a lifetime supply of cookies."

Tom stood and patted his rock hard stomach. I tried not to whimper. It had been a long time since I'd had access to his bare muscled chest.

"I think I'll pass on the sweets," he said, "but I'll take some sugar to go."

Still lost in my pectoral musings, I looked up, puzzled. Tom planted a soft kiss on my surprised lips. "It could be a few days or even weeks before we wrap up this case."

"Need any help?" My lips curved, assuming the answer would be a resounding no.

Tom surprised me. He grinned and chucked my chin. "I can't believe I'm saying this, but keep your ear to the ground and listen to any rumors going around about Spencer's death. You never know when gossip can lead to fact."

In a small town like Placerville, that was a certainty. I sped back to work intent on my gossip-finding mission. One thing was certain. The sooner Tom wrapped up this homicide, the sooner he could wrap me in his welcoming arms.

CHAPTER FOURTEEN

When I returned to my desk, I discovered my boss had plans for me that did not include gossiping with bank customers and employees. I had forgotten that the victim had served on Hangtown Bank's Board of Directors. Mr. Boxer requested, or rather ordered, me to write a press release detailing Spencer's contributions to the bank and voicing the deep loss the board felt over his senseless death.

My goal was to present the bank and Spencer in the best possible light, so I spent several hours searching the internet. After reading one article after another, I wondered if Darius Spencer ever slept. The man served as a director on three other boards besides our bank. He participated on a multitude of local committees and was the founder and current chairperson of a non-profit that worked with disadvantaged youth. He owned a successful investment and insurance company. I was curious how he planned to handle all of those responsibilities if elected, but that question would remain unanswered.

Janet Spencer and I had chatted occasionally during our Zumba classes. I knew the couple had two children in college, one daughter and one son. I could sympathize with her children's loss. I was only ten when a drunk driver crashed into my father's car, killing him instantly. As if losing a parent wasn't distressing enough, those poor kids would have to deal with the notoriety of their father's denigrating demise.

One recent *Mountain Democrat* article included an interview of Spencer as well as other Main Street proprietors regarding their thoughts on the restoration. Spencer enumerated in detail the grand improvements in the works. I smiled when he mentioned the name of his contractor. I hoped for Hank's sake that he'd be able to continue his work. The successful reconstruction of a historical building could lead to some nice contracts in the future.

Some day he might even catch up on the back child support he owed me.

Toward the end of the article, I discovered not everyone in the community was enamored of Spencer's big project. Doug Blake, of Blake's Bookstore, located next door to the hotel, grumbled about the noise, dirt and commotion. Abe Cartwell from Antiques Galore complained the scaffolding was an eyesore, and he thought it hurt the tourist trade. Abe ended his comments on a positive note, though, stating the hotel should eventually draw more business to the town.

Their remarks caused me to consider whether someone disliked the scaffolding so much that they decided to hang Spencer in protest. That seemed a wee bit extreme but then murder always is. According to the reporter, Spencer originally promised the renovation would be completed in the fall, but obstacles had arisen which might delay completion until the following year. The setback only added to the anti-Spencer sentiment.

I needed to discuss the remodel with Hank, but I had a feeling he might be the instigator of said obstacles. Still, I felt proud of his decision to finish the job properly without resorting to shortcuts or cheap solutions. Although I assumed Tom and his detectives would interview anyone who had publicly derided the victim, I made a note to share the article with him the next time we connected.

After all, he had delegated me to the gossip patrol.

I finally whipped out a glowing press release detailing everything Darius Spencer had done for the town and for El Dorado County. Despite some bad press, the man had been an important presence in our community. I left out any negative comments from people unhappy with the deceased, a much larger list than I'd first realized. As far as I was concerned, Spencer could rest in peace.

I pulled into the studio parking lot shortly before seven. Since Hank remained temporarily unemployed, he'd decided to pick up the kids from school then take them to a River Cats baseball game in Sacramento. The kids enjoyed spending time with their father, and since their summer break began the next day, this would be a nice way to celebrate the end of the school year. I only hoped Hank remembered to monitor Ben's hot dog and cotton candy consumption.

Otherwise, I would be the parent cleaning up the grisly aftereffects.

Jammin' Dance Studio was only a fifteen-minute drive from my house, which meant I couldn't use distance as an excuse for not attending on a regular basis. They offered classes in tap, Zumba fitness, hip-hop, and belly dancing. Despite the murder investigation that had interrupted our Hawaiian vacation, Liz and I had still managed to consume more high calorie tropical concoctions than we could burn off during our trip. Once we returned home, we vowed to support each other by signing up for an exercise class together.

Last December Liz had forced me to take ballroom dance to learn a choreographed foxtrot routine for her wedding. With those grueling lessons under my belt, the steps to Zumba were easy enough to follow. Occasionally, when the rest of the class swiveled to the right, I moved to the left, but by the end, we always came together.

A blast of cool air greeted me as I entered the studio, a sign that owner and teacher, Kay Lenhart, expected us to work up a sweat tonight. The rest of the students, including Liz, mingled and chatted at the front of the studio. I didn't see Janet Spencer, but I hadn't expected her to attend tonight's class so soon after her husband's tragic death.

It had only taken one Zumba class for me to learn that I, the mother of two children, one of whom arrived in my hospital delivery room at Mach Ten speeds, needed to make a pit stop before jumping up, down, and around the dance floor. The ladies' room, located in a different building, was locked so I waited outside.

The door opened and I moved aside to greet Janet Spencer, dressed in black as befitted a new widow. Although a black sports bra trimmed in hot pink with matching spandex shorts didn't exactly comprise my definition of "widow's weeds."

"Janet, hi, um why are you—?" I sputtered in confusion. "I'm sorry. I didn't expect to see you in class tonight. How are you doing?"

She dropped her gaze and toed the floor with the right shoe of her silver-toned Nikes. When she looked up, tears quivered in her gray-blue eyes.

"I'm okay. Originally, I didn't plan on coming tonight," she said, "but Kay called to share her condolences and talked me into attending class. She's a firm believer that dancing can cheer up anyone."

I thought about it. I supposed our Zumba class could provide a brief respite from Janet's troubles, although if my spouse had been murdered, I'd be home compiling a list of suspects. I guess everyone deals with grief in a different manner.

Some turn to swiveling. Others turn to sleuthing.

"Do you have any idea when the memorial service will be?" I asked.

She shrugged. "Not really. They still have to complete the autopsy before Darius's body can be released to the funeral home."

"I'm so sorry for your loss. I still can't believe someone would go to those lengths to um—"

"To humiliate my husband?" Her voice rose. "And our family?"

My face colored. "Well, it was a little extreme. Are you concerned about your own safety or that of your kids?"

Her eyes widened. "Oh, my. I just assumed one of Darius's enemies finally did him in."

I barely repeated the word "enemies" with a question mark, when the blast of a raucous samba beat echoed from the studio. Janet rushed off to join the students, and I finished my original mission before I lined up with them.

I squeezed in next to Liz whose hands and legs seemed in perpetual motion. The best thing about Kay's Zumba class was the students could tone it down or rev it up depending on their age or physical condition. After three months of her classes, my body felt more fit than it had since my last pregnancy—a mere eight years earlier. One of these days, I might even be as toned as my mother.

Once class ended, I dragged myself to the side of the room, reached into my tote bag and chugged all sixteen ounces from my water bottle. Janet left a few minutes early, possibly to avoid any more sympathetic or curious glances from the other students, or nosy questions from me. I would have loved to learn more about her husband's enemies. That could prove useful information for my favorite detective.

Liz and Kay chatted next to the CD player so I joined them. Kay complimented me on the improvement in my technique.

"Laurel, you're doing so well," she said, "you should dance with the group during the Wagon Train festivities."

"Since I'll be wearing that ridiculous saloon girl outfit, I think not," I replied. "All it would take is one Zumba spin to the right and that dress would be spinning to the left. I wouldn't want to distract the stagecoach drivers."

"Is Janet performing with the group?"Liz asked.

Kay shook her head. "She dropped out. I thought dancing might take her mind off Spencer's murder, but Janet said a public performance wouldn't be appropriate." Kay sighed. "That poor woman has gone through so much with that man."

My eyes locked with Liz's. "What do you mean?"

"I really shouldn't share Janet's dirty laundry," Kay mused.

Oh, yes, she should. Dirty laundry can be a detective's best friend.

"Laurel is helping the police with their investigation," Liz informed Kay. "So anything you tell us could assist them in solving the murder."

I raised both eyebrows at her comment but nodded at Kay. "I'm sure Janet would be grateful for the help."

Kay looked around the studio to ensure no one hovered nearby. "Janet and I have been friends for years, ever since she enrolled her daughter in a tap class I taught. Marriage to Spencer hasn't been easy, but she hung in there for the kids' sake. When he told her he wanted to run for office, she became apoplectic."

"A lot of women would be excited about the opportunity," Liz remarked.

Kay shook her head. "Not Janet. She worried about negative publicity impacting her and the children. Then something happened that really freaked her out."

Kay dropped her voice, and Liz and I both moved closer. "One afternoon, not too long ago, Janet received a phone call. Her caller ID indicated a private number so she has no idea who it was, but the caller said if her husband didn't withdraw from the election that not only Spencer, but her entire family would be in danger."

"That would bloody well freak me out," Liz said. "Spencer must not have been scared since he didn't drop out of the race."

"Spencer told Janet not to worry," Kay said. "He told her politicians get crazy calls like that all the time. He'd even received some phone threats at his campaign headquarters."

I crinkled my brow as I mulled over Kay's words. "I wonder if Janet told the police about the threat. I'm sure they have ways to track down the caller these days."

Kay tapped her finger on her chin to the beat of the music. The petite dancer could never stand still without tapping at least one appendage. "Now that I think about it, Janet said Spencer figured it was his opponent."

I tossed my head and beads of sweat flew off my brow landing on Liz's designer workout top. She scowled at me, but I ignored her. "Tricia Taylor would never lower herself to making threatening phone calls," I said.

"But her husband might," Liz interjected. "Lars is a developer so his interests were completely at odds with Spencer's no-growth platform. What happens now that Tricia won't have any opposition for the primary?"

Both women looked at me.

"She wins," I said.

CHAPTER FIFTEEN

By Friday, I was more than ready for my workweek to end and the weekend to begin, even if it proved to be another romance-free Saturday night. I hadn't connected with Tom in the last two days other than a few brief texts between us. I knew he was busy, but I was eager to share some of the information I'd discovered regarding Darius Spencer.

I was even more eager to share some kisses with him.

I arrived at work wondering what "fresh hell" Mr. Boxer would have in store for me. I opened my bottom drawer to stuff my purse inside and discovered the baggie with the "Spencer" modified flyer inside. The odds of there being any useful fingerprints on it seemed slim, but it would provide an excellent excuse to lure Tom over for a quickie kiss.

Tom took my call and said he would arrange for someone to pick up the flyer. He sounded distracted, but if I were responsible for catching the killer of an important member of the business community, I'd be preoccupied myself.

Seconds after I hung up, Mr. Boxer buzzed and asked me to join him in his office. The invitation didn't sound optional, so I grabbed a legal pad and headed for the stairs. My boss worked on the second floor executive level. The management team occupied glass-fronted offices furnished with shiny mahogany desks and matching credenzas. Framed black-and-white prints of scenes from Placerville's nineteenth century heyday lined the hallway. I stopped to look at a few photos featuring such luminaries as John Studebaker, who wheel-barrowed his way to fame, and former President Ulysses S. Grant. The nostalgic memorabilia made me wonder if Gran had any old photos of my great-great-grandfather.

When I noticed Mr. Boxer glaring at me from his doorway, I stepped up my pace and followed him into his office. Large cardboard packing boxes covered the floor of the huge and normally immaculate room. His bulbous nose twitched as he gazed in distaste at the dusty, slightly battered cartons. I sensed that before this meeting ended, I would wish for the ability to twitch my nose and make the boxes disappear from sight.

Mr. Boxer lowered himself into his massive navy leather chair. I sat in the far less comfortable visitor chair, pen poised to take notes. He gestured at the haphazard stack. "Yesterday Mr. Chandler decided Hangtown Bank should participate in the Wagon Train decorating contest. He feels it will boost employee morale after that nasty event earlier in the week."

I assumed the nasty event Mr. Boxer referred to was Darius Spencer's hanging. I uncrossed my legs then crossed them again, wondering what my involvement would be. I could devise a cheerful flyer or memo to boost the staff's spirits.

"So, there you go," he said, pointing at the cartons.

There I go where?

I tried not to look confused, but that proved to be impossible. "I'm unclear how you want me to help with this project."

He jerked a thumb at the boxes. "You're in charge of decorating the bank for Wagon Train week. These items have been stored offsite since the last time the bank participated. You'll have a small budget to work with in case you need to purchase additional things."

"You have got to be kidding," I said, then promptly regretted my words. If there was one thing Mr. Boxer was not, it was a kidder.

"No," he said, drawing the word out into three syllables. "I'm not. But you have an entire week to complete the project. If necessary, you can request assistance from other employees."

My eyes lit up with relief that I would have extra help.

"When they're on break," he clarified. "We certainly can't take valuable staff away from their regular workload."

Meaning that my work didn't have value? I opened my mouth to protest then closed it just as quickly. I needed this job. Not only did

I have two children to feed, if Hank didn't get back to work soon, there could be another mouth at the dinner table in the near future.

Mr. Boxer requested I remove the boxes from his office at once, so I went in search of some assistance. Stan's cubicle was empty indicating he was on his break. I zipped through the mortgage department cubicles and entered the staff break room.

Stan stood at the counter stirring a cup of coffee, chatting with one of the other underwriters.

"I need your help," I said to him.

He scanned me from the top of my loose-fitting aqua blouse to the bottom of my beat-up straw wedge sandals.

"I can see that," he replied. "When do you want to go shopping?"

I tried to look affronted, but Stan was right. In the last three months, I'd dropped eight pounds due to my energetic weekly workouts. My old summer clothes looked less appealing on me than potato sacks.

Or even potato skins.

"A shopping expedition would be wonderful, but it will have to wait a week or two. I need your expertise to help decorate the bank for Wagon Train week."

Stan frowned. "I'm really more into Art Deco than nineteenth-century furnishings."

I mimed a goodbye to our co-worker and pushed Stan out of the break room. "Anyone can do Art Deco. But how many people can successfully design Wagon Train deco?"

It took almost an hour for Stan and me to carry the cartons from Mr. Boxer's office down to mine. Since my office had originally served as the bank's supply room, one wall retained storage shelves, which we used to stack some of the boxes. The rest we piled on the floor leaving a narrow path from my desk to the door. We decided to sift through the boxes over our lunch break and then determine what else we needed. Stan left my office and seconds later Deputy Fletcher knocked on my office door.

The good-looking deputy grimaced at my mess.

"I hope these boxes aren't the evidence Tom sent me over to pick up?" Fletch asked.

"No, they're my problem, not yours." I reached into my drawer and pulled out the baggie. "Someone hung this flyer on the bulletin board next door. I doubt it has any merit but thought Tom should check it out. Are you helping investigate Spencer's murder?"

Fletch shook his head and dropped into the side chair. "I kind of hoped they'd utilize me in homicide for this investigation, but I haven't been involved at all. I did hear they may be close to an arrest."

"That's great news. Do you have any idea who it is?"

"Nope. They've been real close-mouthed on this one. The department is still short one detective since they promoted Lieutenant Hunter last February, which is why I hoped to move up the ranks. But they've brought in a couple of detectives from Sacramento County instead."

"Hey, you'd be a great investigator," I said. Fletch may have been a football star, but he'd also been a member of the national honor society with me. He definitely wasn't a dumb jock, like a certain former classmate turned ex-husband.

"Thanks for the vote of confidence." Fletch stood, the giant baggie in hand. "So are you managing to keep Hank out of trouble?"

I sighed with so much gusto the evidence bag floated out of his hand. "I didn't think once we divorced that keeping an eye on him would still be included in my job description."

Fletch bent over to retrieve the baggie. "Hey, the guy misses you."

"Yeah, well, maybe you can entertain him for a change."

He laughed. "Sure, I'll give him a call and we'll go out."

The deputy had one foot out the door when I had a thought. "Fletch, are you working on that Clarkson cold case?"

He shrugged. "Sort of. Tom asked me to check on that old bullet."

"Can you determine the weapon from a bullet that's over a century old?"

He put his hand up. "Only if we retrieve the original gun and match it up. But this bullet is somewhat distinct. It looks like a Minié ball, developed during the Civil War, which was widely used by a variety of guns. Prior to the invention of this conical shaped bullet, ammunition consisted of small spherical balls."

Fletch must have noticed my glazed look because he quickly ended his historical ballistics lecture. "Basically this bullet narrows the time period to sometime between 1862 and mid to late 1870's. I didn't think this case was a priority though."

"My Gran is in a tizzy thinking she could be the granddaughter of a murderer, and I'm worried it could impact her health. So proving someone else did the deed is a huge concern for me."

"I'll see what I can do. Maybe if I solve the cold case, it will help me get that promotion."

"I'll owe you big time if you can prove no one in my family had anything to do with Clarkson's death."

"You got it," he said with a wave, almost ramming into someone standing in the doorway. Speak of the ex.

"Hey, Fletch, man," Hank said. He and Fletch did some kind of goofy knuckle bump thing.

"What are you doing here?" Hank asked Fletch as he perched on one corner of my desk and winked at me. "Is Laurel in trouble again?"

I glared at Hank. "Get your butt off my desk. And why *is* your sorry bottom in my office anyway?"

"I hoped you had some pull with your, um, 'boyfriend.'" Hank did air quotes. "Janet gave me the okay to continue the remodel. The crime scene tape is gone, but both doors are padlocked." Hank turned to Fletch. "Do you have any idea how much longer before I can gain access?"

Fletch's radio squawked before he could answer Hank's question. I told Fletch he could use the empty office next to mine to take the call. A few minutes later, my cell rang. I smiled when I saw Tom's name on the line. I made a shooing motion to Hank, who eventually got the hint and left my office.

"How's the case going?" I asked, feeling a tingling sensation in my lady parts, which always responded to the sound of Tom's voice. I wondered if Pavlov had ever done a study on that kind of reaction.

"The case has taken an unusual turn," he said. "Deputy Fletcher told me Hank is in your office."

"He dropped by to see if I would ask a favor of you. Hank needs access to the hotel so he can begin work again. I don't want to influence your investigation, but the sooner he gets back to remodeling the hotel, the sooner he's out of both of our hair."

A heavy sigh resounded over the line. "He may be out of your hair sooner than you anticipated. Hey, I need to go. Please remember that I—"

I heard shouting in the background. "Aw, crap," he said. "I'll call you tonight."

Fletch poked his head around the corner of my office. "Where did Hank go?"

I shrugged. "I'm not the boss of him. I have no idea."

Fletch cursed then galloped down the hallway heading for the teller area.

What was going on with the Sheriff's Department? They all sounded over-caffeinated today. Out of curiosity, I decided to follow Fletch. I reached the bank lobby, which as usual on a Friday, was wall-to-wall with merchants and seniors.

Friday was also cookie day!

I grabbed a Nutter Butter. It couldn't compete with Gran's cookies but would do in a crunch.

I chuckled at my silly pun then flung open the bank door. Doug Blake, the bookstore owner, almost mowed me down in his effort to get inside and to the section cordoned off for our merchant customers.

Once out the door, I paused on the sidewalk, looking to the right then to the left where Fletch and Hank stood next to the Hangtown Hotel, a few doors down from the bank. They appeared to be in a heated discussion. Their conversation was probably none of my business, but that had never stopped me before. It also looked like they could use a mediator.

I'd only taken a few steps in their direction when the shrill cry of a siren brought me to a halt. A dusty white sedan bearing the imprint of the El Dorado County Sheriff's Office rocketed down Sacramento Street. Its tires squealed as the car rounded the corner, nearly taking out a bystander waiting to cross Main Street.

The car pulled into a vacant parking spot in front of Antiques Galore, across the street from where Hank and Fletch stood. They stopped arguing to stare at the new arrivals. Two men, one in a suit and another in uniform, jumped out of the car and crossed the street.

Geez. Was someone robbing the bank?

No, that couldn't be the case because the officers were heading away from the bank, striding toward the Bell Tower. Some shoppers stopped to watch the men. Others scurried in the opposite direction. Something I should have done myself. Instead, I watched a deputy stop in front of the Hangtown Hotel, grab my ex-husband's forearm and twist it behind his back.

Then he handcuffed him.

CHAPTER SIXTEEN

If I hadn't seen it with my own eyes, I never would have believed it. My ex-husband Mirandized on Main Street then shoved into the backseat of a squad car. I darted between two SUVs crawling down the street, their drivers gawking at the scene, paying no heed to pedestrians attempting to cross to the other side.

The squad car flashed its left turn signal and pulled out seconds before I reached it. Through the dust-spotted rear window, Hank's frightened eyes met mine. He mouthed the words "help me" as the vehicle merged into traffic.

Fletch busied himself with pedestrian traffic control, attempting to persuade the numerous bystanders to go their merry way. Not being in a merry mood myself, I marched up to the deputy and punched him on his khaki-clad arm.

His hand instantly moved to his holster. When Fletch realized who'd hit him, he had the decency to look abashed. "Sorry, I didn't find out about the arrest until I got that radio call."

"Some friend you are, Deputy." I spat out the words. "What was that all about? Why did they handcuff Hank?"

Fletch put a hand under my elbow and tried to lead me down the street. "Do you want to get some coffee so we can talk?"

"I don't have time for chit chat. Why did they haul my husband away?" I shook my head, so rattled I wasn't thinking clearly. "I mean my ex-husband. I have a right to know what's going on." I ducked around Fletch then noticed a short man with a brown goatee and a zealous gleam in his eyes loping down the sidewalk in our direction.

"Before my kids and I find out in the local paper. Here comes Neil Schwartz from the *Mountain Democrat*."

Fletch whipped his head around. "Shoot, there's no way I'm going to be responsible for telling the paper they arrested Hank for murder. That's the lieutenant's job."

I froze, my stomach feeling as if I had swallowed a fifty-six ounce slushie. "You're not serious."

Fletch nodded. "Dead serious."

"But Tom didn't say anything to me." Not one single word.

"Oh, c'mon, Laurel, you can't expect Tom to share stuff like this with you."

"He's had no problem sharing my…" I said then stopped. My personal business was none of Fletch's business.

Fletch led me to the gelato café a few doors down. He ordered a small cup of chocolate for each of us. I told him that I felt too upset to eat, but he insisted on treating. He must have thought the frozen dessert would cool me down. We took our bowls to the back of the restaurant and sat at a corner table.

"So you have no idea what evidence they have on Hank?" I stared at the gelato as if the frozen dessert could miraculously provide answers to my questions.

"Nope. I'm not even sure Tom has been kept abreast of everything. From what I've heard around the office, I think he was concerned about a conflict because of your relationship with him. That's why he brought in investigators from Sacramento County."

I dipped into the gelato to be polite. It did make me feel better— for all of two seconds.

"I don't understand how Tom could arrest Hank without discussing it with me first. What does that say about our relationship?"

Fletch looked confused. "But you don't even like Hank."

"That's irrelevant." I frowned at the deputy. "Plus now that Hank's been arrested, who's going to look for the actual murderer?"

CHAPTER SEVENTEEN

Despite my protestations that I was too upset to eat any gelato, I managed to finish every bite. With my brain and body re-energized, I jumped out of my chair with new resolve. I had an ex-husband to get out of jail. Then I peeked at my watch. And a job to get back to before my boss noticed my disappearance.

I thanked Fletch for the gelato, gave him my cell number and asked him to call when he had any news he felt he could share. He encouraged me to contact Tom for more details, but I was still too annoyed to call my boyfriend.

I realized that as head of the homicide division, Tom had no obligation to keep me informed of his crime-fighting activities. But I also felt, however irrationally, that Dear Abby would concur that proper etiquette decrees your boyfriend should warn you when he's about to arrest your ex-husband.

I shoved open the door to the bank and found the lobby devoid of customers. And cookies. Only a few crumbs littered the trays. I trotted down the hallway hoping my lengthy absence had gone unnoticed. I zipped through the doorway, completely forgetting about the boxes Stan and I had carried in earlier. I crashed into a stack of cartons knocking one of them over as well as myself.

Seconds later, Stan found me sprawled on the floor with a mountain of fake gold nuggets and coins strewn on my lap and around the carpet.

"Did you decide to decorate without me?" he asked. He lent me a hand and pulled me up off the floor.

"No, only moving too quickly," I said ruefully. "I have some urgent business to attend to."

Stan picked up the fallen box and started repacking it. "Like getting Hank out of jail?"

"You heard?"

He stuck the carton on top of a shorter, sturdier stack of boxes then sat down. "Mary Lou saw his arrest on her lunch break." Stan looked at me. "Did you see that one coming?"

I glared at him. "Of course not."

"Don't forget Hank punched Darius Spencer at the fundraiser."

"Yeah, but they worked everything out. Hank didn't mention any issues other than Spencer being a cheapskate."

"Well, sweetie, your ex isn't the most communicative of men, is he?" Stan crossed his legs, brushing off a minuscule fleck of gold from his pressed taupe trousers.

"True." I sighed. "Hank either under-communicates or over-communicates."

"Maybe he and Spencer over-communicated together and got into another fight. Didn't Hank mention a problem with some cost-cutting measures Spencer wanted to implement that would affect the safety of the building?"

"Yes, but that's not a good reason to murder someone."

Stan cocked his head. "So there are good reasons for murder?"

I threw my hands in the air. "You know what I mean."

"Have you talked to your honey?"

"I'm not sure I still have a honey," I corrected him.

"Did you and Tom have an argument over Hank's arrest?"

"Tom and I haven't spoken," I said, my voice chillier than the gelato I'd eaten earlier.

"Hey, you can't blame the man for doing his job."

"His job entails arresting the right person. There are a lot of people who didn't care for Darius Spencer."

Stan grinned. "So it looks like another case for us. I hope my detecting skills haven't gotten rusty since Hawaii."

From what I could recall, the extent of Stan's detecting on the Big Island consisted of him infiltrating his scrawny body into a troupe of super-sized Samoan dancers supposedly in search of clues. But at this point I would take what I could get.

My cell rang with my mother's ring tone. I dug into my purse and caught it before she hung up. I flicked my head in the direction of the door. Stan amazingly got the hint and left my office.

I hit the green answer button and greeted my mother with a dejected hello.

"I gather from your tone of voice you've heard the news about Hank," she said.

"I had the honor of watching him get cuffed then thrown in the back seat of the squad car. How did you find out? It only happened a little while ago."

"Tom called Robert earlier today to get his advice."

"Gee, it would have been nice if he'd asked me for some guidance," I grumbled. "Do you or your husband have any idea why they think Hank killed Spencer?"

"Tom may have shared that information with Robert but, if so, he didn't choose to pass it on to me. I assume my husband would prefer that I stay out of police business."

"Hank is the father of your grandchildren," I pointed out. "That makes it *our* business."

"True." Mother giggled. "Maybe I can seduce Robert into revealing something to me tonight in bed."

Ick! I closed my eyes hoping she wouldn't feel the need to reveal anything further to her daughter—like their favorite position.

"Okay, Mom, why don't you, um, implement your plan," I replied, trying not to visualize any nighttime frolicking between the couple. "And I'll work on mine."

I hung up the phone and leaned back in my chair. Maybe I was looking at this situation the wrong way. If Mother could use her womanly wiles on her husband, perhaps the same method could work with my detective.

It was time that I embarked on an undercover mission.

Forget the trench coat and deerstalker hat.

My next stop would be Naughty Nellie's.

CHAPTER EIGHTEEN

I had barely hung up the phone when bank employees began wandering into my office to commiserate with me. While Facebook and Twitter might represent the new information highway, small town gossip frequently outpaced online avenues. By day's end, I felt grateful my tiny office only held room for a couple of gossip girls at a time. The one bright spot in this disastrous day was a personal visit from the bank president.

Having been embroiled in a murder investigation himself five months ago, Mr. Chandler lent a sympathetic ear to my situation. He stopped by to see how I was holding up. His gesture touched me, although I realized it might have something to do with me providing him with a "get out of jail free" card last year.

Now I needed to figure out how to do the same for Hank.

I asked Mr. Chandler if I could leave early and he agreed. I needed to discuss Hank's arrest with my kids before they heard about it through the media. Although the odds of my children watching the evening news were low, the odds of someone posting the arrest on Facebook were high. Mr. Boxer seemed unsympathetic about my situation, but he could hardly overrule the bank president. I promised my boss I would come in early on Monday to begin my new project and that seemed to pacify him.

I left work and drove to Greenhills, our semi-rural subdivision located six miles west of downtown Placerville. My cell rang when I was less than a mile from home. Rather than risk an accident trying to locate my Bluetooth, I decided to wait until I reached the house to return the call.

I hit the remote door opener and pulled into the two-car garage of the Craftsman-styled home built shortly after Jenna's birth. Seconds later, the door leading into the house opened, and my two kids sprinted across the garage.

"Mommy, Daddy's in trouble," yelled Ben.

I opened the car door, grabbed my purse, and eased myself out. Ben flung himself at me, almost knocking me over.

Jenna hovered behind him. "Did you hear what happened to Dad?" Her eyes were red-rimmed and dried tears streaked her freckled cheeks.

I hugged both kids and with an arm around each of them, led them into the house. Despite my stomach feeling as if it was tied in multiple knots, I attempted to maintain a calm demeanor as we walked into the kitchen and sat at the table. "How did you learn about your father?" I asked.

Ben pointed at his sister. "Jenna saw Daddy on TV."

"I turned on *Ellen* to catch her Taylor Swift interview," Jenna said. "During the commercial, that woman broadcaster, the one with the real short skirts—"

I interrupted her. "You mean Leila Hansen?"

Jenna nodded. "Yeah, the slutty looking one. She announced the sheriff had arrested the 'Hangtown Killer' and that more information would follow on the six o'clock news. Then they showed Dad being walked into the jail with two deputies by his side." Tears rolled down her cheeks, and she made no effort to staunch the flow.

I stood and grabbed a tissue from the box on the counter then kissed her on the forehead. As if being a teenager doesn't provide enough angst, murder kept intruding into her life.

"Why would anyone think Dad killed Mr. Spencer?" Jenna asked.

"I wish I knew," I said, shaking my head slowly. "I spoke with your grandmother, and she's hoping your grandfather can find out more details from Tom."

Assuming Mother didn't get too distracted herself tonight. Sometimes it irked me a little that my baby boomer mother had more passion in her life than I did.

Prior to Hank's arrest, I'd thought Tom and I were finally making progress on the romantic front. But his career continually interfered with our relationship coming to a climax—so to speak.

"Why don't you call Tom and ask him why they put Daddy in jail?" questioned Ben, his green eyes that so resembled his father's wide and concerned.

"Well, I don't think I can do that."

"Why not?"

Why not, indeed? Certainly in the course of their investigation, the detectives must have interviewed plenty of people with opinions about Spencer's possible killer. Why didn't they bother to interrogate the ex-wife of the primary suspect?

I hugged my son. "You'll make a better detective than your mother someday. And, you're right, it's long past time that I called Kristy's father."

Before I could call Tom, the home phone rang and I recognized his cell number on Caller ID. I picked up the cordless phone and headed for the stairs and my bedroom.

I took a deep breath so I wouldn't feel compelled to blast the man on the other end.

"I bet you never want to see me again," said Tom, his voice low and apologetic, his comment unerringly accurate.

"That thought crossed my mind once or ten times today," I replied.

"Look, I wish I could have warned you, but I've never experienced a situation like this before. I need to ensure everything is correctly handled and processed."

"I realize your predicament, but I still don't understand why you didn't give me advance warning, or at least ask my opinion."

"No one else is so closely tied to a suspect. I couldn't take a chance on you warning Hank and him taking off. Leaving the area or even the country."

"Hank would never disappear like that," I argued. "And he would certainly never kill someone."

"You never know what sets people off."

"Tom, I know Hank didn't do it."

"That's your emotions talking."

"Obviously I'm emotional about it. But from an intellectual standpoint, Hank doesn't hold up as a killer."

"We have evidence that says otherwise."

"What kind of evidence?" Maybe I could weasel some answers without resorting to a trip to Naughty Nellie's. Although I was somewhat curious as to how naughty Nellie's nighties were.

"I can't share that information with you," Tom said through what sounded like gritted teeth, a frequent occurrence in our rocky relationship.

"You'll have to release your evidence to Hank's defense attorney, so you might as well share it with me. I'll find out sooner or later."

"It doesn't work that way."

"It will, if I have any choice in his attorney. Do you know who Hank hired?"

"I'm not sure. Detective Hennessey is the lead detective. He's on loan from Sacramento County, but he'll be working with the El Dorado County District Attorney's office."

"I don't suppose Brian..." I began.

Tom interrupted. "Don't even think of getting Brian involved. And I have no idea which Deputy DA will get assigned the case."

"So...?" My head spun with unanswered questions about Hank's arrest.

"So, are we good?" Tom asked.

ARE WE GOOD? Was he serious?

"With the investigation closed, I can keep our date tomorrow night." Tom's voice softened. "Any chance the two of us can be alone?"

"Since you've locked up the kids' weekend babysitter, what do you think?" Could he hear the frost dripping over the line?

"Look, Laurel, I really want to see you. We need to discuss this face to face, not over the phone."

"Well...," I hesitated.

"It's been a long time since I held you in my arms," he coaxed. "I've missed you."

My girls perked up at his tender words. So much for my resolve.

"Okay, we'll keep our date tomorrow night," I agreed. I mentally vowed to stay cool and composed during our time together. I'd firmly resist Tom's toffee brown eyes, full lips, muscular chest, and born-to-wear-tight-jeans tush.

And I had exactly twenty-four hours to figure out how I would actually do that.

I'd barely hung up the phone when it rang again. I didn't recognize the number, but since it belonged in our area code, I answered it. When the operator asked if I would accept a collect call, I knew immediately who was on the other end.

"Thank goodness I got you," Hank said. "I worried one of the kids would pick up the phone, and I didn't want them to know what was going on."

"It's a little late for that. You made the evening news tonight."

"This is a freaking nightmare. Are Jenna and Ben okay?"

"They're upset, of course. But more important, how are you?"

"How do you think I am?" Hank's tone sounded as bitter as week-old espresso. "I'm in a cell near a drunk who's been singing 'Home on the Range' nonstop for the last three hours. I've got to get out of here."

"Have you hired an attorney?"

"They said I don't qualify for a public defender. That I make too much income. That's a laugh," he said, although I could tell from his tone that he was closer to crying than laughing. "So what should I do? I don't hang out with criminal attorneys. Can you help me?"

"Bradford or Brian might have some suggestions as to a good defense attorney. I'll see what I can find out. Anything else?"

"Just pray for me."

"Do you have any idea what kind of evidence they have against you?"

"No. It must be some kind of stupid mistake."

"Tom and I are having dinner tomorrow night. Maybe he'll share something with me."

"You're still dating that jerk?" Hank sounded more horrified than if I were dating a zombie. "After he arrested your husband? I bet he threw me in jail to get me out of your life."

"Ex-husband," I corrected. "And I'm as upset as you are. But this has to be some kind of mix-up."

"Let's hope so," Hank said. "If not—"

I heard a click followed by the dial tone.

CHAPTER NINETEEN

It didn't surprise me that Mother's vast database of real estate clients included an attorney or two who specialized in criminal law. Bradford chimed in with a list of defense attorneys he'd butted heads with in the past. A few of them, he grudgingly admitted, were darn good at their jobs.

After reviewing the list, I placed a call to Rex Ashford, the top defense lawyer in town according to both Bradford and Brian. My rooster clock chimed twelve times in the background, each chime sounding louder and surlier than the last, reminding me it was midnight. I assumed Rex wouldn't respond until the morning, but criminal attorneys apparently keep odd hours. He picked up on the third ring.

I shared everything I knew about Hank's situation with Rex, which took all of about thirty seconds. Since he practiced in Placerville, he already knew about the case. He promised to contact the Sheriff's Office immediately to determine what evidence they possessed. Then he would meet with Hank as soon as possible the following day.

"It isn't often, Ms. McKay, that I receive a call from a woman looking to hire an attorney on behalf of her ex-husband," he said. "Usually they want me to find a way to put their ex-husband *in jail*, not get him out."

"Well, we're one big dysfunctional family. I should probably inform you that Detective Tom Hunter and I have been dating the past few months. That may have complicated the situation a tad."

"You and Hunter are together?" Rex roared with laughter. "This case is getting more and more interesting."

The attorney continued to chuckle as we hung up. As I climbed into bed, I realized we'd never discussed his fee structure. I suspected criminal defense attorneys made more in a few hours than I made in a week. Maybe he'd give a discount for the most entertaining case of the year.

I closed my eyes and tried counting sheep, but my busy brain decided to count the funds in my savings account instead. I finally realized it would be easier to solve the case myself than it would be to find the money to pay for an attorney. A Saturday morning visit to the Main Street businesses might provide a few answers to my many questions. It also might provide me with a hot outfit to entice my even hotter detective into divulging a detail or two about his latest homicide case.

I woke the next morning even more exhausted than the night before. I scrutinized my cheeks in the mirror, hoping the tiny lines creasing my face were due to me hugging my pillow all night and not a sign of my impending fortieth birthday.

The men in my life were certainly not helping me age gracefully.

The kids remained asleep, so I crept down the stairs into the kitchen. I brewed coffee then went outside to retrieve the morning paper. A few minutes later, I sat at the table with a cup of hot Kona coffee and a bowl of bran flakes in front of me. I flipped through the reams of advertising and finally pulled out the main section of the *Sacramento Bee*, which for some reason always ended up buried among the ads. I grabbed my spoon, turned the front page over and immediately dropped the utensil on the floor.

It had been several years since I'd gazed at my ex-husband over the breakfast table. This morning Hank faced me from the front page in full handcuffed ignominy.

The headline read *Hangman Arrested in Hangtown Homicide*.

The reporter spent several paragraphs detailing Darius Spencer's candidacy as well as his numerous community activities. The article said the victim had hired Hank to remodel the Hangtown Hotel. That was the sole mention of my ex. Not a scrap of information on the reason for Hank's arrest. Nor any mention that he'd formerly been married to *moi*. A fortunate omission but likely a short-lived respite. The odds of a reporter calling the ex-wife for a comment were increasing by the minute.

I shoved back my chair with so much force it smacked against the wall. Then I dumped my untouched cereal down the drain. If I didn't help Hank get out of jail, my children could be scarred for life.

This mother was not about to let that happen.

There was little time to waste. If I wanted to pick up any gossip, the first place I should start would be the Hangtown Bakery where I could find hot donuts and even hotter gossip. I had a feeling Hank and I would need all the help we could get.

An hour later, I sniffed the soothing scents of cinnamon, chocolate and coffee permeating the air at Hangtown Bakery. A hint of something else tickled my sensory memory bank. A voice cackled from the rear of the large room, and nostalgia flooded my being as I recognized the familiar scent.

Mothballs and magnolia. My grandmother's favorite perfume combined with the smell of her closets brought back memories of my youth, playing hide and seek with my brother in the nooks and crannies of her house. Gosh, I hated to think of her selling that beautiful old Victorian. It might be time to chat with my mother and see if I could talk her out of listing Gran's property.

You can't put a price on childhood memories.

Gran waved at me from her table in the rear. I squeezed between the crowded tables to join her and her friends. The three Miss Marples from the historical society blinked at me from behind their thick glasses. If not for their jogging outfits, each in a different pastel color, I'd never be able to tell them apart.

"Just the person we wanted to see," crowed Gran. "We might've found our killer."

Thirty pastry-eating, coffee-drinking heads turned in our direction. Subtlety was not Gran's motto.

An unoccupied chair sat at the table next to Gran's. The young couple making googly eyes at each other ignored me when I asked to borrow it. I squeezed the wooden chair between Gran and Miss Marple One, the tallest of the trio.

Gran seemed perturbed by my lack of enthusiasm. "You don't look all that excited about our discovery."

"Oh, no, that's great," I said. "One less dead body for me to worry about."

She patted my palm with her own small hand. "I saw the article about Hank's arrest in the paper this morning and called your mother. Barbara said you had the situation under control. How are my great-grandkids taking the news about their father?"

"Not well." My eyes started to tear. All three Miss Marples reached into their oversized purses to offer me an assortment of embroidered hankies. I didn't want my mascara to permanently stain the starched white linen, so I reached into my purse for a tissue to handle any cosmetic damage.

"I hired an attorney for Hank last night," I said, "so hopefully he'll be out of jail soon."

"Those bozos at the Sheriff's Department couldn't find a killer if he walked into their office and confessed," Gran declared to her friends.

"Don't forget I'm dating the head bozo."

"Oops." She turned to the Miss Marple to her left. "Looks like we have another mystery to solve."

"Oh, no, you don't," I said sharply. "The only murder you're allowed to investigate is your grandfather's case. So what did you find out?"

The Marples leaned in, their fluffy white heads bobbing as Gran spoke.

"You remember how those officers were all hot to close the case 'cause they found Harold's watch in the mineshaft?"

I nodded, remembering how awful I'd felt when Fletch shared that news.

"We've been reading some old *Mountain Democrat* newspapers, and they mentioned a couple of stagecoach robberies that occurred on the route from Virginia City to Placerville."

"Did Black Bart rob them?" I smiled thinking of the unarmed bandit who was so terrified of horses he robbed his victims on foot, leaving behind a poem to commemorate the occasion.

She shook her head. "Old Bart held up more than his share of coaches but not in El Dorado County. And these holdups were in the 1860s, more than a decade before Bart's time. They never figured out who robbed the stagecoaches. But someone also sneaked into homes and boarding houses. Folks lost coins, jewelry, tools and other valuable stuff. In fact, when George Clarkson disappeared, most people figured he was the culprit and he'd vamoosed with the loot."

"So how does this information help my great-great-grandfather?" I twisted around to see if the line at the counter had diminished. I was going to need some fresh coffee in order to follow my grandmother's convoluted logic.

"Maybe someone stole Harold's watch," chimed in the smallest of the Marple triplets. "And it somehow landed in the bottom of the mineshaft."

I mulled over their remarks. Their theory seemed somewhat farfetched, but I didn't want to put a damper on their detecting. "Not bad, ladies. If nothing else, it should muddle things enough so the Sheriff's Office doesn't close the case immediately. I doubt it's a high priority anyway, not with Darius Spencer's murder needing to be solved." I rested my face on my palms. "Or maybe that's no longer a priority if they think they've arrested his killer."

"There, there, child," Gran murmured in the same soothing tone she'd used on the numerous occasions when she'd bandaged my scraped knees and elbows thirty odd years ago. "The girls and I are here to help you."

"I don't want you doing anything dangerous," I instructed the women. "But I suppose a little gossip gathering couldn't hurt."

Gran's blue eyes, handed down to every generation of my family, sparkled with pleasure. "That's the spirit. We'll infiltrate the Ladies League and the Hangtown Guild. Dig up a little dirt. That will be more fun than digging in our gardens. Right, girls?" She winked at her friends and they winked back—in unison.

I knew I should forbid my grandmother and her friends to get involved. But I figured they couldn't get into too much trouble. If my childhood memories served me right, Gran had a knack for determining when someone lied to her.

The senior snoopers were officially on my payroll.

CHAPTER TWENTY

No sooner had Gran and her posse departed than a former bank employee entered the bakery. I hadn't seen Rose Garcia since she'd left Hangtown Bank to assist with Tricia Taylor's supervisorial campaign. Rose's short black bob seemed to have acquired more silver threads in the past six months.

After Rose placed her order at the counter, she scanned the room. Since customers occupied all of the tables, I waved her over.

She set down her scone and coffee, and I stood to hug her. Rose had worked in the HR department, but when Tricia asked her to help manage the campaign, she didn't hesitate to quit her job.

Sunlight streaming through the window made the sugar dotting her blueberry scone glitter brighter than the diamonds sold at Randolph's Jewelry. My stomach growled in appreciation.

"Sounds like you need a pastry refill," Rose said, biting off a chunk of her scone.

"I've yet to make it up there. Be back in a sec." I dashed to the counter before anyone else could walk through the door. With a cup of coffee in one hand and a glazed cinnamon twist in another, I rejoined her.

"How are you enjoying your new position at the bank?" Rose asked.

My doleful expression provided the answer to her question. "Mr. Boxer is a bit of a bear to work for."

"That's what his last employee said when we did her exit interview," she said. "We chatted with him about his communication skills, but it sounds like they could still use some improvement."

"Well, I've made a gaffe or two along the way." I told Rose about my Hanging Man flyer mishap.

She laughed then began choking. Chuckling while eating a scone is not a recommended activity.

I prepared to wallop her back when she stopped coughing. "Oh, Laurel, that's the funniest thing I've heard in days. I needed that. Running a political campaign has been a far more negative experience than I'd envisioned."

"How so?"

"Oh, I guess I'm naïve when it comes to this stuff. Since Tricia and I have been friends forever, it seemed an easy decision to assist with her campaign. It's just..." She stared out the window at the Saturday traffic crawling down Main Street. "I didn't realize how influential her husband would become. Or his cronies."

"Regarding some of Tricia's political positions?" I asked.

She nodded. "Tricia and I seemed in complete agreement when we first planned her campaign. I classified her as a moderate, primarily interested in improving the county's finances, keeping roads, parks, etc. well-maintained, working with agricultural and business interests to best represent them."

"Initially, I thought that, too," I said, "but she seems to have switched to an ardent pro-growth position. We could use some new businesses in this area, but with the drought impacting our water supply, and the current traffic congestion on Highway 50, I don't think we have enough resources to handle the type of residential growth she's envisioning."

Rose swallowed the last dregs of her coffee then grimaced. I couldn't determine if her expression was due to the bitter brew or her employer's opinions.

"Tricia's husband, Lars, suffered significant financial losses when the real estate economy went bust," Rose said. "He still owns huge tracts of vacant land he bought over a decade ago. He wants to develop it into high-density housing, but Spencer and his supporters were against any new development in our district."

"How does Spencer's death impact Tricia's campaign?"

"Unless someone attempts a write-in campaign, which hardly seems likely with the election in ten days, Tricia will be the only candidate for that district."

I tried to think of a tactful way to phrase my next question but decided that was impossible. I'd go with the Laurel McKay blurt-it-all-out approach.

"You don't think Lars had anything to do with Spencer's murder, do you?" I asked.

"Of course not." Her voice rose. "I'm shocked you would even suggest it. Plus they already arrested someone. I didn't catch his name, but he's a local contractor."

"That contractor is my ex-husband."

Her eyes widened. "Are you surprised he did it?"

"Hank did not kill Darius Spencer." I thumped my empty coffee cup in emphasis. "I don't know what evidence the police possess, but they have it completely wrong."

Rose didn't appear as convinced as I was. "Well, I suppose they could be mistaken."

"Have you run across anyone else who had it in for Spencer? Besides Tricia and Lars."

Rose bristled at my comment. "Tricia didn't have it *in* for the man. Obviously they didn't see eye to eye on growth in this county, but she didn't dislike him."

"Well, someone detested him enough to kill him. Maybe someone else disagreed with his position."

"Hmm, I suppose that's a possibility." She gathered the remains of her breakfast. "Some of Tricia's supporters are a tad rabid about their right to develop their property. Especially Phil McKinley, the owner of the Six Springs project. But I can't imagine anyone murdering someone over a housing development."

"Could you keep me posted if you hear anything? This is such an ordeal for my children."

"You poor thing. I'll keep my eyes and ears open." Rose looked at her watch. "I've got to get going. Tricia has a speech tonight at the Summer Festival fundraiser. These events are tough. I've put on ten pounds since her campaign started."

I gazed down at three tiny crumbs, the remains of my cinnamon twist. Detecting wasn't helping my diet plan either.

I walked out of the bakery and stared at the throngs of pedestrians cramming the sidewalks. Weekends provide a busy tourist trade for Placerville since Highway 50 takes travelers directly from Sacramento to the south shore of Lake Tahoe. You can bypass the downtown, but why do that when well-stocked antique stores line both sides of Main Street? Not to mention excellent dining options. And sweet shops.

Someone must have passed a law making it mandatory for gold rush towns to have a candy store on every block. A decision I heartily agreed with. I darted into the Candy Strike Emporium, packed as usual. Their homemade truffles and fudge were a must-have purchase.

Even though it wasn't my face on the front page of the paper this morning, I still felt like people were staring at me. I hoped I was just overly sensitive due to my new status as the divorced wife of a suspected killer. Our situation had *Lifetime* movie written all over it.

I gnawed on a piece of fudge while I ambled down the sidewalk. Maybe if I stared at the scene of the crime, some wonderful deductive thought would pierce my confused brain. Although crime scene tape no longer covered the building, several onlookers peeked into the windows. There couldn't be much to see other than dust, plywood and tools. Maybe they hoped an apparition or two would flit through the empty rooms.

From my perspective, a paranormal killer would be a definite improvement over my former husband being jailed.

I stared at the metal and wood scaffolding from the opposite side of the street. How had Spencer been killed before the murderer strung him up? Would a woman have enough strength to do the deed?

Maybe two people colluded in his death. That would have made the task much easier. Had Tom or the detectives considered they might be looking for a couple of murderers. If so, then Hank would have needed an accomplice.

Omigosh. Could that be why I'd received so many strange looks? Did people think Hank and I were in cahoots?

Shoot. We hadn't *cahooted* together in years.

Someone jostled my elbow, and I almost dropped my fudge. Doug Blake, the silver-haired bookstore owner steadied me.

"Sorry, Laurel," he apologized. "I'm trying to avoid the crowd over there, but it's almost as busy on this side. Crazy situation, huh?"

"I still can't believe someone murdered Spencer," I replied.

Doug snorted. "I can't believe it took that long for someone to knock him off."

"What?"

"Spencer gave time and money to the community," Doug said. "I'll grant him that. But he was one of the most arrogant, deceitful men I've ever run across. He was a wheeler dealer with the cards always stacked in his favor."

"Did he wheel and deal you out of anything?"

Doug took his black-rimmed glasses off, reached into his back pocket and pulled out a handkerchief. He remained silent while he cleaned both lenses. I waited, hoping he would feel compelled to fill the silence.

"What's done is done," Doug said. "Spencer is gone and Main Street is better off for it."

"Do you have any idea who might have wanted him dead?"

"I could give you a legal pad full of names, but it's not my concern. And it shouldn't be yours since they already arrested, oh…" Doug's voice trailed off when he realized who he was conversing with. "Hey, I was sorry to hear about Hank. He was so excited about this renovation."

"Yes, he was, and there's no way he would have killed Spencer."

"I can't see it myself. Although I heard him badmouthing Spencer that night right before he was killed. Well, it was actually in the wee hours of the morning."

"What are you talking about? Hank came to my house for pizza Monday night."

"He might have shared a pizza with you earlier in the evening, but he was raising heck at the Liar's Bench around midnight. That guy doesn't hold his liquor too well."

"Who else did you see in the bar?"

"It was pretty full that night. The Sacramento Kings were playing the Lakers, and the game went into double overtime. Every time the Kings tied it up with the Lakers, Lars bought a round of drinks for everyone. Trying to drum up votes for his wife, I guess. I was glad I could hoof it home instead of worrying about getting into my car."

I gnawed on my lower lip. "Did Hank drive himself home? It doesn't sound like he was in any shape to do that."

Doug pointed across the street again. "I remember Hank mentioned something about sleeping it off in the hotel. Said he had a sleeping bag and camping gear in his truck."

If Hank spent the night in the hotel, how did he sleep through someone killing Spencer and hanging him on the scaffolding?

I felt like I'd been sucker punched when I realized the cops might be right.

Maybe Hank *had* done it!

CHAPTER TWENTY-ONE

As I strolled down the sidewalk, I thought about Doug's comment regarding Hank. I simply couldn't fathom my ex as a killer, so instead I mulled over the news that the Liars' Bench bar had been crammed full of potential suspects the night of the murder. Of course, just because the men were fans of the Sacramento Kings didn't automatically make them killers.

It merely meant they were *optimists*.

Doug hadn't mentioned anything about the victim being in the bar that night. If Hank had badmouthed his boss then Spencer most likely wasn't present. I wondered how the killer lured Spencer to the hotel.

Or did the killer find out about the five a.m. meeting between Spencer and Hank?

Was there any possibility the victim was fooling around with another woman? If so, wouldn't he prefer a fluffy bed as opposed to a sawdust-filled tryst?

Perhaps Spencer was being blackmailed. Or he was blackmailing someone else.

Or maybe I'd drunk too much coffee and eaten too much sugar this morning.

I glanced down at my watch. I'd picked up useful tidbits from both Doug and Rose. According to Rose, Tricia's husband, Lars, and his developer partner, Phil McKinley, were unhappy with Spencer's no-growth platform. According to Doug, more people disliked Spencer than not.

Including Doug.

With my brain swirling with suspects, I decided to stop detecting for now. If ever an occasion justified retail therapy, this was it. I passed by Antiques Galore, one of my favorite stores. Although depression-era glass, bone china, and other collectibles normally filled the front windows, Abe Cartwell, the owner, had created a pioneer theme this week that displayed a set of valuable-looking antique pistols.

I entered the store, hoping his antiques might help me formulate some ideas for decorating the bank. Abe waved at me from behind his ancient brass cash register, where he counted out a stack of bills to a tall customer with graying hair and moustache, who stood on the opposite side of the counter. The man shoved the money in a beat-up brown wallet, which he placed in the back pocket of his faded jeans. He tipped his straw cowboy hat to me then strode out the door.

Abe came out from around the counter. "Laurel, it's been ages since I've seen you." He grabbed my hands in his large calloused ones and peered into my face. "This business with Hank got you down?"

I nodded and sniffed. "It's been tough, especially for our kids seeing their dad on the TV screen—in handcuffs."

Abe's black handlebar moustache bobbed under his hooked nose. "I can't imagine Hank committing murder, much less hanging Spencer out to dry."

"Doug Blake told me Spencer made quite a few enemies. People with better reasons to kill him than Hank."

Abe aimed his bald spot, surrounded by a ring of black curls, at the door. "Take Scott Shelton, the cowboy who just left. I can't think of anyone with a bigger grudge against Spencer."

"He looked familiar, but I couldn't place him. What was his beef with Spencer?"

"Hah. Good one." Abe smacked his thigh and hooted. "Scott owns a cattle ranch near Coloma, but he also owned the Hangtown Hotel before Spencer took it away from him."

"How and why did Spencer do that?"

"Scott couldn't get any of the banks to finance a building needing so much renovation, so Spencer loaned him the money," said Abe. "It was one of his investment company's side businesses. When Scott couldn't make the payments, Spencer foreclosed."

"That's tough. Scott must have been devastated about losing the building."

"If this occurred a hundred years ago, Scott might have challenged him to a shootout at high noon." Abe pointed to the gun display in his windows. "It's been tough for him financially. He's been leaving stuff here on consignment ever since he lost the building. Scott needs the money to purchase supplies for the ride down the hill. It's a grueling trip physically and not inexpensive either."

"Scott's participating in the Wagon Train?"

Abe nodded. "He's gone every year since he was a babe. Scott's father helped found the Wagon Train more than sixty years ago. The old man was probably rolling in his grave after Scott lost the Hangtown Hotel to Spencer. The Shelton family originally owned that property then lost it in the Depression. Scott bought it back when the previous owner needed to sell for financial reasons. He had great hopes for bringing it back to its former glory."

Interesting tidbit. Could the man whose failure might be causing his father to spin in his grave also be the man who put Darius Spencer in his?

CHAPTER TWENTY-TWO

That evening Tom and I sat across from each other in a romantic corner booth at Pappa Giannis, one of my favorite Italian restaurants located in nearby Cameron Park.

I sipped from a glass of Lava Cap chardonnay and nibbled on the restaurant's hot buttery garlic bread, carbs to die for. Not a particularly romantic food choice since anyone within kissing distance would keel over from my breath, but the delicious bread was worth it. Plus it didn't look like I'd be getting close and personal with my detective tonight. Not the way our conversation had progressed so far.

"Isn't there one tiny bit of information you can share with me?" I implored him.

"Laurel, I'm trying to stay as removed from this case as possible," he replied. "I don't want Hank's arrest to create any issues between us."

"It already has. I know you won't agree, but I don't feel like I have a choice. I need to free Hank from jail, whether it's with your help or not." I waved my hands to illustrate my point and my garlic bread flew across the table landing on Tom's plate.

"Oops, sorry. I hope you don't arrest me for assaulting a police officer with a gluten-filled weapon."

Tom drank half of his cabernet and remained silent. I couldn't.

"What kind of example would I be setting for my children if I leave their father languishing in a cell? Hank's attorney will eventually have access to the evidence. Why not speed things up and share a tidbit or two with me? We could trade information."

Tom leaned across the table and I bent forward, hoping my new teal-blue scooped neck top would distract him into sharing some clues.

"How about we trade kisses instead?" he said with a sexy smile that normally would have had me drooling in my wine glass.

But tonight I refused to get distracted. I threw out my first piece of evidence for the defense.

"I discovered the Liars' Bench Bar was packed with men watching the Kings game the night Spencer was killed," I said.

"And we found out Hank went into the Hangtown Hotel not long before Spencer's murder."

"I'm sure that's a coincidence. How did Hank explain his presence?"

Tom sighed. "I shouldn't share this, but your ex-husband claims he didn't enter the hotel until five forty when he discovered Spencer's body."

"So there you have it."

"Jake at Hangtown Bakery saw Hank enter the back door of the hotel a little after two a.m."

I sipped my wine while I processed his information. "Hank had been drinking all night. Maybe he was confused about the time."

"Was he also confused about hitting Spencer on the head?" Tom said. "We found Hank's fingerprints on a two-by-four."

"Of course, his fingerprints are on lumber. Hank is doing a lot of the renovation work himself to save that cheapskate Spencer some money."

"But why were Hank's fingerprints on a two-by-four that had Spencer's blood on the opposite end?" Tom asked.

Our server chose that moment to deliver our entrees, gnocchi for Tom and pasta alla Vodka for me. After Tom's last remark, I needed a pitcher alla Vodka. My ex-husband had a lot of explaining to do.

After our uncomfortable dinner and short silent drive back to my house, Tom pulled his car into my driveway. We sat in silence—two stubborn people, each waiting for the other to make the first move.

Tom reached for my left hand. His fingers gently traced a circle on my palm before they started working their nimble way up my arm. I trembled at his touch. I needed to have a heart-to-heart talk with my erogenous zones, many of which I hadn't known existed until I met the sexy detective.

Tom began to kiss me, starting at my wrist then working his heart-escalating magic up my forearm, creating a magnetic force that caused me to slide closer to him.

I might have principles, but I am not a statue. He tucked one of my errant curls behind my ear, and my resolve melted faster than ice cream on a hot summer's day. I turned to meet his eager lips, my breasts pressing into his chest. I could feel his heart pumping, and the hardening of his...

Ouch. Darn that gearshift.

I pulled away, panting. A wise decision since every window of my house appeared to be open.

Tom blew out a breath. "I'm glad you're not mad at me."

I waited a few seconds before replying. "I know this is a big case. Considering Spencer's involvement in our community, I'm sure a lot of pressure has been put on you and your team to solve it quickly."

Tom reached for my hand and turned to me. "I'm relieved you can sympathize with what I've been going through. Hank would not have been arrested if the Sheriff didn't feel one hundred percent certain. The District Attorney is comfortable with the evidence the detectives brought to him. I realize it must be horrible to discover your husband is a killer. Maybe they argued, and it got out of control. Hank admitted to the detectives he'd been drinking heavily that night."

"In fifteen years of marriage, Hank never once laid an angry hand on me. And, difficult though it may be to believe, I can occasionally be annoying."

Tom chuckled at my comment.

"What I can't figure out is why someone hung Spencer on the scaffolding," I said.

"It might have seemed like a good idea at the time. When people are under the influence, they commit some strange acts. Trust me, when I worked in San Francisco, I saw things far weirder and more disgusting than Spencer's corpse hanging over Main Street."

I shuddered, contemplating the hideous crimes Tom had confronted in the past. What must it be like to face reminders of the uglier side of life on a daily basis?

"I wish you could look at this from my point of view," I pleaded with Tom. "Other than a younger brother on the east coast who Hank hasn't seen in years, he has no family besides the kids and me. Someone has to be there for him."

Tom volleyed a shot back to me. "He must have friends he can count on."

"Of course, he does. But it's not the same."

"Hank is one lucky man to have you in his camp. Not many ex-wives who were dumped for another woman would be this supportive."

"Guess I'm just a softy," I said, "although it helped when he admitted leaving me was the dumbest thing he ever did."

Until now. I sincerely hoped my loyalty toward my children's father didn't prove to be one of the biggest mistakes of *my* life.

"Laurel, I assure you we have the right guy," Tom said firmly. "You need to let this go."

"Look, I promise to stay out of your way. But you have to know that I'll do whatever it takes to help Hank. I have to for the kids' sake."

"I admire your loyalty," Tom said, his eyes glimmering with concern. "But keep in mind if the detectives are wrong and Hank didn't murder Darius Spencer, then there is a killer out there who will do anything to prevent discovery."

CHAPTER TWENTY-THREE

Sunday morning I temporarily shifted from detecting mode into domestic diva mode. Every year I invite family and friends over for a pre-Memorial Day celebration. Even though Hank's arrest dampened my mood, I didn't want to cancel our get-together.

Jenna attempted to maintain a stoic front, but occasionally I noticed tears glistening in her eyes as she helped dust and vacuum. My heart went out to my poor daughter, making me feel helpless. Ben adopted a proactive approach. He pinned Bradford's old badge on his Spiderman tee shirt, grabbed a pen and small pad of paper and proceeded to search the house for clues. Pumpkin followed in his wake, evidently not worried about that old "curiosity killed the cat" adage.

I didn't want to discourage Ben from detecting since it kept him and the cat occupied. Plus, his search eventually led to the discovery of two missing G. I. Joes, an old tube of mascara and a melted Milk Dud.

At the supermarket, I purchased burgers, hot dogs, buns, and beverages. My guests insisted on contributing appetizers and salads. I wasn't certain if their offers reflected on my culinary abilities, but I'm all for delegating when it comes to domestic duties. The fewer hours I spent slaving over a stove meant the more time I could allocate to my investigative checklist.

With a few minutes to spare before my company arrived, I ripped a couple of pages out of Detective Ben's notebook and created a short list of my own suspects.

Tricia and Lars Taylor. Political opponents of Spencer's no-growth policy. Were they willing to win the election at any cost so Lars could pursue his own commercial development?

Phil McKinley. The rabid pro-growth subdivision developer.

Janet Spencer. The spouse must always be included as a potential suspect. Especially one rumored to have an unhappy marriage.

Any of the Main Street proprietors who didn't approve of Spencer's renovation plans. That could be a long list or a list of one—bookstore owner Doug Blake.

Spencer foreclosed on several people, including my mother's client and Scott Shelton. Could there be others that he'd brought to financial ruin?

The more suspects I added, the more dismayed I became. This investigation might require an army of amateur detectives. Fortunately, my crack team or as Tom might refer to them, my crackpot team of detectives, were gathering here today.

Mother and Bradford were first to arrive with Gran huddled in the back seat of their SUV. Mother did not condone her own mother's hot rod purchase, so she had restricted Gran to daytime driving and within the Placerville city limits. When Gran took to the road in her convertible, her matching red boa flying in the breeze, the locals knew to give her a wide berth.

Bradford beeped open the rear power door of the car, reached in and pulled out two large covered bowls. He handed them to Mother and Gran then grabbed a six-pack of beer in one hand and a shopping bag in the other. From the doorway, I could hear Gran and Mother arguing as they walked down my sidewalk. I sensed Bradford might need the entire six-pack before this day ended.

Gran thrust her salad bowl in my hands. "Laurel, please inform your mother to butt out of my business and mind her own beeswax."

Yeah, right.

Mother's face suffused with anger. "Maybe if you'd maintain some decorum, I wouldn't need to get involved in your beeswax. You've created a very sticky situation for me."

Bradford threw me a half-hearted smile and followed his wife into my house. I debated whether I was brave enough to get in my car and take off, leaving the women to squabble the night away without any help from me, something they'd been doing since the day I was born. The flavorful aroma of my grandmother's honey-baked beans made my decision for me. They were too good to pass up.

The kids must have heard our guests' arrival because they were already downstairs hugging Mother, Gran and Bradford. I made room in my refrigerator for the salad bowls and brought out some appetizers—chips, salsa and my homemade guacamole, prepared with a super-secret ingredient that I will take to my grave.

Or sell for a large sum of money.

We moved outside to the back patio, shaded by the wide overhang Hank astutely insisted on adding when he designed our home. I couldn't deny that my ex-husband knew how to build a decent house. My family settled into cushioned chairs around my glass-topped table.

Memorial Day weekends are notorious for their erratic temperatures, ranging from triple digits in the valley to below freezing in the Sierras. Today we enjoyed a postcard-perfect azure sky with the thermometer hovering in the mid eighties. A light breeze tickled the birch trees, which swayed together in perfect unison.

Mother and I chose chardonnay for our beverage of choice while Gran helped herself to one of Bradford's pale ales. Gran noticed Mother's gaze directed at the bottle gripped in her wrinkled hand.

"What's your problem?" she said. "I'm not driving so I may as well be drinking."

Gran leaned back, resting her Donna Reed pageboy bob against the back of the cushioned chair while her gaze roved around my tree-filled backyard. "This is nice, Laurel. Once your mother forces me out of my own house, I might move in here with you. It would be a sight better than living with all of those old folks at Golden Hills Manor."

Bradford snorted but wisely kept his silence. Jenna and Ben threw me matching frantic looks.

Before I could tactfully decline my grandmother's invitation to become my bunkmate, Mother chimed in. "Half the residents at Golden Hills are friends of yours, Ma. Wouldn't it be wonderful if you didn't have to get in your car in order to play bridge or bunco? Plus all of your meals would be prepared. You wouldn't have any maintenance issues to worry about—no broken heaters, leaky plumbing or skunks hiding under your front porch."

Gran scowled at her daughter. "Better the skunks you can see than the skunks you can't."

Whoa. Was that a metaphor? Or had Gran drunk a little too much ale?

"Speaking of skunks," I interrupted with possibly the world's worst segue, "I've learned quite a bit about Darius Spencer. The man appeared to be a workaholic involved in numerous community activities, but he doesn't seem all that popular in certain circles."

"That's what the gals and I discovered," Gran announced with a triumphant smile.

"Yes, but did you have to ask every Main Street store owner if they wanted to string Darius up?" Mother carped at her. "If you're going to help Laurel, you need to use some tact."

"Tact don't loosen tongues. You gotta catch 'em off guard to find out what they really think; otherwise, they clam up."

Mother's face turned the same shade of burgundy as my chair cushions. She looked like she wanted to make Gran clam up on a permanent basis.

"So what did you learn, Gran?" I asked.

"The gals and I stopped at the stores where Tricia posted her flyers," she said. "We figured those owners might have a beef with Spencer."

"Makes sense," I agreed.

"That's what I told your mother. The BBQ Bonanza planned to open up another restaurant in Shingle Springs, but Spencer's no-growth plan would keep the small shopping center from ever getting built."

"I don't suppose they admitted to killing him." I chuckled at my silliness.

"Nope." She shook her head, reached into the pocket of her elastic waist jeans and pulled out a lime green piece of paper. "But they gave me a twenty-five dollar-gift certificate to pass along to the killer, should I happen to run across him or her."

"That's disgusting," said Mother.

True, but also fascinating.

"Anything else?" I asked, hoping Gran had picked up a more useful clue, although the gift certificate was a nice find.

"Spencer was on the Historical Architectural Rules Committee."

I shook my head. "It doesn't surprise me. That man participated in every committee around."

"I'm getting the impression he only involved himself in things that could benefit him personally," said Gran. "Were you aware that the former owner of the Hangtown Hotel building tried to remodel it? The council deemed it unsafe, so he couldn't get a permit to do the work."

Mother's eyes lit up. "Did Darius Spencer have something to do with denying the former owner a permit?"

"Yep." Gran sipped her beer and licked her lips. "When the owner found out he couldn't renovate it, he had no choice but to let the building get foreclosed on by the lender. Guess the name of the lender?"

"Darius Spencer," yelled Bradford. He shrugged as three pairs of eyes glared at him. "Hey, I am a retired detective."

Gran's information corroborated what Abe had shared with me yesterday but with the additional twist of the permit denial.

"My suspect list keeps growing longer and longer." I glanced at my watch. "I wish Rex would call with an update. I feel awful about Hank sitting alone in a cell when he should be here with his family."

Mother shot me a curious look. "Laurel, even if Hank wasn't in jail, you wouldn't have invited him over for Memorial Day, would you?"

"No, I guess not, although..." My voice tapered off as I considered her question. Who would have thought that my ex-husband landing in jail would have brought us closer together than we had been in years?

My home phone rang, startling me, but providing an excellent excuse to escape my mother's question regarding Hank. I ran into the house and picked up the phone, grateful to shove my confused feelings back where they belonged—hidden deep in my subconscious.

CHAPTER TWENTY-FOUR

The defense attorney couldn't have timed his call any better.

"Hi, Rex," I said. "Do you have any news?"

"Probably not the news you'd like to hear from me. Because of the three-day weekend, Hank's arraignment isn't scheduled until Wednesday morning. They may refuse to grant him bail if they think he presents too much of a flight risk."

"That's plain silly," I sputtered. "Hank wouldn't take off and leave us behind." Although I had to admit recent history indicated otherwise.

"It may not make a difference. Even if they granted bail, it could be a million dollars for a murder charge. When bail gets that high, the bondsman will require not only the $100,000 fee but also a million in collateral to guarantee the bond. Do you have that kind of collateral?"

"Hank doesn't have enough collateral to get a mortgage on a doghouse, and I'm barely above water on my own home loan."

So the answer to that question would be a resounding no.

"What now?" I asked.

"It's only been two days since he was arrested, so I haven't received the case file yet. On Wednesday I'll find out if Hank will be charged with first-degree murder or a lesser charge, like manslaughter."

"Since someone hung Spencer from the scaffolding, there's no way his death could be an accident, is there?"

"Not hardly, although several witnesses in the bar noticed how intoxicated Hank became. The fact he was under the influence might be mitigating circumstances."

This was sounding more and more like a bad episode of *Law and Order*. I was ready for a commercial break.

"What kind of sentence are we talking about?" I asked.

"Twenty-five years to life. With time off for good behavior and overcrowding that could bring it down to fifteen."

Fifteen years or more for the father of my children to wear an orange jumpsuit? That didn't work for me.

"Have you discussed this with Hank?" I asked.

"Yes. Hank claims he's innocent. This is far too early in the process, but he informed me that even if they offered a plea deal down the road, he wouldn't accept it."

"Of course he's innocent. Don't you believe him?"

"In my line of work, you don't choose to believe or disbelieve. All you can do is to try to get the best deal possible for your client."

Shoot. What if the District Attorney was a friend of the victim and pursued the case to the max? Hank could be sentenced to life in prison.

I sniffed as miniature waterfalls coursed down my cheeks.

"I'll call you when I have some news," Rex said. "Until then, try to stay positive."

"Thanks." I attempted to wipe my cheeks dry with a tissue. "I realize you're trying to do the best you can. When can I get in to see Hank?"

"Visiting hours are from one to three every afternoon and also two evenings a week."

That was good to know. I was off work on Monday so my day was free to spend with the man who was not.

We hung up as the front doorbell rang. I walked into the foyer, threw open the door and flung myself into Liz's arms. After a comforting hug, I offered to help Brian with his load. He handed over a glass plate piled high with something that appeared to be both chocolate and frosted, a combination guaranteed to be a hit at this house.

"I'm so glad to see the two of you," I said as we entered my kitchen. I scanned all four walls in search of a place to hide her dessert from the kids until after dinner. Both of my children had inherited my chocoholic gene and were genetically blessed with an internal chocolate GPS system.

"I'm especially pleased to see Brian," I commented after hiding the dessert behind a stack of towels in the laundry room.

Brian's eyebrows rose. Being the intelligent counselor that he is, he instantly caught on. "I can't help you with Hank's case."

I put my palms up as if protesting his comment. "I wouldn't think about asking you for help."

Liz and Brian snorted in tandem. How well they knew me.

"No, honest. I have a legal question for Brian."

"And it has nothing to do with Hank's arrest?"

Geez. Those deputy DAs are a suspicious bunch.

"No, it's kind of a 'what if' question. It came up on an episode of *Castle* the other night."

"Hey, if you're looking to educate yourself about proper police procedure, you won't learn it from that show."

Liz chuckled. "Sorry, honey. Laurel and I aren't watching the show to pick up any crime scene tips. We only watch *Castle* because of Nathan Fillion. What a cutie." She followed her remark with two smacks, leaving a pink lipstick trail on her husband's cheek.

With Brian in a hopefully improved and less suspicious mood, I charged ahead. "So at what point would a prosecuting attorney offer a plea deal?"

Brian cocked his head, and I could almost hear his brain in action sifting through different case files. "There could be a variety of reasons. The Deputy District Attorney might feel they needed a stronger case to take it to trial. Occasionally there are extenuating circumstances related to the defendant."

"Do people ever take a plea deal if they're innocent?" I asked.

"Sometimes if it makes sense, their attorney may advise them to do so. Every case is different."

"Darling," Liz said to Brian, "You have to do something to help Hank. Even if he is a butthead, he's Laurel's butthead and, more importantly, Jenna's and Ben's father."

Liz was no fonder of Hank now than she was twenty years ago when we met at a fraternity party at the University of California at Davis. That night both of our dates drank themselves silly, and we bonded over the three-mile walk back to the dorms. We've been best friends since.

Brian remained silent, only opening his mouth to ask for my corkscrew. I pulled out wine glasses for them, which he filled from the bottle they brought. He took a sip, swirled it around his palate and swallowed.

I wondered if the wine had loosened Brian's tongue and his legal inhibitions or if his wife's affectionate nuzzling of his ear had anything to do with his next remark.

"No promises. I can't get involved with the case itself. I could get fired for interference, and I'm sure you don't want that."

Nope. I certainly didn't want Brian to lose his job any more than I wanted the kid's father to lose his freedom.

Or his own life.

CHAPTER TWENTY-FIVE

Sunday had ended up as a wonderful bonding experience with my family and friends. Even though Hank had never been a favorite with any of them, especially after he deserted me for Nadine, they all agreed we needed to help him for the kids' sake. The first stop on that path was to visit him in jail.

I dithered in my bedroom wondering what one wears to visit an ex-husband in jail if there is a chance she could run into her current boyfriend. I decided Dear Abby would tell me to focus, and not on my clothing. I threw on a sleeveless white top and a red floral skirt, a combination far cheerier than my mood. The El Dorado County Jail is located near the Placerville library, so I contemplated picking up some books for Hank to help occupy the long days and nights. But there could be a heck of a fine if I couldn't return them on time. Would they even be allowed? Had anyone ever tried to hide a weapon inside a book?

It turned out to be a non-issue since the library remained closed on Memorial Day. I would visit Hank empty-handed, although hopefully leave with some worthwhile information.

The county jail was larger than I anticipated. They snapped my photo, checked my ID and my purse, which I placed inside a locker. After decades watching crime shows, I should have realized I couldn't bring it in with me, although the closest thing to a weapon inside my purse was my lipstick wand.

I met Hank in a room divided into six partitioned areas filled with inmates and their visitors. We sat across from one another completely separated by a glass window. He wore an orange jumpsuit far too large for his frame. The circles under his eyes were as dark and large as Oreos.

I could feel my eyes start to tear, but I was determined to remain strong. The jail only allotted one hour for visitors, so we needed to make the most of every minute.

"You look beautiful," Hank said into the phone on his side of the glass.

I smiled and wiped away a stray tear as I answered via my own phone. "What woman wouldn't look beautiful in these surroundings? Are they treating you okay?"

"Yeah, I get my three meals." Hank sighed.

"Rex said he's still waiting for the case file. He hasn't seen the evidence they have against you."

"I don't care what they say they have. I'm innocent," Hank shouted then lowered his voice when the guard's head snapped to attention. "You have to believe me."

"I do, of course, I do. But why did you lie to me about going back to the hotel that morning?"

He slumped in his seat. His dark-blond hair brushed against the collar of the jumpsuit. Hank needed a haircut before he approached the bench for his arraignment.

"I didn't want you to find out I got drunk again," Hank explained. "I was upset with Spencer. And fuming about you and Hunter being together. I didn't intend to drink that much, but Fletch and Abe each bought me a beer. Then Lars and one of his builder buds started buying rounds whenever the Kings scored. It wasn't until the bar closed and I weaved my way to the truck that I realized I shouldn't be driving."

"Good thinking."

"Maybe not in this case." He shrugged, the over-sized jumpsuit flopping with his movement. "If I'd made it home and not entered the Hangtown Hotel, I might not be sitting in a cell."

"Doug Blake said you told him you were going to sleep it off in the hotel."

"Yeah, I always keep my camping gear in my truck. Since Spencer and I were meeting in a few hours that seemed the most prudent thing to do. I hauled my sleeping bag into the building and shoved it into a corner. Threw my hat on the floor next to it. I felt thirsty and kinda dehydrated, so I went back to the truck to get the water jug I keep behind my seat. Once I climbed into the back, I felt woozy. I guess I passed out. I didn't wake up until five-thirty and freaked out, worried I'd missed Spencer and he'd fire me for good this time."

I stared at my ex-husband for a full minute before responding. "That is the sorriest alibi I've ever heard."

"Yeah, that's what my attorney said. And the cops."

"Tom also said your fingerprints were on a two-by-four with Spencer's blood at the base."

Hank's expression grew puzzled before he cried out, "Oh, geez, that must have happened when I straightened up some of the lumber. I was worried Spencer would get annoyed if the place looked like a mess." He blinked back tears. "Guess I'm screwed, huh? Make sure you tell the kids how much I love them."

If my purse had been handy and Hank wasn't trapped behind a barrier, I would have whacked him on the head with it.

"Hey," I said. "We're not going down without a fight. If you didn't kill Spencer, then someone did. And I'm not about to let them pin it on you."

CHAPTER TWENTY-SIX

The next morning I moped around the office, unable to accomplish anything constructive on the marketing front or my own personal front. My sandaled heels practically wore a hole in the industrial strength carpet from trekking back and forth to the break room.

By eleven o'clock, after traipsing past Stan's cubicle a dozen or more times, he jumped out of his chair and barricaded my path.

"What is going on with you?" he asked.

My hand wobbled with java jitters, so Stan grabbed my full cup before I spilled it all over the gray carpet. He set it on his desk.

"Sit," he ordered. And I did.

"Talk."

And I did. I shared the latest update about Hank's arraignment scheduled for the next day and his insistence on his innocence. Stan can be a goofball at times, but his work as an underwriter requires him to be analytical, which makes him the perfect confidant. He's excellent at both jobs.

"So your grandmother spoke to some of the Main Street shop owners over the weekend?" Stan asked.

"A few. She got the impression Darius Spencer wasn't too popular around here."

Stan mulled that over. "Odd that a man so disliked would run for election as a Supervisor."

"She only spoke with a few store and restaurant owners. I'm sure there are plenty of people who supported him and his no-growth platform."

"I guess we don't need to concern ourselves with the no-growth people then," Stan said. "It's the pro-growth people who are the likeliest to have wanted him out of their cumulative hair."

"No one would kill someone over a political platform," I objected.

"Heads of state have been assassinated over political issues," Stan reminded me. "Someone as active as Spencer could have annoyed a multitude of suspects." He tapped his pencil against his palm before he pointed it in my direction. "You're right. This is enough to turn someone into a coffee-swilling addict."

My hands and head shook in agreement. When I spotted my boss coming toward us, my shakes increased to a 4.0 trembler on the Richter scale.

"Laurel, I haven't noticed any Wagon Train decorations up yet," Mr. Boxer said. "When do you expect to be finished with that project?"

Hmm. The more accurate question might be when was I starting it? I'd been slightly distracted, but I doubted I'd earn any brownie points mentioning my personal problems.

"Laurel and I were discussing our time frame," said my quick-thinking friend. "We plan on spending our lunch hour viewing the storefront windows on Main Street to ensure we don't duplicate anyone's decorating theme. Hangtown Bank needs to have the best window display in town."

"Precisely," Mr. Boxer agreed. "Mr. Chandler expects the bank to win first place in the contest. Carry on."

We watched as Mr. Boxer's charcoal pinstriped back retreated down the corridor.

"Whew," Stan said.

"I owe you one."

"You owe me at least a hundred something or others, but don't worry about it. How about we actually do what we told your boss. Grab a bite to eat and ogle the window displays."

"Sounds like a plan."

Half an hour later, Stan and I strolled along a sidewalk crowded with shoppers. The Wagon Train's official arrival in Placerville was twelve days away, but the town had already dressed itself for the occasion. An enormous banner welcoming the Wagon Train hung across Main Street. The historic Bell Tower, whose original purpose was to sound fire alerts, stood tall and proud in the small town plaza, festooned in red, white and blue ribbons. Although some shops and restaurants on Main Street chose not to participate in the decorating contest, the majority of them displayed true pioneer spirit. Our bank would have some stiff competition this year.

Hangtown Bakery, located across from the Bell Tower, displayed one of Darius Spencer's flyers in their window, so we guessed the owner was on the low-growth side of the political hedge dividing the two groups. One of their servers, dressed in a nineteenth-century costume, identified her character as Lucy Wakefield, the original Pie Lady of Placerville. She rattled off the names of an array of tasty looking fresh-baked pies.

"Lucy was quite the entrepreneur," Stan remarked as we shared a slice of apple pie à la mode, with an emphasis on the mode. "Supposedly she baked 240 apple pies a week and made a fortune selling slices to the miners. She earned over $25,000 in two years."

"Wow. That would have been a lot of dough," I said to Stan who groaned at my pun. "I bet she made more than most of the miners."

"Could be. She was granted the first divorce in El Dorado County by an all male jury."

"Did she remain single?" I asked.

"A year later, she ended up marrying a much younger man who'd testified on her behalf at her divorce trial."

Interesting that Lucy remarried so quickly after her divorce. Females can be such softies. After Hank left me, I vowed to eschew men for the remainder of my days.

How easily a cool dude with hot kisses could change one's perspective.

Jake, the stocky bakery owner, came out from the back to help clear the tables. I threw my own litter in the garbage, walked over and tapped him on his shoulder.

The black-bearded man whirled around, his arms laden with dirty plates and cups. He smiled when he recognized me.

"Hey, Laurel, what's new?" His smile reversed into an "aw shucks I made a stupid remark" wince. "Sorry, that came out wrong. How's Hank doing?"

"Not well, as you can imagine. I visited him at the jail yesterday."

Jake dumped the dishes on a table. "I can't tell you how sorry I am."

"Sorry you told the detectives about Hank going into the Hangtown Hotel?" I folded my arms over my chest and shot an angry look at him.

"Hey, I was merely doing my public duty. The cops asked if I saw anything unusual when I arrived at the bakery that morning. I couldn't lie about something so important," Jake said. He moved to another table and began clearing the dirty dishes.

"Did you see anyone else out at that time?" I asked, but Jake must not have heard me. I tapped him on his shoulder to get his attention. "What time do you normally get in? I know bakery owners need to rise early. Just like your pastry."

Geez. I shook my head. I couldn't stop the bad puns from coming. Must be all the sugar I'd consumed.

"I usually arrive between two and two-thirty," he said. "We open at six and it takes a few hours to prepare hundreds of muffins and scones for the early birds."

Geez. Was I ever glad I'd chosen banking, not baking for a career.

"Would you call me if you remember anything else? Especially something that might help Hank."

Jake promised he'd let me know if anything came to mind, so I left him my home number and email address and returned to our table.

On our way out the door, Stan and I stopped to scan the short biography the bakery had posted about the Pie Lady. One of her famous quotes made me laugh. Lucy told a friend that if she desired a husband, she could easily find one, "with any amount of fortune as they are as thick as toads after a rain."

Stan chuckled. "Speaking of toads, or rather, toadies." He pointed at the sign on the red brick building to our left. We stood in front of Spencer's campaign headquarters, located a few doors from the stately white, hundred-year-old county courthouse.

"Spencer can't still be up for election," I said. "Or did his staff forget to remove him from the ballot?"

"I've heard of cases where a candidate died, and his spouse jumped in and took his spot," Stan said. "I once read about an election where the voters disliked a candidate so much they voted for his dead opponent."

"Dead guys winning elections is definitely scary. Do you think Janet Spencer is considering running in her husband's place?"

"Let's find out." Stan pushed open the door, and a bell tinkled our arrival. The small space consisted of six basic IKEA-style desks, a counter along the wall covered with printers and other office equipment, and a multitude of empty paper cups emblazoned with the Hangtown Bakery logo. Maybe that's why Jake posted Spencer's flyer on his bakery window. His business must have prospered from the candidate's coffee-guzzling staff.

Since it was almost noon, it wasn't surprising the desks were unoccupied. A tall woman, who looked to be in her late twenties, appeared in a hallway leading from the back of the building.

"Can I help you?" she asked, undoubtedly assuming we were tourists looking for directions to one of the numerous historical landmarks located throughout Placerville.

"Oh, um, we are, or were supporters of Mr. Spencer. We wondered what was happening since he..." My throat tightened as the vision of the politician, a noose around his neck, claimed my thoughts.

"Gone," said Stan with a quick save. "Is someone running in his place?"

"Yes, although we haven't broadcast it in the media yet," she answered, her face reddening.

I wondered if the young woman's blushing was due to her fair complexion or because of some irregularity with the new candidate.

"Aw, c'mon..." Stan glanced at her nameplate and urged her cooperation with a conspiratorial smile, "Anita, we promise not to give it up."

Anita smiled at Stan's silliness. "Nice try, but you'll have to wait along with everyone else." She walked over to a desk and glanced down at a pile of papers. "The announcement will be in tomorrow's *Mountain Democrat*."

"How wonderful someone could fill Spencer's shoes so quickly," I commented. "Not that anyone could ever fill his wingtips as adequately as Darius could..." My voice trailed off as my shoe scenario sent a confused expression to her face.

"You must have been devastated by his loss," Stan said.

Anita's strawberry-blond ponytail bobbed up and down as she nodded. "The staff couldn't believe what happened to Mr. Spencer."

"I still can't stop thinking about him," I said then suddenly started choking.

"Are you okay?" asked Stan.

I sent a frantic look to the young woman. "Water?" I gasped.

She turned and headed down a hallway that presumably led to a kitchen or at least to water that wasn't piped in from muddy Hangtown Creek.

The minute Anita disappeared, I zipped over to her desk and picked up the piece of paper she had glanced at earlier.

Stan reached my side in seconds. "What's that?" he whispered.

"Shush. It's the press release. Let me read." I skimmed the announcement, ignoring all the blah blah blah remarks to arrive at the name of the new candidate—Chad Langdon of Mountain High Winery.

Stan peered over my shoulder. "Chad Langdon. How interesting."

A long freckled arm reached out and snatched the press release from my hand. "Do you still want the water?" Anita's hazel eyes shot daggers at me over a full glass of H2O.

"Of course, thanks for your concern." I drank all eight ounces in an attempt to display the appropriate amount of gratitude.

She frowned disapprovingly at us. "If you don't have any more questions, I have a lot of work to do."

Stan and I thanked her profusely and left her to get on with her duties. Once out the door, we discussed the media announcement.

"So Chad wants to take Spencer's place," I said. "That makes sense. A winery owner would have a vested interest in agriculture and tourism, maintaining the culture and financial solvency of this county."

"I wonder why he didn't run in the first place."

"Managing a winery is a huge job. Maybe Spencer's constituents persuaded Chad to run after Spencer died." I stopped. "Or maybe someone else did."

I pointed toward the steps of the courthouse where the new candidate and the former candidate's wife stood engrossed in conversation. And based on the rapt look on her face, possibly in one another.

CHAPTER TWENTY-SEVEN

"Would it be rude to interrupt them?" Stan asked me. A few pedestrians directed dirty looks at us for halting in the middle of a sidewalk teeming with two-footed traffic. With my children's father in jail on a murder charge, discretion took a back seat to detecting. I grabbed Stan's arm and race-walked toward the animated couple. Janet noticed our approach and turned to greet me.

"Hi, Laurel," she said. The widow was appropriately dressed in black. And white. And lime green. The floral print sleeveless top and Capri outfit accentuated her toned Zumba-practicing body. The bronze highlights in her new sleek haircut gleamed in the sunlight.

Stan put out his hand and introduced himself as my coworker. Chad pumped Stan's hand with the fervor of an about-to run-for-office candidate. He then tried to lead Janet away.

I delayed their departure by giving her a comforting hug. "You're looking much better."

Talk about an understatement. Janet looked ravishing as well as radiant. Her cheeks colored as she glanced at Chad. "I'm trying to get on with my life."

Obviously.

"When is the memorial service?" I asked.

"They finally released my poor husband to Collier's Funeral Home." Janet said, her voice calm, her mascara-lashed eyes bone dry. "The service will be Thursday night. I hope you'll attend."

"Of course, I'll be there to support you." And sniff out some suspects.

"I understand you're running for Supervisor," Stan said to Chad.

Chad's heavy dark brows drew together. "Where did you hear that bit of gossip?"

I could see the "oops" register in Stan's eyes.

"Oh, somewhere on Main Street," I said, waving my hand airily in all directions. "You know how news travels in this town."

"I haven't officially decided on a write-in campaign yet, so I would be deeply appreciative if you wouldn't spread that rumor any further."

Stan mimed zipping his lip. If only Chad knew how worthless that gesture was. Stan could spread gossip faster than a Twitter feed.

"Of course, we won't." I assured Chad. "But you'd be a wonderful candidate."

"Chad is the perfect person to step into the vacancy," Janet gushed. "I'm sure Spencer would be the first to approve."

She made the sign of the cross then peered up at the sky. I followed her gaze. Was she searching for Spencer's spirit? Or focusing on the last place where her husband had been seen.

Swinging in the wind.

"I think my cousin would be pleased I'm providing a choice for his constituents," Chad said.

The smile Janet beamed at Chad made me wonder if he'd also taken Spencer's place in his master suite. Is that what they meant by politics making strange bedfellows?

Chad said goodbye, turning to leave, when I remembered a comment the winery owner had made the night Spencer and Hank fought.

"Say, Chad, when I saw you at the Cornbread and Cowpokes event, you mentioned something about a loan question for me. Is there anything I can help you with?" I asked, curious how I could assist the possible future supervisor.

With a bland expression on his face he replied, "I got the answer to my question. Thanks for asking, and don't forget to vote." He winked and with his hand against Janet's back, guided her down the street.

We watched as the couple entered campaign headquarters. I wondered if Anita would mention that a couple of sneaky supporters dropped by and snatched a surreptitious peek at the press release on her desk.

Stan glanced at his watch. "We better get back to work, but let's walk by Antiques Galore on the way. I bet they have a great window display."

We crossed the street then passed by the Candy Emporium without stopping inside. If that wasn't a crime, I didn't know what was. But we were short on time and, after our bakery stop, long on calories.

We reached Antiques Galore and Stan's eyes widened at the display of matching antique Colt guns Scott had sold to Abe. "I would love to own an authentic set of pistols," he mused. "They would really set the tone for my Wagon Train outfit."

Yes, they would, especially if they came with a red-fringed holster.

By three that afternoon, I realized my list of murder suspects was longer than my list of suitable Wagon Train decorations. It had been ten years since Hangtown Bank last participated in the contest. Most of the stored items were so worn they looked as if they had crossed the Sierras with the Donner Party. Moths had noshed on a box full of wool cowboy hats, and it appeared that a mouse or two had nibbled their way through some of the straw items.

Mr. Boxer frowned when I shared the bad news, but after he personally pawed through the remaining boxes, he relented and provided some petty cash to buy extra decorations. I put together a list of items that might give the bank a shot at winning the contest.

Bales of hay strewn throughout the bank would take up a lot of space. My friend Vicky Parsons owned a ranch in Gold Hill, a few miles outside Coloma. She might have some bales she could spare. Also, bridles, saddles and other horse tack to add to my equine theme.

And if I could borrow a horse to tie to a lamppost the trophy would be a lock.

I arrived home a few minutes before six. Jenna had assured me dinner would be on the table. With school out for summer break, someone needed to watch Ben. Babysitting combined with domestic chores made for a perfect summer job for my daughter.

The sound of two chattering voices emanating from the family room piqued my curiosity. I discovered Kristy Hunter and Ben playing a video game. Despite their mismatched sizes and gender, the eight-year-olds enjoyed each other's company. Fair-haired Kristy was only a few inches shy of my height. Ben was undersized for his age, although what he lacked in inches, he made up for in energy.

"Kazoom, I got him," crowed Ben, his Play Station control in hand.

I yelled hello to both children. Engrossed in their game, they nodded their heads, acknowledging my presence. An exotic and savory fragrance lured me into the kitchen.

"Something smells yummy," I said to my daughter who stood at the stove stirring a large pan loaded with chicken and assorted vegetables.

"It's my own recipe," Jenna replied. "I'm calling it California Curry, a milder version of the original recipe."

"You can name it whatever you want. I can't wait to try it." I pointed in the direction of the family room. "What's Kristy doing here?"

Jenna placed the lid on the pan and turned to face me. "Tom called. His mother had an eye appointment and Kristy's grandfather needed to drive her to Sacramento. Tom asked if I could watch Kristy and I said yes. I didn't think you'd mind."

"Of course not. Anything to keep Ben occupied."

"Exactly." Jenna's grin displayed her orthodontic-perfected and financially crushing set of teeth. "I also invited Tom for dinner."

I raised an eyebrow at her initiative. "Did he accept?"

The doorbell rang answering my question. I trotted to the front door and flung it wide open. The man standing on my doorstep may have been partially responsible for putting my ex-husband in jail, but I couldn't deny my attraction to him.

He shoved his hand through his wind-whipped hair and hesitated, as if trying to gauge my reaction to his presence. Then he smiled that sexy smile I could never resist.

My heart executed two double back flips and some other invested body parts applauded with wicked abandon. Tom's arms reached for me and I moved into his welcoming embrace. He smelled like a lime daiquiri and tasted even better.

The fireworks I felt from his smoldering kiss were hotter than the curry Jenna would be serving for dinner. They were louder too.

Thirty seconds into Tom's embrace I broke away when I realized we had an audience of two kids providing surround sound fireworks with their portable video games.

"Hi, Daddy," said Kristy.

Tom removed his arms from around me and shifted them to his daughter.

"Can I stay and eat dinner with Ben?" she asked, snuggling against her father's broad chest.

"We can both stay," he said, "but as soon as dinner is over, we need to go home. I have a lot of paperwork to catch up on."

Jenna announced dinner and led us to our formal dining room. She'd set the table with the gold-trimmed wedding china that normally appeared only at holiday functions. I began to have an inkling Jenna had cooked up something besides dinner tonight.

The California Curry turned out to be a nice surprise, flavorful but not overpowering. The spices simmered on my tongue instead of burning my taste buds.

"Terrific meal," Tom said to my daughter. "You must have inherited your mother's cooking skills."

Jenna choked on her water but politely refrained from telling Tom that the only person who raved about my culinary expertise was Ben, whose gourmet favorites included hot dogs and pizza—the kind delivered to our doorstep.

"I'm glad you enjoyed the meal," said Jenna. "I realize you've been working long hours trying to get our father released from jail."

I gagged on my iced tea. My daughter really was a chip off her mother's block. I managed a straight face while I waited for the detective's response.

His right shoe bumped against my left sandal. If Tom expected me to come to his rescue, he could be waiting until we served breakfast the next morning.

"So how come you arrested Ben's dad?" asked Kristy, turning a puzzled look to her own father. "Did he do something bad?"

Tom cleared his throat as four pairs of eyes stared at him. "Detectives don't decide if people did bad things. That's what juries are for, and technically, I didn't arrest their father. The Sacramento detectives handling this case made that call."

Jenna's dropped fork clinked against her china plate. "But you didn't do anything to stop them, did you?"

I felt horrible that Jenna had maneuvered Tom into this awkward discussion although her train of thought was hurtling down the same track as mine.

Tom pushed his plate aside, but he didn't shy away from meeting her accusing gaze. "There's evidence you don't know about, Jenna, evidence I can't possibly share with you. Since I'm dating your mother, the county hired outside help to ensure there was no conflict of interest. Based on their discoveries, they had no choice but to arrest your father. I'm as sorry as you are about the situation."

Jenna rose from the table, her body rigid. "Yeah, right. If you really cared about my mother," her voice shook, "and us, you wouldn't rely on their so-called 'evidence.' You'd try to find the real killer."

She flounced out of the room. The sound of the kitchen screen door banging shut indicated her departure from the house. I hoped the cool night air would calm down her redheaded temper.

Ben and Kristy exchanged glances but remained silent. Tom stood up from the table, holding a plate full of his unfinished dinner. "It's time to go, Kristy. Let's take our dishes to the kitchen and leave."

Tom and his daughter placed their plates on my tiled counter. Then Kristy grabbed her backpack from the family room and mumbled a quiet goodbye to Ben. I followed them to the front porch. Tom told his daughter to wait in his car while we said goodbye.

"Sorry about the grilling," I said. "My daughter is sneakier than I realized. I'll get her so she can apologize."

"No, it's okay. I hope Kristy would defend me just as fiercely as Jenna's doing for her dad." He tried for a smile. "I'm not even going to comment about any resemblance between mother and daughter. I'm in enough hot water to fill a hot tub."

"You can't blame my kids. This is a monstrous situation."

Tom looked down at his feet. "Look, I truly feel powerless at this point, but I've seen the evidence and it's a solid case."

"You don't feel the detectives acted prematurely in arresting Hank? Did they interview every potential suspect? From what I've gathered, enough people disliked Spencer to fill a town hall meeting."

"Laurel, you know as well as I do that merely because there's enmity between two people, it doesn't turn one of them into a homicidal killer."

"So you're just going to sit and do nothing despite a list of suspects longer than Ben's Christmas list?"

Tom put his arms around me. "My hands are tied. Don't you realize that?"

I stepped back from his embrace. "I'm trying, but it isn't easy. And I hope you can understand I'll continue doing whatever I can to free Hank."

Tom's eyes darkened as they locked with mine. "Not that long ago you couldn't stand the man's guts. Has something changed between the two of you?"

"Of course not," I protested, "But..."

The shriek of a car horn startled us before I could expand on my reply. Kristy waved at her father to hurry up.

"You better go," I said to Tom. "Your daughter is waiting for you. And my daughter needs her mother more than ever right now."

CHAPTER TWENTY-EIGHT

The next morning, I woke with my cotton sheet wrapped around me and my blanket on the floor. My bedtime antics were burning off calories faster than my Zumba class. In my opinion, tossing and turning all night attempting to sleep is *not* the highest and best use of a king-size bed.

I reflected on my problematic relationship with Tom. Maybe I should resign myself to spending the rest of my life as a single woman, growing old with my kids and making weekly visits to my ex-husband in prison.

I groaned thinking about the arraignment today. I'd told Hank when I visited him in jail that I wanted to go to the courthouse to show support, but he'd been resolute about me not attending the brief hearing. Hank said seeing my tearful face in public would be too traumatic for him. Plus it could take hours for the court to process their huge caseload.

Instead, I would occupy my time getting my bank errands out of the way.

I whipped up a blueberry protein shake and poured it into a travel mug. Then I grabbed my purse and headed to the garage. Mornings were so much easier with the kids out of school.

The drive down Green Valley Road lightened my somber mood. The snow-tipped Sierras smiled a sunny good morning at me as I headed east toward Coloma. My favorite winery bordered Vicky's property, but they weren't open this early. Depending on how Hank's arraignment went, I might want to curl up in their tasting room later today.

The Prius hugged the twisty curves of Gold Hill Road. To the right, miniature horses grazed and galloped along the fence. With their short legs, they'd be ready for a nap by the time they rounded the property. After my sleepless night worrying about the men in my life, a nap sounded fantastic.

I drove down the long gravel driveway to Vicky's farmhouse-style residence. She met me on the front porch, a mug of coffee in each hand.

"How well you know me." I chuckled as I reached for the steaming cup.

"I know Mr. Boxer, too." She grimaced. "And I don't envy your job."

I glanced around her white-fenced property, at the colorful roses climbing up the latticework of the covered porch, the bucolic pastures in the distance. "Maybe someday I can afford to retire too. What a way to spend your days."

"Hey, it's not all sunshine and roses. Most of the time I'm either shoveling hay or shoveling shit." She cracked a smile as we reached her large red barn. "But I do love my four-legged friends."

Vicky introduced me to her equine family. She lent me some spare horse tack I promised to return as soon as the contest ended. We squeezed three saddles and two hay bales into my car, all my Prius could handle and strapped one additional bale to the roof.

"You should stop at Scott Shelton's ranch next door," she said. "His family has owned that place for over a century. As I recall, he has some interesting antiques in the house. He might let you borrow them."

"I've never been formally introduced to him, but we bumped into each other at Antiques Galore last Saturday when he sold some guns to Abe…" My voice trailed off as I realized I shouldn't discuss Scott's financial woes with his neighbor.

"That's okay. Scott's had it tough since he lost the Hangtown Hotel. He feels like a failure."

"Do you know him well?"

"Yes and no." She gazed in the direction of her neighbor's ranch. "Scott's a typical strong silent cowboy type. Doesn't stick his nose in anyone's business and expects others to do the same. But when

CINDY SAMPLE

Brad is out of town on sales calls, I can always count on Scott to help me with this place if necessary."

"That's the kind of neighbor you need. Is there a Mrs. Scott Shelton?"

Her eyebrows veered upward. "Not for a long time. But he's a little old for you. And aren't you seeing that good-looking detective?"

Yes and no.

"Hey, speaking of my neighbor." Vicky pointed at the gray truck moving up her driveway, a cloud of dust following behind. The driver parked next to my overloaded Prius, which now looked more dusty beige than periwinkle.

Scott extended one long denim-clad leg out of the cab of his truck. A black lab stuck its curious head out the window, greeting us with a lonely woof. The rancher motioned at his pet. It lay down in the passenger seat as quiet as a sleeping turtle. His dog appeared better trained than my son.

"Morning, Scott," Vicky said then introduced me to her neighbor.

"We crossed paths last Saturday in Antiques Galore," I added.

Scott merely nodded and turned to Vicky. "I have to leave a day earlier than expected to get the rig over the hill, so you'll need to watch Polly starting tomorrow."

"Is Polly your dog?" I asked.

"She's his favorite mare," Vicky answered for him. "Polly is pregnant so she doesn't get to go on the Wagon Train this trip. But there's always next year."

Scott frowned. "We'll see. This could be my last ride. I'm thinking of selling the homestead and moving to Alaska. Someplace not so crowded."

"Scott, I can't believe you'd sell your family home," Vicky exclaimed.

He stared at the ground. "Too many snakes in this part of the country."

I wondered if the reptiles the cowboy alluded to were the ones who crawled on the ground. Maybe a compliment would encourage him to open up. "I've always admired the people who participate in the Wagon Train year after year. I'd like to try it myself sometime."

"Takes dedication, hard work and money." His sharp gray eyes assessed my well-filled lacy white top and flowered skirt. His gaze

134

eventually landed on my three-inch wedge sandals. "Not much fun for a city gal."

I bristled at his assessment. Liking cute shoes didn't automatically proclaim me a wimpy city girl. I tried to come up with a brilliant rebuttal, but he mumbled goodbye and sauntered back to his truck.

"Not the friendliest guy in town," I muttered.

"Aw, did he hurt your feelings, city girl?" asked Vicky, falling into a fit of giggles.

I frowned then joined in. "I prefer to think of myself as an urban cowgirl. But maybe it's time to get some manure-kicking boots to demonstrate my country roots."

On that note, Vicky and I hugged each other goodbye. With my car crammed full, I decided to forego stopping at Scott Shelton's ranch for additional antiques. It sounded like he had enough on his mind without this city gal annoying him.

I drove out Vicky's long driveway then turned right on Cold Springs Road toward Placerville. The hay bales in my car smelled heavenly for all of three minutes until I began to sneeze and the interior of my car turned into hay fever hell.

So much for riding in a covered wagon. I was relegated back to wussy wimp status. Scott Shelton didn't have to worry about me annoying him on his Wagon Train journey.

After hauling all of the items from my car into my office, I checked to see if any other marketing duties awaited my attention. A new "to do today or else" list prepared by Mr. Boxer glared at me and I glared back. I whipped out a flyer extolling the bank's hot rates on our CD accounts and another one for a new loan program. Once I completed those two exciting projects, I picked up the phone to call Gran.

The phone rang seven times before she answered.

"Hold your horses, toots," she said. "I need to put my hearing aid in."

I waited almost four minutes before she got back on the line. "What took so long?" I asked.

"Oh, Judge Judy is on and I wanted to see if she gave the jackass who sued his mother any money."

"Well...?"

"Well, what?"

"Did the jack... er, did the plaintiff win?"

"Nope. That is one smart judge. We could use her in this county."

I wagered if Judge Judy heard the charges against Hank, she'd have him out of jail by the end of her show.

"Hey, Gran, I'm decorating the bank and many of our supplies are eroded and corroded. Do you have any memorabilia I could borrow? Anything that would fit in with a gold mining or western theme."

"Your mother's been bugging me to get rid of the stuff stored in the shed. How 'bout I check it out and call you back."

"Thanks. You're the best. But don't go lifting anything too heavy. Promise?"

She muttered something about young whippersnappers and bid me farewell. My grandmother had been an active woman all of her life, first raising my mother and my uncle then working as a bookkeeper. After retirement, she became involved with a variety of community activities, including the historical society. She fought the physical realities of aging with every tool she could—including weekly Tai Chi classes.

I'd missed a call on my cell while chatting with my grandmother. I checked voicemail and discovered a message from Hank's attorney. I hoped he had good news after the arraignment. Assuming good news was even an option.

I called Rex back, but he'd left the office. His secretary promised to have him return my call.

A few minutes later, my cell rang again, but it was neither the attorney nor Gran.

"Hello, luv, what are you up to?" asked Liz.

"My life seems to be on perpetual hold. I'm waiting for the attorney to call back with an update on Hank's hearing and waiting for Gran to call back with an update on old crap. Waiting for Tom to call back and admit he's full of ..." My voice petered out as Liz's throaty chuckle floated over the line.

"My word. You are in a pissy mood today. Is there anything I can do?"

"Can you talk your husband into finding out what evidence the prosecution has on Hank?"

"Hah," she said. "I have a better chance of winning the lottery than getting anything out of my tight-lipped husband. I take it you haven't been able to crack your boyfriend's code of silence either."

"I'm not sure I still have a boyfriend. Hank's arrest has driven a huge wedge between us."

The phone remained silent for so long, I thought we'd lost our connection. Then Liz said, "You don't suppose Tom is jealous of Hank, do you?"

I snorted. "Don't be silly. What does Tom have to be jealous about?"

"Hank hangs around you and the kids a lot. At least, he did before they arrested him. Which I'm sure Tom had nothing to do with."

"If Tom's detectives hadn't thrown my husband in jail, I could have dealt with the situation."

Liz waited a few seconds before replying. "You realize you referred to Hank as your husband?"

"A slip of the tongue. You know what I mean."

"I may know what you mean, Laurel," she replied. "But do you?"

CHAPTER TWENTY-NINE

I spent the remainder of the afternoon completing a variety of minor tasks while I waited for a multitude of people to return my phone calls. My best friend's implication that I still had feelings for Hank gave me heartburn. When his attorney called back to inform me that the court would not grant Hank bail, my gastric inferno reached volcanic proportions.

I phoned Gran several times, but she never answered. My request must have prompted her to clean out her shed. Or she tired herself out and fell asleep. By six, Gran still hadn't called back. As I walked to the parking lot, an uneasy feeling waged war with the flames burning in my belly. If something happened to my grandmother while she searched for stuff for me, I would never forgive myself.

I gobbled two pastel-colored Tums found in the bottom of my purse that I hoped were no more than a decade past their expiration date. I called the kids and told them to eat dinner without me then aimed the Prius east toward Bedford Street.

A few minutes later, I parked on the street in front of my grandmother's Victorian. As I walked to her house, I reflected on the happy childhood memories spent there. After my father died when I was ten and my brother, Dave, was twelve, my mother supported us on her real estate commissions. She worked long hours, including nights and weekends, so we spent many hours under Gran's watchful supervision.

The two women may have been polar opposites, but they remained united in one thing—their love for my brother and me.

I blinked back tears as I realized our family home would eventually belong to some other family. Yet, realistically, neither Mother nor I wanted to move into the hundred-year-old house. I enjoyed my rural subdivision, and the kids were happy with the schools in our district. After they wed, Bradford and my mother had purchased a single story contemporary style home in an adult community in El Dorado Hills, which suited their needs.

I banged on the door twice then turned the knob. Unlocked as usual. I walked through the house calling her name. No answer. I went out the back door and traipsed over to her detached two-car garage. She'd remembered to lock the garage, but when I peered through the window, her Mustang sat in its place, the crimson exterior sparkling as the sun's rays shone inside.

If her car was here, Gran must be at home, unless one of her friends had stopped by to take her out to dinner. It seemed peculiar she hadn't called me back, but she could be so engrossed sorting through stuff in the shed that she didn't realize how much time had elapsed.

My great-grandfather had located the building, almost the size of a small barn, a distance from the house. I studied the dense weeds that had overgrown the path to the shed before my gaze shifted to a dozen vultures circling above me. The realization that the large black birds were undoubtedly salivating over tonight's dinner, completely creeped me out.

Even from this distance, I could see the partially open shed door. That niggling feeling refused to disappear. What were a few scratches on my calves compared to my relief once I assured myself Gran was okay?

The star thistle played havoc with my bare legs. I began to realize why my mother wanted to relocate Gran to a retirement community. This property was a handful for an elderly woman to maintain. As soon as I returned home, I would arrange for someone to cut these weeds. They were a fire hazard as well as a hiking hazard.

I pushed on the shed door. It squeaked open, revealing a dark, musty interior. I threw the door open wide hoping the waning sunlight would improve visibility.

A weak voice cried out. "Who's there?"

"Gran?" I shouted. "Where are you?"

"Way in the back. Be careful. There's a lot of stuff in here."

I eased my way through the shed, my eyes finally adjusting to the dimness. The sides of the shed contained built-in wood shelves crammed full of boxes. Stacks of cartons covered the cement floor leaving a narrow maze for a path. I bumped into an old rusty lawnmower, nicking my toe on the rotor and causing me to rethink that tetanus booster I kept putting off.

If I'd previously thought an *Antiques Road Show* visit might be in our family's future, I was sadly mistaken. This shed needed the "We Haul Your Junk" guys to move in for a month or two.

"I'm coming," I called out. "What happened?"

"You'll see." Gran sounded subdued, far from her normal ebullient self.

I bumped my knee on another antique/really old semi-rotting object and cursed the lack of a flashlight.

The niggling feeling exploded into full-blown anxiety when I saw Gran lying on the hard concrete floor. In the semi-darkness, she looked dangerously pale. As I bent over, she attempted to raise herself to a sitting position. She winced in pain and dropped back down.

"Don't move." I crouched next to her. "How did you get hurt?"

"After you called, I came out here to see what kind of stuff had been stored. As you can see, your great-grandparents were pack rats. They never threw anything away. I guess they figured with all of this space why bother. Our phone conversation reminded me of some items we had in the house when I was growing up. Things that could be worth some money."

"Like what?"

She gave me a blank look. "I can't remember now."

I leaned closer, fearful she might have internal injuries. "Did you hit your head?"

She tenderly touched her scalp. Fortunately, for her, a curly auburn wig protected her hard head. "I don't think so, but my memory isn't what it used to be."

She sent me a defiant look. "But don't go sharing that with your mother."

Her memory might not be what it used to be, but she was still my feisty Gran. I looked at the open boxes surrounding her, their contents scattered on the floor. A pile of dusty books lay off to her right.

I pointed to the mess. "So what exactly occurred here?"

"Sometimes I can be an idjet." I chose not to agree or disagree with her. In my opinion, it's our constitutional right to be an idiot every now and then.

"I was having a swell time going through the boxes, sorta like a treasure hunt. I couldn't quite reach the top shelf, and I didn't want to walk all the way back to the house for my stepstool, so I decided to stand on that bucket over there." She pointed to a four-gallon metal bucket that wouldn't have been sturdy enough for a toddler to stand on much less an eighty-eight-year-old osteoporotic granny.

"When I stretched my left arm," she said, "the bucket tipped over. Then I tipped over."

"Geez, Gran. Do you think you broke anything?"

"Not sure, but it hurts too much to walk. I began to think I'd die here."

I looked at her *Red Hats Rock* tee shirt. "Where's your Alert button? You're supposed to wear it at all times."

She glanced down at her chest. "Oops."

Yeah, oops. "I left my purse and cell in your house, so I'll have to go back to call the paramedics. Do not move without them checking you first. Did you crack a rib or anything?"

She flinched as I gently touched her ribs.

"Hang in there," I said. "I'll have them here in a jiffy."

I bumped and bounced my way through the shed, relief coursing through me that Gran was okay, hopefully with only minor injuries. Once my mother heard about this accident, she would be relentless in her mission to relocate my grandmother.

Much as I hated to leave Gran alone in the dark, I didn't want any snakes to turn the shed into a temporary timeshare, so I shut the door behind me. The western sky resembled an impressionist painting, a swirl of pink, mauve and varying shades of blue. Twilight can be a beautiful time, but it did not improve the visibility. I could barely see the house from here. With rattlesnakes on my brain, I decided to forego traipsing through the weeds. Even though my journey would be longer, the path around the tree-lined perimeter of the property might be easier and safer.

I jogged down the dirt path, anxious to reach my phone and a rescue team. My eyes remained glued to the trail, watching out for creatures either slithering across the path or coiled along the side, prepared to strike at any intruders. Engrossed, with my eyes gazing down, I failed to notice an unexpected guest until a deep growl startled me.

My head jerked up and I froze. A pair of topaz eyes glinted from a distance of fifteen feet. The eyes belonged to a cat. But not the kind of creature you want curled up on your lap while you read a cozy mystery.

This spotted cat could devour my multi-colored kitty as an appetizer before it moved on to a bigger and more satisfying entrée.

Me!

CHAPTER THIRTY

I stood still. My heart palpitations sounded louder than an arena full of Sacramento Kings fans, and I wondered if the mountain lion could hear them. Could it sense my fear?

The animal inched closer, its fierce gaze never leaving mine, as if assessing the high caloric content of a busty soccer mom. Based on his lean and wiry frame, he could devour me in one claw-licking bite.

Desperate thoughts flashed through my brain. What did the experts recommend when encountering a mountain lion? Could I outrun a fleet-footed cat? I glanced at Gran's house, which seemed at least a mile away from my current location.

Considering that I'd come in last during my high school track meet and currently carried an additional thirty pounds, that did not seem like a practical solution.

Should I make myself small and curl up into a ball?

Hah! It would take a lifetime of dance classes for me to do that.

Suddenly a recent article in the *Mountain Democrat* about a twelve-year-old boy who pulled out his trumpet and scared a mountain lion away came to mind.

I didn't have a trumpet, but I did have Zumba.

The mountain lion growled so loud it resembled the full-throated roar of the king of the jungle. Someone wanted dinner. His front paws bunched up as he prepared to pounce.

And so did I, putting my Zumba lessons to the test. I rocked to the right and I swiveled to the left. I swung my arms up, down and all around. I jumped forward and back while simultaneously belting out the words that accompanied this particular routine—"I Will Survive."

The mountain lion froze in place. I could swear he cocked his head as a puzzled look appeared in his eyes. He stared at me for a full minute before he wheeled about and disappeared into the woods.

The same response I received the last time I sang this song at karaoke. Only that time I'd emptied out an entire bar.

I waited thirty seconds before I ran down the path, hoping I'd scared the feline intruder into another county. My heart pulsed so fast I worried the paramedics would need two stretchers, one for my grandmother and one for me. When I finally reached the house, I threw open the back door to the kitchen and grabbed my phone with relief.

I dialed 911, and the operator promised the paramedics would arrive at the property in less than ten minutes. Not until I dropped my cell on the tiled counter did my recent experience fully hit me.

I slid onto the floor with my arms circling my legs and rocked back and forth. That encounter felt much too close for comfort. Gran didn't know it yet, but I planned on joining Team Barbara's Relocation Effort. My grandmother needed to move somewhere safe—where her fiercest opponents were across the bridge table and not in her backyard.

The dispatch operator excelled at her job. An ambulance screeched to a stop in exactly nine minutes. I quickly ended my cell phone call with my mother to meet the men at the front door and explain Gran's situation. I warned them about my recent stare-down with a king-sized kitty. The younger EMT blanched at my encounter, but his dark-skinned partner didn't appear fazed. He radioed the Sheriff's Department about a mountain lion sighting in town. After he hung up, he confided that mountain lions were so prevalent in the area that the authorities usually didn't follow up unless someone or something had been eaten.

So not reassuring.

With the two men accompanying me, carrying high-powered flashlights in their hands, our trip to the shed was like a walk in the park. Bob, the elder paramedic, examined Gran, checking her blood pressure and other critical stats. At first, she resisted the stretcher, but when I shared my close encounter of the most terrifying kind, she acquiesced. I'd brought her a couple of bottles of water and a granola bar which would hopefully tide her over until she reached the hospital.

The drive to Marshall Hospital took less than five minutes. Gran convinced the EMTs to pull out all the stops. We arrived at the emergency room entrance with lights flashing and sirens screaming. We held hands the entire time, although after my cat meet-up, I wasn't certain who was comforting whom.

I climbed out of the back of the ambulance and waited while the men removed my grandmother. She assisted by barking out her own directional commands. At one point, Bob and his partner looked frustrated enough to unload Gran onto the gurney and leave her outside the entrance.

A familiar-looking SUV pulled into the circular drive before we entered the lobby. With Bradford in the driver's seat, Mother exited the car the minute he put it in park and rushed to her own mother's side.

"Ma, what have you done now?"

"No biggie," said Gran, brushing off her concern by waving her away. "I had a small fall. That's all. Go on back home."

"There is no such thing as a 'small fall' at your age. I can't imagine what you were thinking."

Gran scowled at her daughter. "I tried to help my granddaughter and also clean out the shed like you asked me to do."

"I never meant for you to do it yourself."

Bradford interrupted their bickering by pulling his wife aside and whispering in her ear. I stayed with Gran, following her to the registration area.

I missed Bradford's comments to Mother, but she remained silent while I assisted my grandmother with her check-in. The emergency room seemed quiet, maybe because we'd arrived on a weeknight. Within minutes, a nurse whisked Gran away, leaving the three of us to twiddle our thumbs and tap our toes in the waiting area.

"Laurel, I can't believe you told Gran to clean out the shed by herself," Mother complained.

"I only asked if she knew of any things I could borrow for the bank, for the Wagon Train decorating contest. I certainly didn't expect her to climb on top of a bucket."

She slumped back into the uncomfortable hard plastic chair. "We have to get her out of that house."

"I couldn't agree with you more," I said, "especially after my mountain lion incident tonight."

Mother replied with a wide-eyed "What?" at the same time the glass doors opened with a whoosh. The tall man dressed in jeans and a navy windbreaker bore a concerned look on his face. He rushed up to me and pulled me into his arms. I rested against the safety of his chest for a full minute before he released me.

"Are you okay?" Tom asked. He seemed to have added a few crow's feet since our dinner the previous evening. "I heard what happened. How did you get away?"

"That mountain lion was evidently not a fan of disco. Or my singing," I said with a wry smile as I plopped back into my chair. "I survived by belting out a few verses of 'I Will Survive.'"

"So you soothed the savage beast." Tom winked at me as he fell into the chair next to mine.

"It's more like I scared the savage beast. I hope it's traveled many miles from Gran's house by now. How did you find out?"

"I heard the call about the mountain lion on my radio and recognized the address as your grandmother's home. When I phoned in, they told me both of you were at the hospital. How's she doing?"

"I don't think she broke anything," I said.

"But not for lack of trying," Mother interjected. "We have to get her out of that house. Tom, there's no reason why I can't list it, is there?"

"I don't see why not. We have what little evidence we found from the mineshaft in the cold case file. The DNA will take weeks to get back since it's not a rush. We could close the file immediately without it."

I sent him a quizzical glance. "Can you close the case without determining the murderer?"

"We could," he said, "although you won't like our findings."

I shifted a few inches away from him so our shoulders and thighs were no longer touching. My brain might be annoyed with the detective sitting next to me, but other enthusiastic parts were cartwheeling with delight at his close proximity.

"I guess I'll have to continue investigating both murders since no one in the homicide department seems interested in finding the real killer in any of your cases."

A frustrated expression crossed Tom's face, which probably matched the look on my own.

"I'm glad you're okay," he said to me. He stood and addressed my mother. "Go ahead and list the house, Barbara. I'll keep the case file open, but that shouldn't interfere with any sale."

"Thanks, Tom," Mother said. Bradford rose and accompanied Tom outside. As his former partner, my stepfather could share wise advice on the subject of dating while detecting. Maybe I should have a discussion with him myself since I sucked at multitasking between the two.

A nurse approached us with an update on my grandmother. She'd bruised one rib and twisted her left ankle. Given her age, they wanted her to spend a night or two to ensure there were no other issues.

Mother and I stopped in Gran's room to say goodnight. She sat propped against a few pillows. Her color looked better, possibly due to the IV attached to her right arm, although her curly red wig listed to the left.

Only one penciled eyebrow remained, giving her the appearance of a cockeyed Little Orphan Annie. "If you've come to bawl me out," she said, "you might as well turn around and leave."

Mother kissed Gran on her cheek. "I'm grateful you're okay."

I plopped down at the end of the bed. "Don't scare me like that again. Promise?"

She nodded, but I could see her crossing her fingers under the bed. Honestly, sometimes my grandmother's behavior was worse than my son's antics.

"You need to go back to the barn," she said to me. "I found a couple of boxes of stuff on the bottom shelf that could work for your bank decorating. Some old gold pans. Even a box of satin shoes and parasols. I'm not sure how valuable that old stuff is."

"I could have Abe appraise it first. He's the most knowledgeable antiques dealer in town," I replied. "If you're sure you don't want to keep it."

"It's not doing me any good sitting in that shed. Hey, did you notice those books that fell out of that box from the upper shelf?"

I thought back to earlier that evening when I'd first discovered her in the shed. "There were a few leather bound volumes scattered off to the side. Are they first editions?"

"No, I think they're..." She stopped when the nurse bustled in to check her vital signs. Gran leaned back, her face etched in a million tiny lines. She swallowed the two pills the nurse handed to her and waited while the nurse logged everything on to a chart. The nurse also suggested her patient remove her wig, but Gran shooed her out of the room saying she'd deal with it after her guests left.

As the nurse disappeared down the hall, I leaned forward, curious to see what else Gran had to say about her discovery.

"So what did you want me to do with those old books?" I asked.

She yawned then looked at me, her confused eyes meeting my curious ones.

"What books?" she asked, before her head dropped, her pointed chin coming to rest on her hospital gown, followed by her not-so-soft snores echoing throughout the room.

We tiptoed out of the room although it wasn't necessary since Gran's snores were loud enough to wake the walking dead. If hospital stays weren't so expensive, my recommendation would be to leave her there for a few weeks so we wouldn't have to worry about her. I mentioned my concern about Gran's recent memory lapses to the doctor, but she assured us forgetfulness was normal and Gran was doing great for her age.

I arrived home, a little after eleven, feeling tired and dejected. My grandmother had been a solid presence in my life for thirty-nine years. She'd always reminded me of the Unsinkable Molly Brown. Gran would have made a great pioneer woman. Other than a few months last year when she flew to the east coast to spend time with her brother who had been diagnosed with terminal cancer, she'd always been there for me.

It was time to reverse our roles. I needed to be there for her.

I discovered my children in the family room, cuddled next to each other, watching television. The kids' eyes remained glued to the screen. When I turned on the light, they both jumped and Ben ended up sprawled on the floor.

"You scared us." He came over and wrapped his arms around my waist.

Jenna put the movie they were watching on pause. "Is Great Gran okay?"

"She'll be fine," I reassured Jenna, hoping to reassure myself.

DYING FOR A DUDE

I ruffled Ben's hair. "Honey, why aren't you in bed?"

"My sister," he elaborated by pointing to Jenna, "invited me to watch a movie with her. An offer I couldn't refuse. I'm learning how to romance a woman."

My head whipped around. "What are you watching?"

Jenna giggled. "*Enchanted.*"

Ah, the story of my life—not!

"Liz called," said Jenna. "She wondered what you're wearing to the funeral tomorrow."

I smacked my forehead with my palm. Between Gran's injury and my lion-taming encounter, I had almost forgotten about Darius Spencer's funeral the next evening. The political candidate had been such a prominent figure in El Dorado County the service would undoubtedly be packed with mourners.

Or people celebrating his demise.

What were the odds the person responsible for his death would also attend?

149

CHAPTER THIRTY-ONE

The next day, my family, friends and I attended Darius Spencer's memorial service, which represented politics at its worst. In her eulogy, Janet Spencer claimed her deceased husband would have been thrilled had he known that his platform would continue. The widow's stiletto-heeled steps seemed springier than I remembered, almost as if Spencer's demise had given Janet a new lease on life.

The widow also announced that in lieu of flowers, mourners should donate to the campaign of Chad Langdon, her husband's beloved cousin and now write-in candidate for the Sixth District Supervisorial seat.

I didn't think the service could get any tackier, but once again she proved me wrong. After her remarks, Janet invited supportive political candidates to address the crowd of over five hundred mourners. An opportunity they could not refuse.

I sat with Mother and Bradford to my left, with Liz and Brian on my right. The largest room in the chapel was wall-to-wall mourners.

And voters.

I crossed and uncrossed my legs. I owned one suitable black dress, a light wool blend, perfect for a romantic dinner in front of a roaring fire, but not for a hot summer evening. After an hour listening to one politician after another extolling Spencer's virtues or, to be precise, his campaign's virtues, I'd experienced enough politicking to last me a decade or two. I stared across the room at the two large Darius Spencer campaign posters flanking the podium, and wondered what Spencer would have thought of this political send-off.

Liz fanned herself with her program then leaned over to whisper in my ear. "Talk about being bored to death."

"Are these candidates as clueless as they appear?" I eyed the crowd of mourners, several of whom chose to listen with their eyes closed. I could use a power nap myself.

"I suppose it would be rude to slip out," I remarked to Liz.

"No one is sneaking out," said my mother, whose sixty-two-year-old hearing had not diminished a tinge. "Some of my clients are here as well as members of the Chamber of Commerce. We can't do anything tacky."

I personally couldn't think of anything tackier than turning a memorial service into a political rally, but I didn't want to annoy my mother who prided herself on her perfect etiquette. Mother could give Miss Manners a pointer or two.

Sometimes it amazed me that my grandmother had given birth to my mother. The two women were complete opposites—my mother was as classy as they come, although she sometimes acted as if she had a stick up her butt. My grandmother belonged in a class of her own and was usually the one prodding said stick.

I breathed a sigh of relief that Gran's injuries kept her from attending the service. Although she was upset that she couldn't help me detect, we were all better off with her spending a second night in the hospital.

I yawned and immediately a refrain of yawns echoed in the rows around me. The political orator at the podium finally realized his audience seemed more captivated by their phones than by him. He bid us farewell and handed the microphone to Janet.

Janet thanked the mourners for coming out to pay their respects and graciously invited everyone back to her house for refreshments. We waited our turn while the widow and other family members walked down the aisle, followed by attendees seated in the front rows of the chapel.

"Do you mind if we stop at her house?" Brian asked Liz. "It would be the polite as well as the politically expedient thing for me to do."

She smiled at him. "Certainly, plus I have a condolence basket of spa items I wanted to drop off for her."

I arched an eyebrow at my friend. "You're bringing spa items to Janet?"

"Can you imagine how much collagen the poor woman has lost due to this tragic crime?" Liz asserted. Then she leaned forward to scrutinize my skin. "You're looking a little dry yourself. Try my new aloe and grape extract moisturizer. It will solve all your problems."

"I need to find a murderer, not a moisturizer," I lamented. "But I definitely want to visit the Spencers' house."

"I'm also dying to find out if Janet wants to list it," Mother said. I threw her one of my "do you always have to be in Realtor mode" looks. She had the decency to look abashed.

"It's an enormous house and a lot of property for a single woman to take care of," Mother defended herself. "Especially with both kids in college. I'm sure she'd love to have someone take it off her hands."

"Let's give her a week or two to mourn before you wave a listing agreement in front of her," I suggested. Sometimes my over-achiever mother's antics made me cringe.

She shrugged and turned her attention to Bradford who, as usual, ignored our mother-daughter commentary.

I gazed at the crowd of people filling the aisles, anxious to escape the overheated chapel. Political candidates and local business owners shook hands and conversed. Doug Blake and Abe chatted as they slowly made their way out of the chapel. Doug's hands flailed in the air. He was either describing something to Abe or trying to turn himself into a human fan.

I ratcheted up the speed on my own program fanning. The mortuary must not have anticipated such a large crowd or their air conditioning needed a makeover. I could use a makeover myself since the sweat beading my forehead had turned my bangs into frizzy corkscrew curls.

As they passed by our aisle, Abe threw me a wide smile, but Doug frowned at me. Was it something I'd said? Done?

Or someone I married eighteen years ago?

Couples passed by our seats, many of whom I didn't personally know, but who appeared to recognize me. After more than a dozen strangers shot curious glances in my direction, I questioned my decision to attend the service in an attempt to seek answers.

I remained positive Hank was innocent of this hideous crime, but until we proved it, I doubted anyone else would agree with me. With the exception of one person.

Darius Spencer's murderer.

CHAPTER THIRTY-TWO

The Spencer estate reminded me of something out of a *Luxury Home* magazine. I didn't know how many acres they owned, but the money squandered on wrought iron fencing alone looked like it equaled my mortgage.

I'd spent so much time running around town on my decorating and detecting missions that I hadn't had time to prepare a sympathy casserole. Since the best caterer in town parked her trucks off to the side of the expansive six-car garage, it didn't look like anyone would miss my runny lasagna.

Not until I trudged three blocks from my parking spot did I realize Janet had arranged valet service for her guests. Weirdest memorial ever!

A young woman in a conservative uniform greeted me and offered to take my purse and put it in a back bedroom. I would have preferred to hand off my panty hose as well. Dumbest fashion decision yet this week. For some reason, I'd decided bare legs were a no-no at a funeral. Now my thighs felt like they'd been encased in hot concrete.

Servers circulated with trays of champagne, which seemed somewhat inappropriate given the circumstances. Not wanting to appear rude, I accepted a glass and wandered through the house in search of a familiar face.

Tricia and Lars Taylor huddled with a dark-suited, heavyset and balding man I recognized as a bank customer although I couldn't recall his name. I assumed the majority of the political candidates present were supporters of Spencer's no-growth campaign. Were the Taylors here to show their respect or spy on their opponents?

Only one way to find out. The heavyset man moved to the bar and began a conversation with a local judge, leaving the Taylors alone. I ambled over and greeted them. Tricia and I brushed our cheeks together in air kiss fashion, and Lars shook my empty hand, the one not holding the excellent champagne.

"A sad situation, isn't it?" I said to the couple.

"Tragic," Lars replied, his florid face as red as the petals on the two dozen roses nestled in a crystal vase behind us. He reached into his pocket for a handkerchief and wiped perspiration from his forehead.

"Spencer was a worthy rival," said Tricia. Her brown eyes looked thoughtful as she gazed around the room, possibly in search of her new political opponent.

"You must have been stunned by his murder," I said.

She sipped her champagne before replying. "Darius and I disagreed on many issues, but we kept it a fair campaign. It's difficult to imagine his life being cut short by a disgruntled employee..." Her voice trailed off and her pale eyebrows lifted to meet her thick blond bangs.

Suddenly she blurted out, "Laurel, I know you and Hank divorced awhile ago, but do you think it's appropriate for you to be here?"

I stepped back, affronted by her bluntness. "Janet and I are friends. I'm here to support her."

Tricia didn't appear convinced, and I wondered how many others in the room might share her sentiments.

"Plus I don't believe Hank killed Spencer," I asserted.

Lars latched on to my forearm. "If he didn't murder Spencer, who do you think did?"

"That's what I'm trying to find out," I replied with so much vigor my champagne danced out of my flute and on to the off-white carpet.

He bleated out a guffaw. "So you're gonna play Nancy Drew and interrogate people? Good luck with that."

"Someone else committed the murder, and I intend to prove it." I finished what remained of my champagne and placed the glass on the table. "I understand a large crowd gathered in the Liars' Bench to watch the Sacramento Kings game the night Spencer died. Weren't you also there that evening, Lars?"

"Me and half the merchants on Main Street." Lars cocked his head to the side, displaying a long, thin scab running from his ear to his jaw line. "It was a noisy crowd that night, and Hank was definitely loopy. He seemed agitated but I dunno why."

I did. According to Hank, he'd been upset about my burgeoning romance with Tom. Spencer's murder had certainly halted any future burgeoning between Tom and me.

"Did you overhear Hank make any specific threats against Spencer?" I asked.

"I didn't pay attention to everything the guy yakked about. I wanted to concentrate on the game." Suddenly Lars snapped his fingers. "Someone else kept yammering on about Spencer that night. Said he'd about had it with his next door neighbor."

"Spencer's nearest neighbor is a half mile away from this house."

Lars shook his head. "Naw, not here. I'm talking about the building next to the Hangtown Hotel."

I tried to visualize that section of Main Street, but before I could respond, Lars pointed to two men entering through the massive double oak front doors.

"That's who—your neighborhood bookstore owner."

CHAPTER THIRTY-THREE

My brow furrowed while I pondered Lars's remark. If I didn't stop sleuthing, I would need a Botox infusion before my birthday.

"Doug isn't thrilled about the construction mess," I said, "but the renovation would have been completed fairly soon, if Spencer were still alive."

Or if Hank weren't in jail, I thought to myself.

"You must not have heard that Spencer terminated Doug's lease," Tricia added.

"But Doug's rented that space for over thirty years," I protested. "Why would Spencer want to get rid of a successful tenant?"

"I guess once Spencer started the renovation, he realized its potential for bringing business meetings and small conventions into town," Lars said. "He wanted the bookstore space for additional meeting rooms and such."

"Doug told us he searched for a new venue," Tricia said, "but the only available spot was a small space in a strip mall outside of town, not exactly a prime location for an independent bookstore. That's why this no-growth movement is so ridiculous."

I ignored her pro-growth sentiment as I gnawed over the possibility that my favorite bookstore owner could be a killer. Doug's store offered a wonderful selection of mysteries for its patrons. He could easily research how to successfully murder his landlord without even leaving his store. And, despite having informed me he'd walked home from the bar that night, he wouldn't be the first murderer to lie to me.

It was so *annoying* when they did that.

Tricia felt compelled to share that Lars had driven straight home after the Kings game ended, giving him an alibi. Although, from my perspective, spousal alibis were always subject to question. She waved to a local Superior Court Judge and walked away. Lars started to follow his wife then turned to me.

"Look, you may enjoy playing detective, but there are some people in this county who might not appreciate you digging up any dirt."

I frowned at him. "People who had something to do with Spencer's death?"

He pressed his beefy palm into my shoulder. "Influential people you don't want to mess with. Trust me." He removed his hand and walked across the room to join Tricia. I could feel the imprint of his heavy hand and even more heavy-handed threat long after he left my side.

Was I starting to make the true murderer nervous? Maybe there was a conspiracy at play, and Spencer's killer had not acted alone. I needed to share Lars's remarks with my family if I could ever locate them. This gala, I mean, memorial reception, must include the back of the estate as well. I decided to visit their guest bath before I wandered the grounds in search of my family and friends.

I tapped one of the servers on his white-shirted shoulder and asked for directions. He pointed down a very long hallway where he indicated a bathroom for the use of the guests. I meandered down a corridor lined with family photos as well as pictures of Spencer shaking hands with virtually every dignitary in the state. He'd even posed with former Governor Schwarzenegger. Both men wore the same smug "I can smoke a cigar wherever and whenever I want to" expressions.

Two doors remained closed, so I knocked on the first one which resulted in an annoyed "I'm still peeing" response. I waited patiently for the guest to relieve herself, so I could do the same. Once I completed that urgent task, I could continue with my own assignment.

After washing my hands and fluffing my hair in the luxurious marble bath, whose accessories probably cost more than a week of my salary, I opened the door onto the hallway. Simultaneously, the door next to the bathroom flew open, and Scott Shelton and I crashed into one another. His black felt cowboy hat went flying but luckily, no one else did.

"Sorry," Scott apologized, helping me maintain my balance. The man moved with the force of one of his stallions. I fortunately remained upright.

He bent over to retrieve his hat while I straightened out my wool dress, which clung to my pantyhose, turning my knee-length dress into a mini. I glanced into the room Scott had vacated. The door opened into a magnificent study, including box-beam wood ceilings and floor-to-ceiling bookshelves lined with leather tomes. French doors led to the gardens behind the house.

"What a gorgeous room," I said to Scott. Then my brain clicked in. "What were you doing in Spencer's office?"

He tapped his hat against his thigh before replying. "Looking for the bathroom."

I pointed over my shoulder. "You were one room off."

"So I see." He looked as if he wanted to expand on his answer but could not come up with a better explanation. After another brief apology, Scott loped down the hall to the great room.

It didn't take a detective to determine Scott had lied to me. What reason did he have for entering Spencer's office? The same reason I had.

None. Which is why I closed the door behind me hoping no one else would enter while I checked it out.

There is a fine line between sleuthing and trespassing, and I really wished someone would clue me in as to that line of demarcation. Maybe someday one of my favorite cozy authors would write a book on *An Amateur's Guide to Sleuthing*.

I paused for a minute questioning my intentions before I persuaded myself that Hank's freedom was at stake. My gaze swiveled around the room. I jumped when my eyes locked with Spencer's. He stared at me from behind a framed 24 x 36 sized campaign poster.

It almost felt like Spencer's eyes were following me around the room, but I had work to do. I presumed the detectives examined all of Spencer's papers. But they may have been so satisfied with whatever evidence they found on Hank that they hadn't bothered analyzing the victim's financial statements. There were no signs of fingerprint powder, crime scene tape or anything official, but Janet

159

undoubtedly would have had a cleaning service remove anything the crime scene techs left behind.

Besides a massive desk and the bookcases, the office included a small drafting table in a corner of the room. A set of blueprints rested on top, so theoretically they were exposed to the public.

I identified the plans as those for the Hangtown Hotel renovation. Hank must possess another set of blueprints, possibly at his apartment, but more likely at the site itself. I couldn't pass up an opportunity like this. Plus technically, as pro bono detective for the defense, I had a right to review them.

At least, that's how I justified my current position. I glanced at Spencer's poster, and I could swear he smiled in approval at my decision.

Or that glass of champagne was causing me to see things.

Over the years, I had reviewed enough appraisals on new construction to feel comfortable reading blueprints. Spencer's decision to remove the wall between the hotel and the bookstore made a lot of sense. Not only would the additional space provide meeting rooms at street level, but there would also be additional hotel rooms on the second floor. Someone had penned multiple notations where the demolition of the wall would occur.

I flipped the pages back to the way I'd found them then walked over to Spencer's desk. Going through his drawers seemed morally reprehensible. Yet there must be a reason why Scott sneaked into Spencer's office.

I wondered if the lanky rancher found what he'd been searching for. He hadn't been holding anything when he bumped into me, but he could have hidden something from sight. Spencer had already foreclosed on the hotel. Did he hold additional paper on Scott's ranch? Could that be the reason Scott mentioned moving to Alaska?

Or had Scott threatened Spencer and now hoped to recover any menacing missives he'd sent the victim?

The sound of voices in the hallway abruptly ended my moral dilemma. I hoped the newcomer was merely a guest who needed to use the bathroom and not a family member on their way to the office. I bumped into the desk and knocked the stack of papers to the floor.

I bent over and grabbed the scattered documents. Putting them back in their original order proved an impossible task, but maybe

Janet wouldn't notice they'd been disturbed. I shuffled them into a pile, glancing at the document resting at the top of the stack.

I squinted at the tiny font on the lengthy grant deed, perusing the more salient terms of the deed. Why would Chad Langdon grant his ownership share in Mountain High Winery to his cousin?

The sound of a low male voice outside the office door spooked me, and the document floated to the floor. I bent over and retrieved it as a female trilled a response. I froze as the glass doorknob slowly rotated.

CHAPTER THIRTY-FOUR

It's amazing how fast I can move when necessary. I escaped through the French door mere seconds before anyone entered the room. The glass door nicked shut behind me, and I cowered with my back against the stucco exterior wall, hoping to peek inside to catch a glimpse of the new intruders.

Three couples, all of whom looked like they belonged on the cover of *Town and Country Magazine,* stared at me. I couldn't think of a reasonable excuse for peering back into the room, so I smiled and asked for directions to the bar. The size zero blond, with an improbable double D chest, turned glazed turquoise eyes on me and pointed toward the gazebo. Based on her tipsy expression, she'd visited the bar a few times herself.

Even though I was thrilled to escape detection, I was annoyed not to have discovered who'd entered the room after me. It could have been another lost soul in search of the bathroom. Or Janet. Or any of the other suspects on my growing list.

I finally discovered my family and friends stationed next to the temporary bar. Smart planning. I didn't need any more alcohol, but I knew from past experience that this caterer served delicious appetizers.

I grabbed a white china plate and filled it with grilled veggies, then offset that healthy choice with a variety of pastry-filled items. It didn't matter what the caterer stuffed inside. If flaky dough covered the item, it landed on my plate. Briefly.

Mother and Bradford stood next to Liz, Brian, and a handsome man in his thirties, attired in a well-fitted expensive charcoal suit.

"It's about time you joined us," Mother griped. "I was beginning to think you walked all the way from the funeral home."

"Ha ha," I said, although it sounded more like hack hack since the mini beef Wellington lodged itself near the top of my esophagus.

I grabbed Liz's glass of champagne and swallowed several gulps of the expensive bubbles. I handed the flute back to my friend.

"Do you need a good thumping?" Liz asked.

My brows drew together. Yes, I did, but I didn't want to discuss my sex life in front of a stranger.

Brian gave me a resounding thwack on the back.

"Hey, cut it out," I yelled at him.

"We thought you were choking, luv. Where have you been? Rex has been dying to meet you."

"Rex? You mean Hank's attorney?" I swiveled my head to the left and right in search of the man who was supposedly the best defense attorney in Placerville.

The tall slender man standing next to Brian put his hand out to me. "It's nice to put a face to a voice."

Wow. For some reason I'd imagined Rex Ashford would be a dignified white-haired chap about my mother's age. Not the dark-haired Chippendale lookalike I'd seen talking to Brian at the Cornbread and Cowpokes event. I wondered if his success was due to him charming the pants, or skirts, off the female jurors.

"Thank you for taking Hank's case," I said. "I know he's innocent, and I've been trying my hardest to figure out who did it."

"Your mother raves about your past sleuthing successes." He winked at me. "Have you come up with any new evidence for me?"

I shook my head. "Nothing substantive. I have a list of suspects who are long on motives and opportunity, but I am sadly lacking in actual clues. Did you receive the evidence file?"

"The DA assigned the case to Camille Winterspoon," Rex said, morphing into attorney mode. "She told me I'd have the entire file by tomorrow."

I turned to Brian. "What's Camille like? Hopefully, she's not one of those bulldog prosecutors."

"I assume you're not referring to me." A sly grin crossed Brian's face. "Camille is more like a pit bull crossed with a lioness."

Rex nodded. "They say she takes no prisoners, but she not only takes them, she gets them sentenced for exceptionally long terms. Sometimes a few years of case work are needed before new deputy district attorneys learn how to negotiate."

"I hate to have her practicing her prosecuting skills on Hank," I muttered.

Rex patted my forearm. "Let me see what I can do to get the charges reduced."

Reduced would be nice. Removed would be far better.

Rex left our group and went off to share his condolences with Janet Spencer, and I updated everyone on my recent discovery in Spencer's office.

Bradford frowned. "You weren't going through the victim's confidential documents, were you?"

Once a detective, always a detective.

"Not intentionally," I weaseled. "I bumped into the desk and the papers scattered everywhere. That's when I noticed the grant deed from Chad to Spencer."

My mother, the vigilant broker, frowned in concentration. "Did you see if it recorded?" she asked.

I mumbled a bad word to myself. How quickly I'd forgotten my underwriting skills. "I didn't notice."

"Too bad," she said. Her gaze veered in the direction of the patio outside Spencer's office. "There are too many people milling around for me to sneak in and find out."

"There will be no sneaking into the victim's office by my wife," Bradford announced firmly.

"Okay," she meekly replied.

"If anyone is going into Spencer's office," said Bradford, "it will be me."

I stared at the retired detective in amazement, and he shot me a conspiratorial grin. Let the force be with you!

CHAPTER THIRTY-FIVE

Despite Bradford's willingness to participate in a little amateur sleuthing, once we returned inside, we discovered the office had become a locked room in our absence. Mother indicated she could find out if the deed had been recorded through one of her sources, so retrieving the document wasn't critical. I wondered what prompted Janet to lock the office, but that would remain her secret. Along with so many others she seemed to possess.

Friday morning I arrived at work, exulting over the end of the workweek. Mr. Boxer promptly squashed my inner celebration by ordering me to complete my decorating project by Sunday evening at the latest. When Hangtown Bank opened its doors Monday morning, the bank's pioneer spirit must be displayed in full gold rush splendor. Or else.

Mr. Boxer left that simple implied threat on my voicemail then announced he'd be leaving early for a weekend getaway in the city. I wondered how the dignified Mr. Boxer relaxed on vacation, but the best I could visualize was an assignation at the San Francisco Opera House or the Museum of Modern Art.

My personal daydream included a torrid tryst on a tropical island with my newly sleek body wrapped in Tom Hunter's arms. Although with my luck, any exotic weekend foreplay would inevitably result in me turning into a sunburned, bug-bitten, dysentery-afflicted tourist.

I shook my head. Thoughts of a future romantic rendezvous needed to go on the backburner for now. Possibly forever, based on the way our relationship was progressing. Or not progressing.

Tom and I hadn't spoken since our conversation at the hospital Wednesday night.

I chewed on my ballpoint pen, finally admitting to myself that I'd behaved poorly that evening. The guy only wanted to do his job without my interference. Maybe it was time to cut him a break.

I dialed Tom's cell, expecting to leave a groveling apology in his voicemail. He startled me by answering his phone.

"Laurel, what a surprise," he said in a tone that sounded more official than personal. "I was about to call you."

"I wanted to apologize for the way I spoke to you at the hospital the other night," I said into the receiver, wishing we were face to face, so he could read my body language.

And maybe do something spectacular to said body.

"I understand. You were upset about your grandmother and your close call with the mountain lion."

"And worried about Hank, of course," I replied.

"Yeah, of course." His tone echoed his frustration over the line.

"Do you have any news about his case?"

"No," he barked, not even trying to hide his irritation with me. "Although Deputy Fletcher's research may have produced something helpful regarding the skeleton at your grandmother's house, if you're still interested in *that* case."

"Of course, I am. If it will help old Harold's situation, it might cheer up my grandmother. She's been in the dumps since they released her from the hospital. Mom put her under house arrest."

That comment finally elicited a laugh from Tom. Something about that man's laugh was so comforting and yet so sensual.

I heard Tom conversing with someone else before he came back on the line. "Fletch wondered if he could stop at your grandmother's house and ask her some questions," Tom said. "He's off duty at five tonight. Do you think she'd mind?"

"Are you kidding? This will provide a terrific pick-me-up for her. My boss already left for the weekend, so I can meet Fletch shortly after five. I need to complete my decorating project by Sunday night, and I hope to find some worthwhile antiques in Gran's shed."

"Okay, I'll tell him you'll see him then. Goodbye," Tom said. Before he could hang up, I called out his name.

"Tom, maybe you can join me at Gran's house tonight. Or stop by my house later. We haven't been alone together all week."

"No, we haven't." I knew him well enough that I could almost hear him running his hands through his thick hair. "Look, Laurel, I've been thinking that maybe we should take a break."

My heart dropped faster than a Six Flags roller coaster. "What do you mean?"

"This situation with Hank is creating too many issues between us, both personally and professionally. You running around looking for other suspects has damaged my credibility in the Sheriff's Department."

I sat in silence, formulating a tactful rebuttal to his comment. "You understand my motives for trying to get Hank out of jail, don't you?"

Tom waited a few seconds before he replied. "I'm not sure that *you* are truly certain what your motives are. I think you have some unresolved issues with Hank which need to be addressed before you and I can proceed any further with our relationship."

"But, but..."

"I have to go," he said. "I'll, um, I guess I'll see you around."

The line went dead.

CHAPTER THIRTY-SIX

The rest of the day passed in a blurred frenzy of activity while I tried to distract myself from the crushing impact of Tom's words. I wanted to hide in a corner and wallow in pity, but instead, I soldiered on, working through the last-minute tasks Mr. Boxer assigned before he left for his fun-filled weekend.

Only once did I give in to my despair. I ran over to the Candy Strike Emporium and purchased a one-pound box of homemade fudge. After I returned to the office, I phoned Liz at her spa, knowing my best friend would have wise counsel for me. According to her voicemail, she would be at a meeting all afternoon and not able to return calls until the evening. Throughout the day, I continued to hope Tom would call back and apologize for his dumb suggestion to take time off from one another. His silence was a deafening confirmation of his decision.

I waddled out of the bank a few minutes after five, having consumed a third of the box of fudge. I eased into my overheated car, pushed the air conditioning to high, and managed to arrive at my grandmother's house in less than ten minutes.

When I stepped on the sidewalk leading to her front porch, I noticed a few patches needing repair. Gran had left her door unlocked, a better option than limping through the house to welcome visitors. I called out her name, hoping she hadn't fallen asleep waiting for me.

"Keep your shirt on," she said, "I'm on my way."

"Stay where you are. I'll come to you." I headed in the direction of her voice, which sounded like it came from the living room, or more accurately, the parlor. This room always gave me the feeling I'd time-traveled back to the early twentieth century. Decades-old blue striped wallpaper covered the walls above white paneled wainscoting. My grandmother had replaced some of the original furniture, but a few of the family ancestral pieces remained scattered throughout the house.

Gran sat in her bentwood rocking chair, her left leg propped on her cherished needlepoint ottoman. An oversized book by one of her favorite authors rested on the mahogany end table. Blasts of cool air from the ceiling vents ruffled the lace curtains covering her windowpanes.

I walked over and kissed her wrinkled forehead.

"How's my favorite granddaughter?" she asked. We both chuckled since I was and would always be her only granddaughter.

I plopped down in a velour wing chair and leaned back, wondering whether to bother Gran with my romantic issues.

"There are two lines on your forehead that need to disappear before they become permanent," she said. "What's your honey gone and done?"

"How did you know?"

"It's as plain as the frown on your face," she replied before pointing in my direction. "And you've left a trail of chocolate clues that anyone related to you would notice."

I looked down at my fudge-spotted blouse. My Gran could read me like her large-print book.

I sighed and blew out my breath. "Tom thinks we should take a break from one another. He feels my involvement in Hank's case has created a negative impact on him professionally."

"Men can be such jackasses."

I loved the way my grandmother never held back an opinion.

"He also believes I still have feelings for Hank." I scowled in her direction. "How can he think such a thing?"

Her crepe-paper thin lips pursed together. "What do you think? Would you take back Hank if they set him free?"

"Of course not." I jumped up and began to pace the scuffed wooden floor. "Hank and I had good years together and bad years together. When he left me, my heart felt as if he'd ripped it in two. But time, as well as Tom, have helped to heal those wounds. Hank and I remain the supportive parents of our two children, but that's the total extent of my feelings for him."

"Alrighty then. I'm sure Tom will eventually realize his true feelings for you. Though the man might need a wee bit of nudging. Say, what'd you do with that corset thingamabob? I thought your fella's eyes would pop right outta their sockets when he saw you in that getup."

We both giggled and almost missed the sound of the doorbell ringing. I sprinted to the foyer secretly hoping Tom had changed his mind and decided to stop by after all. Instead, Fletch, dressed in casual clothes, stood on the stoop smiling. My face must have appeared crestfallen because he immediately asked what was wrong.

"Everything is fine," I said, my lower lip trembling. "I hoped Detective Hunter might be accompanying you."

Fletch looked puzzled. "The lieutenant didn't mention anything about coming along. Do you want me to call him?"

"No, he, I mean we— Never mind." I blinked hard to make sure no stray tears wobbled down my cheeks. "Tom said you had some questions for my grandmother."

"Yeah, I've been doing some research on her backyard case. I hoped she might have some personal information about your family that could help clarify a few things."

I escorted Fletch into the living room where he shook hands with my grandmother then perched his six-foot-two frame on her hard-as-a-horse's-rump original horsehair sofa.

"So what'd you find out, young man?" Gran asked. "Did you clear my granpappy's name?"

"Not yet, but maybe with your help I can," Fletch responded, his blue eyes twinkling.

"You bet your boots I'll help. Honey, get this fine man a cold beer." She peered at Fletch over her wire rims. "Unless you'd like a soda?"

"I'm officially off the clock," he said. "That beer sounds great."

"I'll have one, too, while you're up," Gran ordered.

I wandered into the kitchen and grabbed two beers as requested and a root beer for me. I delivered the beverages to Fletch and Gran, popped the top of my can of soda and listened in on their conversation.

Gran rocked back and forth in her chair, looking like she was a million miles away. Or eighty years away, lost in childhood memories.

"So you wondered if Granpappy supported the Confederacy?" she asked Fletch. "He grew up in Kentucky, but I don't know what his political leanings were."

I threw a perplexed look at Fletch. "Did the two sides fight in California during the Civil War?"

"No battles were fought here," he said. "But there were people sympathetic to the Confederate cause. They tried to recruit soldiers as well as raise cash, especially near the end of the war."

"Oh, yeah, those Confederate fellas even pulled off a stagecoach robbery to help their cause," said Gran. "I forgot about that one."

"You're kidding," I said.

"Nope," she replied. "The robbers lucked out because two stages were traveling together. They not only got two Wells Fargo strongboxes, loaded with gold, but large amounts of silver bullion from Carson City. That's one of the reasons they named it the Bullion Bend Robbery."

Fletch added, "They left a receipt on behalf of the Confederacy saying they were using the money to outfit California recruits."

"If you have to get robbed," I said. "I guess a polite bandit is preferable. Were they caught?"

Gran shrugged, but Fletch nodded. "The robbers escaped to the Bay Area, but the sheriff and his men recovered the majority of the money they hid in this county. Later the authorities arrested most of the gang and brought them back to Placerville for the trial. One of them went to prison, another they hung here in town, and the rest got the case moved back to Contra Costa County. Those men all got off scot-free."

"What?" I yelled my dismay that a life of crime could pay.

"Yep," said Fletch. "And oddly enough, they ended up becoming pillars of the community. Fascinating, isn't it?"

Fascinating indeed! It made me wonder if any of the current pillars of Placerville was involved in criminal activities.

"Okay, this is interesting, but what does it have to do with our property?" I asked.

"Sorry, I get excited about these old stories," Fletch replied. "Besides the bullet the mobile crime scene unit found in the mine shaft, a couple of other things were pulled out that the techs shoved in the evidence file. The guys didn't have any idea they were historically significant."

"Like what?" I edged forward in my seat. Now we were getting some place.

"Like a silver coin minted in 1864. That would indicate the body couldn't have landed in the shaft any earlier."

My phone rang and I jumped. I reached into my purse and pulled out my cell hoping to see Tom's name appear on the screen. No such luck, although I was glad Liz couldn't see my doleful expression when I realized it was her and not my detective returning my call.

"Thanks for calling back." I walked into the kitchen out of earshot of my grandmother and the deputy.

"Of course, luv. Tell me, what has your detective gone and done?"

"He thinks we should take a break. He says I've embarrassed him by trying to get Hank out of jail."

"Well, you have created a bit of a sticky wicket for him at work."

"If his detectives had done their job properly and arrested the real murderer, I wouldn't need to stick my nose in his affairs," I responded with a huff.

"Hey, don't get in a snit. I'm on your side, sweetie. What can I do to help?"

"Can you or Brian talk some sense into him? Maybe explain my position better than I can?"

"No, I think that's something only you can do. But you'll have the opportunity tomorrow night."

"What are you talking about?"

"Oh, dear. Did I forget to tell you Chad Langdon asked the Sassy Saloon Gals to entertain at an impromptu event at the winery tomorrow? The proceeds go to the Benefit the Kids charity, so it's definitely for a worthy cause."

"I guess as long as it doesn't benefit Chad's political pockets, I'm in." I blew a robust sigh into the receiver. "But what does this event have to do with Tom?"

"Your honey is on the board, remember? I'm sure he'll feel obligated to attend."

I mulled over Liz's information. "Okay, but I'm not wearing that tortuous corset again."

She sighed and I could almost sense her disapproving frown. "Whatevah," she said, enunciating each annoying syllable. "I'm sure you can find an equally suitable but more comfortable top in one of the stores in town. Check out Redneck Bling. The blingier the better, I always say."

Right-o as the Brits would say. Liz offered to pick me up at my house the following evening and I agreed. Even if I failed to woo my detective back into my life, at least I'd help improve the coffers of a worthy charity.

I returned to the parlor to find Gran and Fletch deep in discussion about some of my forebears' exploits.

"I can't imagine Granpappy rooting for the Confederacy, or getting involved in that Bullion Bend stick-up, but you're welcome to go through the shed. Remember your goal is to prove old Harold innocent." Gran looked at me. "Laurel, can you take this nice young man out back and let him look around?"

I nodded. I needed to rummage through the shed myself to find items for the bank. Plus if a four-footed oversized kitty showed up again, a man with a gun would be standing next to me. Although somehow I sensed Fletch and his weapon would not be nearly as terrifying to the mountain lion as my karaoke performance had been the other night.

CHAPTER THIRTY-SEVEN

We traipsed through the weeds, which seemed to have grown another foot since my last foray. By the time we arrived at the shed, tiny star thistle burrs coated his jeans and my slacks. Fletch had wisely worn leather cowboy boots. I had unwisely worn sandals and my toes were complaining about my poor fashion choice.

Fletch shoved open the heavy door then halted in the doorway. "Whoa."

"Scary, isn't it?" I said.

"I don't suppose any of this stuff is categorized by time period?"

I almost fell on the floor laughing, but I didn't want to land on any creeping critters. Battling the cobwebs hanging from the windows and rusty farm equipment sufficed as disgusting enough.

"I don't think the shed has been a top priority for my grandmother." I scanned the stacks of boxes crammed everywhere. "Nor anyone else in the family."

"Do you have a game plan?" Fletch asked.

"How about we head for the nearest bar?"

Fletch laughed, but my remark wasn't entirely in jest. It would take more than a couple of hours—more like a few months—to wade through the clutter.

We spent the next hour sifting through the contents of various boxes and cartons stored in the shed. We caught up on the latest news of our high school classmates, marriages, divorces, new additions. Fletch informed me his mother, whom I vaguely recalled from our early years, had moved to Florida. Actually, I remembered her excellent peanut butter cookies more than the woman herself.

I could almost visualize my tombstone. Here lies a woman who never met a cookie she didn't like.

As we chatted, the pile of discarded trash grew exponentially. Mice had nibbled on the old books and newspapers that looked like they could have been interesting reading.

If you had absolutely nothing else going on in your life.

I sorted through the old volumes. Some I would donate to the Friends of the Library monthly sale. Others landed on the discard pile. Fletch helped me lift a large, heavy box that had been stored on the top shelf. When I dug inside, I discovered a treasure of family memories.

Several dusty journals and leather-bound photo albums had somehow managed to escape turning into a critter buffet. I grabbed a scratched wooden folding chair and plunked down. It squeaked its disapproval—a noise I optimistically attributed to its age and not the fudge I'd consumed earlier in the day.

Slowly turning the pages of one album, I smiled at the sepia photos of my grandmother as a small child. I assumed the pictures were of Gran since the petite blond woman holding her hand looked like a pint-size version of my own tall and elegant mother. I found it interesting that many of our family traits skipped generations. My personality resembled my grandmother's far more than my mother's, much to Mother's dismay. And I definitely had not inherited my mother's OCD genes.

"Can I help you go through those journals?" Fletch asked.

"No, that's okay. You've spent enough time researching this case. I think my daughter will enjoy learning more about her family history. Plus it might take her mind off her father."

Fletch threw me a sympathetic look. "I stopped and saw Hank a few days ago. He told me he's counting on you to find out who the real killer is."

I sighed so deeply the inch of dust on the album powdered my nose and cheeks. "My life is a disaster. My boyfriend, or ex-boyfriend, based on our conversation this morning, says my interference has created issues with the Sheriff's Department. But my kids are traumatized by their father's arrest. What if Hank ends up in prison just because no one bothered to ask the right questions?"

"You've got a lot on your plate, that's for sure." Fletch rubbed his chin, leaving a dusty gray shadow behind. "Look, I can't promise you, but let me see if I can learn anything helpful. I mean, a man can't just let his old quarterback sit in a cellblock, can he?"

"No, he can't." I jumped up and hugged the deputy. "You've officially..." I stopped when I caught his expression, "okay, unofficially joined Team Hank."

A neighbor's rooster crowed an early wakeup call the next morning. I rolled over and peeked at the clock. Six thirty on a Saturday morning was far too early for this mother to rise and shine. My arms felt sore from hauling the old books and gold mining stuff from Gran's shed to my car.

After my return home, I'd stayed up well past midnight reading my great-great-grandfather's journals. Despite Harold's spindly handwriting and the faded ink, his description of his younger days kept me turning pages until my eyes refused to stay open any longer. While the information proved interesting from a historical standpoint, it didn't answer any burning questions about the body in the bottom of the mineshaft.

Oh, well. Mr. Bones had remained hidden for more than a century. A few more days or years would not make a difference in anyone's life. Except for Gran, who was desperate to learn the truth about her grandfather's past.

And my mother, who wanted the property on the market yesterday.

A half hour later, Jenna slid into one of the oak spindle-backed kitchen chairs. The mouth-watering scent of the Kona coffee I'd brewed must have wafted its way upstairs. Her eyes appeared redder than mine were.

"You're up early," I said to her. That was my subtle way of asking why she wasn't sleeping until ten like usual.

"I had a nightmare." She rubbed her eyelids so hard I thought her tender skin would peel off. "About Dad. I dreamt that some old guy with a badge, strung him up on the gallows. When they let it drop, Dad fell and...then I woke up."

I reached for her slim hand and stroked it. "Did you and Ben watch a western last night?"

She shook her head. "No, it's probably because I leafed through the newspaper to check out the Wagon Train activities next week. I guess my subconscious mixed the two thoughts together. When can we visit Dad?"

"He told me he doesn't want you kids to see him in jail. Plus he's optimistic he'll be out any day now."

"But what if they don't let him out and he goes to trial? There's no possibility Dad can get the death penalty, is there?" Her face was so ashen her freckles looked like they'd been painted on her cheeks.

"Of course not. He'll get off. He has to..." My voice petered off as I wondered what would happen if Hank did not get out of jail.

If I couldn't prove my ex-husband did not kill Darius Spencer.

I slammed my mug down, and the lukewarm liquid slopped on to the table. A guilty verdict was not an option. Maybe I should stop my subtle approach to sleuthing and start accusing some of the more likely suspects. Would I upset someone enough to confess to his or her crime?

Hardly. It was far more likely I would become the next victim. But it was beginning to look like that was a chance I needed to take.

I told Jenna about Harold's old journals, and she jumped at the chance to help solve at least one mystery. With that project delegated, I would have more time to shop and sleuth along Main Street this morning.

My costume search began at Redneck Bling. The store lacked bustiers, but it definitely did not lack bling. I selected a long-sleeved red sequined top, a pair of dangling earrings and a matching set of inexpensive rhinestone bracelets to adorn my wrists tonight. The jewelry reminded me of Hank's handcuffs. I stuffed the bag in my purse and switched my brain into detecting mode.

Next stop—Blake's Books.

Doug had acted peculiarly toward me ever since the police arrested Hank. I wondered about the reason for his unusual behavior. This might be the perfect opportunity to confirm Tricia Taylor's comments regarding Spencer's proposed expansion.

I pushed on the door and two tiny bells tinkled overhead. Snowball, the oversized long-haired white cat, stretched luxuriously across a pile of books in the window display. She threw me a sleepy-eyed look then furiously began licking her toenails.

If you're going to sit in a store window all day, you better make sure your claws are clean.

My own claws might need sharpening in order to pry information out of Doug.

The proprietor walked behind his counter and dropped a stack of leather-bound books on the glass surface. I gazed at the volumes, stymied for an appropriate segue into my investigation.

"Are those local history books?" I asked.

"Yes," Doug said before moving the pile to a shelf behind him.

"Could I take a peek at them? Did you hear about the skeleton found in my grandmother's backyard? Gran is petrified her grandfather may have killed his former partner. My job is to figure out who this pile of bones really is. And how he ended up in that boarded-up mineshaft."

Doug relaxed his shoulders and expelled a long breath. The proprietor seemed relieved we'd found a dead guy in Gran's backyard. He turned to the pile and selected three volumes.

"These books all deal with the history of the gold country." Doug laid the books in front of me. "Is there a particular incident you want to research?"

"I'm not sure. Based on a wee bit of evidence, the Sheriff's Department thinks the victim might be George Clarkson. He and my great-great-grandfather owned a mine together. Clarkson supposedly disappeared in 1864. Everyone thought he ran away, but no one knew why. There were rumors he might have committed a robbery or two."

Doug grabbed the volume on the bottom of the stack and opened it up. His index finger traced the Table of Contents. He flipped pages until he found the one on gold rush miscreants. I leaned over so we could pore through it together.

"This chapter goes into some detail about the local criminal element around here—a few of the more famous bandits like Bloody Dick Crone and Rattlesnake Dick."

I chuckled and Doug broke into a wry smile. "Hey, they really existed. I didn't make them up."

"I'm laughing because I may have dated a dick or two," I elaborated. "My ex-husband excluded from that description."

Doug's face grew serious. "So how is Hank faring?"

"Not well. I hope you don't mind me asking, Doug, but are you angry with him?"

The vein in his temple pulsed, and he waited a few seconds to reply. "Hank and I did have words a few weeks ago."

"Before Spencer was killed?" I asked.

He nodded.

"Did it have anything to do with Spencer's plans to expand into your store?"

Doug stepped back, his eyes indicating surprise and a trace of something else. Fear?

"Did Hank tell you about the expansion?"

"No, Tricia and Lars Taylor mentioned it. They seemed to think it enough of a motive for you, to um…" My voice trickled off into an uncomfortable silence broken by the tinkling of the welcoming bell.

Doug forced a cordial smile at the newcomers who asked for the mystery section. He pointed to the left rear of the store. Once the couple had moved on, he eased himself onto his stool.

"Three weeks ago, I received a thirty day eviction notice. For this store where—" Doug grew angry, his volume increasing enough to catch the attention of the mystery fans. He wiped dots of perspiration from his forehead and lowered his voice so I could barely hear him.

"I've spent my entire life building up the reputation of this store. Without any thought of the consequences for me or my business, Spencer decided he could tear it all down. The day I received that eviction notice, I stormed into the hotel. Hank admitted he'd promised Spencer he wouldn't tell anyone about the expansion plans. He'd even kept it from me, whom Hank has known for most of his life. I blew up at him then marched down to that asshole's campaign headquarters, ready to—"

CHAPTER THIRTY-EIGHT

I never found out whether Doug threatened Spencer or not. The young couple walked up to the counter and plopped several new mysteries next to his cash register. My eyes landed on—*The Weed That Strings the Hangmans Bag* by Alan Bradley. With a huge inventory of mysteries, Doug was privy to numerous methods of silencing the man who threatened to take his livelihood away.

But did he? And if he did, why would he take the trouble to string Spencer up?

When two chattering families burst into the store, I realized the answer to my questions would have to wait. Although I might learn something valuable at my next stop—the jail.

I went through the usual drill of handing off all of my belongings, including my new earrings, which the guard deemed sharp enough to utilize as a weapon. Hank's skin appeared sallow, possibly due to the day-glo orange uniform he wore, or poor nutrition from his nine-day stint at the county bed and breakfast.

Orange is the New Black—the reality show version.

It was difficult to smile, but I forced a toothy grin at my ex. "Are they treating you okay?" I asked.

"Yeah, sure, it could be worse," he replied, his voice barely audible.

"The kids say hi."

Hank's face perked up at the mention of our children. "I can't believe I'm sitting in a dark cell all day when I could be playing ball with Ben and helping Jenna with her homework."

This probably wasn't the time to remind Hank that Jenna's academic prowess already surpassed his. My job description involved boosting his morale.

"I went to Spencer's memorial on Thursday. You should have seen it. Tacky, tacky." I shared an abbreviated version of the chapel service as well as the reception held at Janet Spencer's house. I also mentioned my attempts to grill some of the suspects on my list.

"Laurel, you need to be careful when you're questioning people," he said, his eyes worried.

"I am." Well, as careful as one can be when attempting to solve a murder. "I spoke with Doug Blake today, and he basically confessed that he threatened Spencer when he got the eviction notice. He seemed angry with you, too."

"Yeah, I felt bad I couldn't give Doug advance notice, but if I had, Spencer woulda fired me. I don't think Spencer wanted the news to come out before the election, in case it impacted his image. Made him seem unsympathetic."

As far as I could tell, Darius Spencer could have used a busload of image consultants. But he didn't need to worry about that now.

"I saw the building plans for the hotel," I said to Hank.

"Did you go to my apartment? How did you get in?"

"I sort of, inadvertently, found myself in Spencer's home office. Long story. Anyway, I can see why he wanted the additional space for his hotel. It makes a lot of sense. But what would Doug have done about moving the book store if Spencer hadn't been killed before the thirty days were up?"

Hank and I stared at each other.

"Doug hung out that night in the bar, along with almost every merchant in town," he said. "I don't recall much, but I think he was throwing down the drinks as fast as me."

"He could have lured Spencer to the hotel for an early morning meeting," I mused.

Hank slowly nodded. "Yeah, but I hate to think Doug would commit murder over something like that."

"We're talking about his livelihood, you know."

"I guess. Say, I've been meaning to ask you something. Will Tricia automatically win the Supervisor election since no one's running against her?"

I shook my head. "No, Chad Langdon stepped into Spencer's shoes." And possibly his bedroom slippers.

Hank frowned. "That's strange."

"Why?"

"Chad isn't a proponent of the no-growth platform. I happen to know he owns a percentage of that huge Six Springs subdivision Phil McKinley wants to develop."

"Is that public knowledge?"

"I doubt it. Chad stopped by the hotel one day looking for Spencer. I showed him around, and he seemed impressed with the workmanship. He mentioned he was a silent partner in that subdivision. Chad said they would be hiring construction superintendents once the county approved the project."

Interesting. Chad Langdon's bedfellows were becoming odder and odder.

"Phil McKinley is a longtime client of Hangtown Bank," I said. "I wonder if the bank is financing the project."

"Could be." Hank dropped his chin on his hands. "Does any of this matter? If the judge doesn't set a reasonable amount for bail, I could be stuck here until the trial. Big Jack, my cellmate, told me I'm cuter than Neil Patrick Harris." Hank's voice grew loud and shrill. "The big oaf refers to me as his *cupcake*. I keep telling Jack I'm not that cute."

The guard grabbed Hank's arms and pulled him away from the glass. Hank threw me an "I screwed up again" parting glance over his shoulder as the officer prodded him out of the room. I blew out of the jail, charged with energy and fear. I needed to solve this case fast.

Before my ex-husband became Big Jack's BFF!

CHAPTER THIRTY-NINE

Saturday evening, my friends and I gathered at Mountain High Winery, admiring the panoramic vista of the Sacramento valley below us, as well as the vista of rich desserts in front of us.

The sun painted the western sky in brilliant shades of pink, rose and coral, presenting the perfect backdrop for Stan and his new iridescent hot pink cowboy shirt. I hoped Stan didn't commit any kind of offense that would land him in jail tonight because Big Jack, Hank's cellmate, would definitely upgrade my friend to full cupcake status.

"I'm probably going to regret this question," I said to Stan as I reached for an iced cookie with thick frosting that matched Stan's western wear, "and this dessert, but where did you find that shirt?"

"Oh, this old thing?" Stan gazed down at his chest with pure adoration. "I got it on eBay for only ninety dollars. What a steal!" I agreed with his assessment except that the eBay seller was the one who committed internet robbery.

I turned to Liz who was either kissing Brian or licking frosting off his cheek. "How much longer before we go on stage? I'm stress eating enough to use up my calorie quota for the month. Are you sure you can't perform without me?"

She checked her slim gold watch. "The Sassy Saloon Gals perform when the Country Rollers take their break in a half hour. Go get a glass of wine. That should calm your nerves."

"I don't know how I let you talk me into performing at this event," I muttered.

"Because you're so charitable and kind?" Liz responded.

Stan smiled and mouthed the word "sucker" in my direction.

It takes one to know one.

I decided to heed Liz's suggestion and wandered over to one of the temporary bars set up on Mountain High's enormous flagstone patio. The winery didn't stint on anything when it came to visitor comfort. I mulled over whether having a supervisor in their back pocket, so to speak, would be hugely beneficial for the family business.

Which made me think about the grant deed for the winery property I'd spotted on Spencer's desk. This plot seemed to be thickening faster than my waistline. There were more questions swirling in my mind than there were guests swirling glasses of the winery's award-winning ruby-red petite syrah. Deep in thought, I didn't notice the heavyset man charging in my direction, a glass of red wine in his hand.

Crash! My dance training came in handy as I spun around, managing to remain upright. Unfortunately, the wine in my attacker's goblet continued to twirl. The heady liquid spilled onto my over-exposed chest, plastering my sequined top to my skin.

"Pay attention where you're going," said the seriously balding, barrel-chested man, scowling at me. The tufts of black hair sprouting from his open shirt shimmered with red wine droplets.

I could match him scowl for scowl. "I'm sorry, but you were the one who charged into me."

He frowned then his gaze dropped to the accident site. "Whatever. Can I help you um, clean up?" he offered, looking like he would welcome the opportunity to lick the spilled wine off my bosom. "Here, let me make it up to you." He dropped his empty goblet on a picnic table. "I'll buy you a glass of wine."

He chortled at his comment and stuck out a sticky palm. "Phil McKinley." I met his wine-soaked palm with my own, marveling at the coincidence of running into the developer Hank had mentioned earlier. Considering that Chad Langdon and Phil McKinley were silent partners, I guess it wasn't that much of a coincidence he would also be attending this fundraiser.

"It's nice to formally meet you," I said, although I could think of better methods of introduction than being splattered with syrah. I grabbed a stack of napkins from a table and proceeded to clean off the wine. "I work at Hangtown Bank, so I've handled some of your construction loans in the past."

"Good bank to deal with," he replied. His beefy arm curled like a boa constrictor around my waist as he guided me back to the bar. "I should stop by more often, sweetcakes, now that I know you work there."

Yuck. It was bad enough that Big Jack was salivating over my ex-husband. Now I, too, had been relegated to the tasty pastry shelf. I shifted and managed to elude Phil's grasping hands. I planned to throw a few questions at him then escape his clammy clutches.

"I heard you're developing a new subdivision the bank will be financing," I said. "How soon will you begin construction?"

He touched an index finger to his fleshy lips. "Just between you and me, we should be good to go by the first of July."

"That's terrific news. So your development has already been approved by the county?"

Phil winked. "In a manner of speaking." We moved to the head of the line, gave our wine choices to the bartender then returned to the patio. A server proffered a tray of garlic and goat cheese appetizers. I nibbled on one, while Phil gobbled down half a dozen.

Specks of goat cheese dotted the developer's pudgy jaw. I handed him an extra napkin while I tried to think of a subtle way to discuss Spencer's murder with him. Scott Shelton, Chad Langdon and Janet Spencer, who never seemed to be more than an inch from the winery owner's side, interrupted our conversation.

Janet wore a stunning emerald-green brocade gown. Her dress perfectly replicated nineteenth-century fashion down to the bustle and lace trimmed sleeves. The costume fit her slim body like a kid glove.

In my scarlet sequined top and satin skirt, I felt like nineteenth-century trailer trash in comparison. Chad wore basic cowboy attire, a plain denim shirt and jeans, looking like a regular fellow—the kind of man you wanted to represent your supervisorial district.

Scott Shelton was imposing in all black—black shirt, leather vest, jeans, boots, and hat. I admired that the Wagon Train participant took his costuming seriously, even in ninety-degree heat.

Phil McKinley greeted the newcomers, nudging the candidate's elbow as he introduced me. "Hey, Chad, buddy, have you met this pretty lady? She works at Hangtown Bank and is going to help with the loan on Six Springs. Say, I didn't get your name, sweetheart."

Chad interrupted before I could respond. "I've known Laurel for years. Her ex-husband, Hank, is the man who killed Janet's husband."

Phil's wine glass hovered an inch from his lips when he received this news.

"What?" He flung his right arm out, and I received my second syrah shower of the day. This was getting ridiculous. Janet reached into a small Mary Frances designer purse and pulled out a tissue for me. I dabbed at my top but only succeeded in adding clumps of white lint to my wet chest. Could this evening get any worse?

"Sorry, babe. Hey, how come you didn't tell me you were married to the guy they arrested for killing Spencer?"

"And how come neither of you informed the voters that Chad has a silent ownership in the Six Springs subdivision?" I replied, pleased to see the startled looks on both Chad and Phil's faces. I hoped my announcement demonstrated that this Sassy Saloon Gal was no slouch of a sleuth.

"Besides, Hank did not kill Spencer." I scowled at them. "And I'm going to prove it."

Scott maintained his tall silent cowboy image, merely lifting a bushy eyebrow in response to my declaration.

I would have loved to stick around and grill the men, but after peering at my wine-soaked top, I could tell my priorities lay elsewhere. "I need to find a ladies room. I'm performing in fifteen minutes."

Chad pointed to a row of green Porta Potties.

Oh, ick.

Janet shook her old-fashioned ringlets at him. "Chad, those are disgusting. Let her use the restroom in the back of the winery. She'll need a mirror to fix herself up."

Chad started to object then changed his mind. "Okay, it's unlocked tonight for the staff's use. The bathroom is in the building where the wine is aged." He pointed to a large building not far from the patio. "It's all the way in the back."

I sent Janet a grateful smile. "Thanks. I'll head over there now."

Numerous guests crowded the patio so I wasted valuable time dodging the partygoers. I finally reached Liz's side. She and Brian were talking to Abe and Rex, but her eyes widened when she saw me.

186

"What the blazes happened to you?" She stepped back and scrunched her patrician nose. "You do know you're supposed to drink the wine and not wear it."

"Ha ha. Love that dry British wit." I grabbed an extra napkin from her hand and fruitlessly dabbed at my top. "Phil McKinley bumped into me and doused me with wine. I'm off to the winery's storage building. Chad said I could use their restroom."

"Well, hurry it up. We're on in ten minutes. Why were you jabbering with Phil McKinley? He's a creepy guy."

"A little sleuthing." I winked at Liz. "I think I'm getting close to cracking the case."

Rex shook his head in amazement. "I wish all of my clients had family so tenacious in proving their innocence."

Abe smiled at me, his handlebar moustache dotted with cornbread flakes. The portly man loved good food almost as much as his antiques. "That Hank is a lucky man to have you looking out for him."

"Yes, he is. See you in a few, Liz," I said to my friend. "Although feel free to go on without me."

She stuck her tongue out at me in a most unladylike fashion. I ignored her and trotted over to the large stucco building. I opened the door and stepped back, my nose overpowered by the plum and fruity scents of the aging wine varietals.

I'd toured a few wineries in Camino, but this operation surpassed the other local wineries in size and output. The enormous silver cylinders reminded me of the machines in the Transformer movies. The ten-foot tall sentries guarded thousands of gallons of the precious liquid. The wine stored in this building must be worth a small fortune.

It felt weird walking through the building alone and not in the company of a bunch of babbling, tipsy tourists. I had only one goal. Find the bathroom, clean myself off and get out as quickly as possible. Lighting proved to be minimal, however, and it took me longer to find the restroom than I originally anticipated. Liz was probably ready to kill me for delaying the performance. Unless they went on without me.

With that cheery thought in mind, I finally spotted a door in the rear that appeared to be gender neutral. As far as I was concerned, almost anything beat a mirror-less, window-less, smelly Porta Potty. I felt around the wall to my right and eventually located the light switch. A forty-watt bulb barely lit the room, but it was better than nothing. It made sense to avail myself of the facilities while I was there. I'd no sooner perched on the cold seat when the lights went out.

Shoot. Did the bathroom switch operate on a timer in order to save electricity? I'd only been in there a few minutes. Or did this blow-out party contribute to the winery blowing a fuse?

After I finished my business and located the sink in the dark, I searched for paper towels but only succeeded in clobbering my head on something hard. Probably the hand dryer. I finally decided my hands could drip dry. I pulled on the doorknob and re-entered the cavernous midnight-black room. The power outage must have affected this building, or possibly the entire winery.

Worried that I might bump into one of the French oak barrels and end up responsible for spilling gallons of the liquid treasure, I crept through the building. A creak sounded behind me, and I spun around. My heart pounded, but I couldn't detect another presence. The chorus of machinery gurgling maniacally in the background did not ease my anxiety.

It was odd the equipment was still operating since there was no power, but maybe they had backup batteries to ensure the fermentation process wasn't interrupted. I walked with my arms outstretched, petrified of crashing into one of the solid metal cylinders. Suddenly a cord caught my ankle, and I fell forward. My palms flew out to brace myself, but my left knee smashed into the unforgiving cement floor. I lay there for a few seconds, trying to catch my breath. I sat up, rubbed my knee and felt something sticky on my hand.

I placed my fingertips against my nose and felt a surge of relief when I sniffed the pungent smell of wine, not blood. I stood tentatively, wincing from the pain in my knee.

I limped forward trying to get my bearings. Where was that doorway I had originally entered? How would I locate it again in the dark? A loud clink of metal against metal almost made me leap out of my heeled sandals. I whirled around, grimacing as my knee protested the sudden movement.

Nothing. Just my overactive imagination.

I wondered if anyone had ever considered filming a slasher movie in a winery. That thought freaked me out so much that goose bumps appeared on my goose bumps.

Just nerves, I thought, giving myself a pep talk. All I had to do was take one baby step at a time and eventually I would reach the opposite side of the enormous building. I remonstrated with myself for leaving my purse in Liz's car so I wouldn't have to worry about it while we were performing. I could have used the flashlight application on my cell phone to light my way or called for help.

The back of my neck prickled with unease. A loud click sounded behind me. I stiffened. The smell of garlic-scented breath against my ear was the last thing I remembered.

CHAPTER FORTY

I woke with my hands tied behind my back, my head pounding louder than a Broadway revival of *Forty Second Street*. I wiggled my fingers and my nails scraped against something metallic. My body lay stretched out uncomfortably on a very hard surface. When I shifted, my head bumped against something solid. I carefully moved in the opposite direction, sliding down almost a foot until my toes encountered another obstacle.

Where was I and how did I get here?

There was minimal space on either side of me, making me feel like I'd been stuffed into a coffin. Was I still in the Mountain High Winery building, or had my captor moved me elsewhere? Would that have been possible with so many people milling around the grounds?

I tried to recall what other equipment winemakers used other than large storage vats or barrels. The only thing that came to mind would be the grape crusher, a ferocious machine that liquefied solid grapes in minutes. The machine performed the task far faster and cleaner than the old method of stomping on grapes.

It was also far more dangerous. Especially if I was trapped inside.

I shuddered as I recalled a tour I'd once taken that included a demonstration of the machine in action. My palms felt clammy as they strained against my cloth handcuffs. My claustrophobia kicked in and I began to hyperventilate.

Calm down, Laurel. I tried to distract myself by contemplating who could have moved me in here and why. *Why* was easy. I must have said or done something recently, perhaps even tonight, which made Darius Spencer's killer think I could be closing in. That was the good news. I possessed some important information about the murderer and possibly his or her motive.

The bad news was that I didn't know what it was.

Even worse than that—not only did I not know *where* I was—neither did anyone else. Except for my attacker.

How much time had elapsed since the blow to my head? Minutes? Hours? Liz and the Sassy Saloon Gals should have noticed my absence by now. Unless my friend assumed I'd bailed on her, something I had threatened to do repeatedly during the course of the evening.

Good thing Liz and I drove to the winery together. I was almost positive she wouldn't leave without me. Almost.

My breathing grew labored, and my heart hammered in my chest. Did my current situation confirm Chad Langdon was the murderer? Who else would have knocked me out and placed me inside a piece of winery equipment?

Silly question. Many people in our county were familiar with the process of making wine. No one could be ruled out at this point.

I squirmed in the constricted space, attempting to slide my hands out of their bindings but to no avail. I tried to remember my Lamaze breathing, but that just reminded me of my children. Tears flowed down my cheeks as the faces of my family paraded before me. I blinked rapidly. Crying would not help. I needed to be proactive.

I began yelling at the top of my lungs and kicked the heels of my shoes against the walls of the steel prison. Even though it seemed unlikely anyone would hear my cries, it was better than lying still with destructive thoughts filling my brain. My screams ricocheted off the metal walls.

Tom was right. I had no business interfering in this investigation. Look where it led me. Now my children might lose both of their parents—one to life in prison and the other trapped in a dark coffin until oxygen and time ran out.

I thought of the burly detective and the wonderful traits he possessed. How gentle and patient he always was with me. His excellent sense of humor. Visualizing his warm brown eyes made me tingle, proving I wasn't dead yet.

If only I could see Tom's smiling face once more, I vowed to never again get involved where I didn't belong.

The sound of people screaming startled my reverie. Brilliant rays of light, brighter than a summer day made me wonder whether I had died and gone to heaven. I blinked, my blurred vision resting on a large figure bending over me. His chestnut hair grazed my cheeks as his soft full lips met mine.

If this kiss wasn't heaven then I didn't know what was.

Shrieks of joy provided a background chorus for our kiss. In shock, I stared at the people surrounding us as Tom helped me to sit up. He refused to untie me until he'd donned some protective gloves. Then he removed the fragment of cloth binding my hands together. My abductor had used a red calico kerchief, similar to the ones worn by a multitude of cowboys tonight. Tom tucked the small article of apparel into an evidence bag.

The detective never left home without them. Especially when his girlfriend was in the vicinity.

He lifted me out of the coffin as if my body were as light as paper mâché. My left leg buckled, but with Tom's arm wrapped securely around my waist, I could stand. The throng of people surrounding us assaulted me with questions.

Liz reached my side in seconds. She hugged me hard enough to crack a rib. I didn't think she would ever release me, but curiosity finally beat out concern. She stepped back and asked the obvious question. "Who did this to you?"

I glanced back at my prison, and my entire body trembled. "I don't know. Someone hit me on the head then dumped me in there." My eyes scanned the people standing around me. I immediately ruled out Liz, Brian and Stan.

Janet Spencer bore a shocked expression on her carefully made-up face. Chad Langdon looked puzzled. Several members of the Hangtown Posse, dressed in assorted western wear, shuffled their booted feet. Scott Shelton stood alongside the men, so he must also be a member. Their expressions indicated concern, but nothing more.

Would the person who attacked me be foolish or arrogant enough to stand in front of me now? That was one question I needed answered.

The second question I addressed to Tom. "How did you locate me?"

Liz answered for him. "I was bloody annoyed with you, missy, when you didn't show for the performance. When the party started to break up and you still hadn't appeared, I knew something must be wrong. We looked all over for you. Then I remembered you were coming here to use the loo. I found Tom and he put together a search party."

She gestured at the Sassy Saloon Gals, a couple of Mountain High employees attired in burgundy polo shirts, several Sheriff's Deputies including Fletch and Chuck Kramer. Even Rex had stayed to help which was nice considering the defense attorney billed at $300 an hour.

My brain was awake enough to compute that mathematical equation and concerned enough to wonder if looking for me counted as billable hours.

Tom squeezed me and I beamed up at him, safe in his arms. "We searched this building but couldn't find you anywhere." He pointed at Stan who bustled to my side. "Then your pal found something none of us noticed."

I must have looked confused, so Stan directed my attention to the floor. "I saw one red sequin in the restroom and then two more on the floor by this scary piece of equipment. They screamed CLUE!"

"You're lucky." Chad stepped forward and pointed at my former prison. "We only use the pulverizer in the fall. It's completely soundproof, so you might not have been found for months."

One of the winery employees chimed in. "Yeah, and if someone pressed the ON button by mistake, you'd have been crushed in minutes."

So I had been trapped, mere seconds away from the pulverizing machine turning me into liquid Laurel.

I looked at Tom and Stan. Then I blacked out for the second time that evening.

CHAPTER FORTY-ONE

Several hours later, I sat in Tom's car, parked in my driveway. I did not intend to tell my kids about tonight's incident. They were worried enough about their father's arrest. The fact that someone intentionally tried to kill me would remain my secret. Assuming the story didn't make it into the *Mountain Democrat*. It was definitely *National Enquirer* worthy.

After my discovery, Tom conducted brief on-site interviews with Chad and the Mountain High Winery staff, but no one had noticed anything unusual. Although it would be difficult to obtain fingerprints from cloth, Tom still hoped the calico neckerchief that had bound my hands would provide a clue.

He urged me to let him take me to Marshall Hospital to get my head checked out, but I refused. He probably figured stuffing me into a hospital bed was the only surefire way to keep me out of trouble.

"Honey, you don't make things easy for me, do you?" Tom said with his hand strongly clasped around mine.

I perked up at his use of the endearment. "So you don't want us to take a break any longer?"

"That was one of my dumber ideas," he admitted.

"You realize that I don't intentionally try to get into trouble."

"I know, and despite your bumbling approach..." I eased my hand away, but he quickly pulled it back to him. He gently kissed my fingers one by one, to ease the pain of his bumbling conversation.

"Sorry. I need to work on my conversational skills," Tom said. "I'm going to admit something to you now."

My heart pulsated and my lady parts tingled like they were holding a going-out-of-business sale as I wondered if Tom would finally declare his love for me.

"I think you may be right about us arresting the wrong person for Spencer's murder," he said.

Not exactly the most romantic declaration, but I would take it.

"Does your conclusion have anything to do with my near-death predicament tonight?"

He turned to me, his face serious. "Yes. Someone wants you out of the way and permanently. My guess is you've stirred things up with your questions and you're making them nervous. Can you think of any other explanation? It obviously was intentional."

"I hate to think it took me being stuffed into a grape crusher to change your mind, but I'll accept your apology."

He quirked an eyebrow at me. "Was I apologizing?"

I tilted my head at him and smiled. "I certainly hope so."

Tom grabbed me in his arms and proceeded to apologize in the most delicious fashion. Although the next time he apologized to me, I intended to move it to the privacy of my bedroom.

Fifteen far-too-short minutes later, Tom walked me to my front door.

"I know I'm repeating myself, but please be careful. Don't go anywhere unless you're surrounded by other people."

"I promise. Since you're going to take another look at this case, I can go back to banking and being a mom."

"I wonder if I should have a patrol car drive by periodically."

"We'll be fine. Now go catch that killer."

After one last ten-toe tingling kiss, I stepped into our foyer. I crept up the stairs, my sandals in one hand and my clutch purse in the other. I entered my bedroom, hit the light switch... and screamed.

CHAPTER FORTY-TWO

A figure lay in my bed, tangled in a sheet and my lightweight summer blanket. Then my daughter sat up. She rubbed her eyes and scowled.

"It's about time you came home, Mother," Jenna grumbled.

I splayed my palm against my chest. Tonight had held one too many surprises. Once my breathing returned to normal, I smiled, secretly pleased at my daughter's concern.

"What are you doing in my bed, honey?" I dumped my purse on my dresser then plopped myself down on my comforter.

"I was worried because you weren't home yet, so I decided to watch television in here. I must have fallen asleep." She stifled a yawn with her hand. "You shouldn't worry your children by coming home so late."

"Sorry, sweetie. The fundraiser went longer than I anticipated."

"How did your dance go?"

How to answer that question without lying to my daughter? "It went well," I replied. According to Liz, the women received a standing ovation, so my remark was completely true.

"Did Ben behave?" I asked automatically, then received a surprise when she frowned.

"Justin's mother called and said he couldn't come over to play with Ben tomorrow."

"Did something come up?" I asked.

"She didn't come right out and say it," Jenna spat out, "but I think it's because of Dad's arrest. It's not fair for people to treat us this way. Lindsay also called and cancelled our shopping trip tomorrow. She used that old 'something came up' excuse, too."

I sighed at the lack of empathy from the other parents while trying to relate to their fears, unjustified though they might be.

"Our life will get back to normal soon." I kissed Jenna on her forehead. "I promise. Now go to bed."

She yawned through a muffled okay, rolled over on her right side and fell asleep in seconds. I didn't mind bunking with my daughter, although first I needed to shower off all the nasty residue from the night's events.

I wanted our normal life back as much as Jenna.

The next morning my head felt like a dozen miners were tunneling from one side to the other. Four Advil tablets did nothing to diminish the pain, making me wonder if I should heed Tom's advice and drive to the hospital. My fingers tiptoed along my scalp, settling on a bump the size of a Cadbury egg.

Then I remembered Mr. Boxer's command that the bank be decorated by tonight or else. My schedule did not allow for a six-hour stint in the emergency room. I brewed a large pot of coffee, hoping the caffeine would quell the pounding in my head. While I nursed my first cup, I mulled over the events of the previous evening. Which suspect most likely attacked me?

In my mind, the top three suspects were Chad Langdon, Phil McKinley and Scott Shelton. I had blatantly announced to the men that I intended to prove Hank's innocence. One of them might have taken my comment seriously enough to remove a potential threat to his freedom.

Chad campaigned on a no-growth platform, yet he was involved in the Six Springs Development. Phil McKinley indicated he'd found a way to get around some of the county subdivision approval requirements. Both of them had substantial financial investments at stake. Either of them could have individually lifted me into the grape crusher or colluded together.

Scott Shelton remained an enigma. Bad guys didn't necessarily dress all in black these days. So did many a fashionista. But the rancher definitely had a grudge against Spencer.

Brooding over my potential list of attackers was not helping to eliminate my headache. Nor were my three cups of coffee. I would never share this with Mr. Boxer, but I welcomed the opportunity to distract myself as well as the kids by decorating the bank.

In less than an hour, the three of us stood on the sidewalk outside Hangtown Bank. My keycard provided access and we hauled in the quaint items discovered in Gran's shed. Quaint might be overly generous. My mother would have classified everything as crapola.

But what seems like crap to one person may be riches to another. The items would help spruce up the bank and that was my primary concern.

My daughter had inherited my mother's artistic and decorating flair, which somehow skipped my genetic composition. Jenna giggled as she paired some of the old bonnets I'd collected with a couple of parasols. My daughter had been so quiet and reclusive since her father's arrest that it was nice to see her sparkle like her normal self.

I debated informing the kids about Tom's decision to take a closer look at Spencer's murder case, but decided to wait until he came up with another conclusion—one that did not involve their father being tried for murder.

We finished decorating in less than two hours. Ben occupied the time by sliding down the hay bales repeatedly. It kept him entertained so Jenna and I could concentrate elsewhere.

"What do you think?" I asked my daughter once we finished.

She scratched her chin with an elegantly shaped index finger. It would have been more elegant if the nails hadn't been gnawed off, a genetic characteristic we shared.

"We need more filler in the main lobby," she said. "Are there any additional things we can use?"

I shook my head, which proved to be an exceptionally bad move. I winced at the pain and said, "Let's hit a couple antique stores. I have some petty cash left, and we might find some bargains."

Ben's face fell. "I hate those stupid stores. That old stuff smells poopy. And it's pro'bly full of cooties, too."

"There are no cooties," I said, although Ben wasn't entirely wrong about the olfactory factor permeating some of the historic Main Street buildings. While most stores bore nostalgic scents such as lemon oil and lavender, there were a couple that smelled moldy or, as Ben so elegantly described it—just plain poopy.

We first stopped at Placerville Hardware, the oldest hardware store west of the Mississippi, dating back to 1856. Crowded floor-to-ceiling shelves lined the maze of narrow aisles offering everything from toilet plungers to gold-rimmed teacups.

I'm firmly convinced there's a dead body stuffed somewhere in the store. They just hadn't discovered it yet.

After I purchased a gold pan and cowboy hat for Ben, we headed over to Antiques Galore. I immediately noticed the change in the window display. The silver pistols no longer rested on the red satin centerpiece. An ornate jeweled bracelet and earring set dazzled sidewalk shoppers.

I pushed the door open, the kids lagging behind me. Jenna checked out an old Victrola record player. I instructed Ben he could look but not touch anything, or else!

Abe waved from behind the counter where he rang up a purchase for a middle-aged couple. I meandered through the store in search of anything old, showy and cheap. Abe specialized in quality merchandise, so the odds of him offering anything fitting the remainder of Mr. Boxer's paltry budget were slim.

Near the back of his vast store, I found a clearance table. A couple of slightly tarnished horseshoes would fit with my theme. A towering pile of books looked ready to fall over, so I restacked them into two piles. I pulled out an oversized pictorial book and rifled through the pages.

The population of Hangtown during the Gold Rush was surprisingly similar to today's population of 10,000 in the city proper, making it the third largest city in the state behind Sacramento and San Francisco at the time. Back then, Main Street consisted primarily of jewelry stores, hotels and at least twenty saloons.

A tad different from the makeup of today's city.

I examined a photo of the original Hangtown Hotel. According to the book, it was quite a showplace, claiming the biggest stage in town until the construction of the Empire Theater. The hotel also boasted the largest number of female companions.

Now how did they define *female companions* back then?

I grabbed my horseshoes and the book and ambled up front. Abe's cash register pinged yet another sale. A cute couple wearing matching yellow polo shirts, khaki shorts, white curls, and satisfied smiles exited the store. I plopped my purchases on Abe's glass counter.

"How are you doing after last night's ordeal?" asked the sympathetic owner.

I gently patted the bump on my head. "Other than my head feeling like a runaway horse stomped all over it, I'm okay."

"You're sure lucky they found you."

I started to nod then settled for a smile. "I'll take a pounding headache over a pulverizing any day."

Abe kindly switched our conversation to something less terrifying than the previous night's misadventure. He held up the horseshoes. "You taking up riding?"

"Nope. Some last minute items to decorate the bank." I pointed to his store windows. "Although I don't know how we'll compete with your wonderful wares. I see you sold Scott Shelton's antique guns."

Abe shook his head. "No, Scott came in and bought them back. Even paid me a commission although I told him he didn't need to."

"He must have hated parting with something so valuable and sentimental."

"Said he came into some money and wanted to wear them on the Wagon Train trek."

"That jewelry set you put in their place is gorgeous," I remarked. "My mother's birthday is coming up. Can I take a look at it?"

The portly owner shuffled over to the window, removed the bracelet and earrings and placed them in front of me.

"Beautiful, ain't it?" he said.

"They look like family heirlooms." I picked up the bracelet and admired the skillful workmanship. When I peered closer, I noticed some minuscule engraving inside the gold band, "To S, love forever, M." Aww, that was so sweet.

"It must have been hard for the owner to part with them," I remarked.

Abe sucked in his breath, but he remained silent. It wasn't any of my business why the previous owner sold the lovely pieces of jewelry. I bent closer to read the minuscule price tag attached to the bracelet.

Ouch. "I don't suppose that third zero behind the three is a mistake?"

"It's a work of art as well as a piece of history."

"I don't disagree, but it's too much for my measly budget. I'll stick with the horseshoes and this book. I'm trying to solve the mystery of the skeleton in my grandmother's back yard."

"Boy, you're a real Jessica Fletcher, aren't you? Maybe you should stay away from sleuthing though. Look how close you came to getting crushed last night."

Geez. Didn't anyone think I looked more like Nikki Heat than the elderly detective from Cabot Cove? I began to reply when a huge crash startled us. Immediately following the deafening sound were the words no mother wants to hear uttered by her young son. Especially when he's surrounded by cut glass crystal and English bone china.

"Oops."

CHAPTER FORTY-THREE

One hundred dollars' worth of broken china fragments later, the kids and I finished decorating the bank. Ben claimed that his run-in with a small curio cabinet was due to him wanting to catch Abe's Siamese cat. When the cat rebuffed Ben's efforts and unsheathed its claws, Ben knew enough to back off. But he forgot to look behind him and crashed into the cabinet.

Abe seemed understanding about the incident, but I felt obligated to reimburse him for the damages and gave him all the twenties in my wallet.

Ben's lower lip puffed out to twice its normal size. "I'm sorry, Mommy. I tried to be careful. That is a very dangerous store for a young child to be in."

Jenna burst out laughing and so did I. Ben was correct. An antique store was no place for a small boy, especially if Ben had inherited his mother's klutzy DNA.

Monday proved uneventful which, considering the incidents of the past couple of weeks, was a nice change. Mr. Boxer actually smiled a good morning at me, so he either approved of my decorations or enjoyed his time in San Francisco. I wondered if his visit included socializing with any "female companions."

I debated calling Tom to see if his detectives were pursuing new leads but decided he would call me if he learned anything new.

I needed to update Rex regarding Tom's and my conversation. Since the lawyer helped search for me Saturday night, he might realize the incident confirmed Hank's protestations of his innocence. Rex already may have set legal things in motion.

My mother called as I was halfway out the door to grab a sandwich. "How is your headache, dear?" she asked. "Are you feeling better today?"

"A little, although I still need Advil now and then. I'm sure it will disappear eventually."

"I believe you've become a headache for Spencer's murderer. Does Tom think you need police protection?"

"He offered to have someone drive by my house in the evenings, but as long as I'm either at home or work I should be fine. The good news is that Tom is having the detectives re-examine the case. After I hang up with you, I'll call Rex and give him an update. Maybe he can get Hank out of jail."

"Funny you should mention Rex's name," Mother said. "Remember I mentioned I would check to see if that deed you found granting ownership from Mountain High Winery to Spencer was ever recorded?"

"Yes. What did you find out?"

"No deeds have been recorded between those two parties. Are you certain you saw Chad Langdon's name on that document?"

"Positive. Almost." My mind raced as I tried to grasp what this meant. "So if Spencer was about to record that deed transferring Chad's interest in the winery over to himself, wouldn't that be an excellent motive for murder?"

"Exactly what I thought."

"Tom needs to find out about this. You didn't do anything illegal to get that information, did you?"

"Don't be silly. I simply networked." She giggled. "But that's not the only thing I discovered."

My ear glued itself to the phone waiting for her response.

"I had my informant, um, I mean my friend, run every recorded transaction involving Spencer's name in the past twenty-four months. Guess who else he foreclosed on?"

"I already know the answer to that. He took back the Hangtown Hotel from Scott Shelton. And Scott is not a happy camper."

"Well, there's one other unhappy person camping out a few doors down from your office."

"What? Who?" Was she going to share her news or turn this into a one-hour primetime special?

"Two months ago, Spencer filed a Notice of Default on a million dollar loan for a property located on Coloma Road."

"And this is important why?" I asked.

"The person who owns the property is your ex-husband's defense attorney."

CHAPTER FORTY-FOUR

Wow. You could have knocked me over with a legal pad. The victim tried to foreclose on Rex Ashford. Who knew?

And that truly was the question. Did the detectives review any of Spencer's financial transactions when they investigated his murder?

"Laurel, are you there?" Mother asked.

"Yeah, just bowled over. I'm not an expert on this legal stuff, but isn't it a conflict for Rex to be representing Hank?"

"I ran that by Robert before I called you. He said it's okay as long as Rex discloses it to Hank and the judge. Maybe Rex felt it wouldn't be an issue and that he was the best attorney to defend Hank. Or maybe it's just an odd coincidence."

I personally think all coincidences are odd, but this particular one leapt to the top of the odd pile for me.

I thanked Mother for her research, and she warned me to keep an eye out for murderers on the loose. My stomach knotted when I recalled Saturday's ordeal. From one standpoint, my almost getting killed benefited Hank since Tom agreed to re-examine the investigation.

But it sure would have been nice if he'd listened to me before I was almost mashed into McKay mulch.

I debated the best way to proceed with the information Mother unearthed. Chad Langdon continued to take the lead on my suspect list. As for Rex, even if he was experiencing financial issues, I simply could not imagine him killing Spencer. I called the attorney's assistant and made an appointment to see him at one-thirty. If nothing else, Rex needed an update on the case.

I opened the frosted glass door of Allen & Ashford, Esq. a few minutes late for my appointment. Rex's young assistant dressed more like a backup dancer for Beyoncé than a paralegal. After following her swiveling hips down the hall, I decided she could show professional dancers a move or two. The young woman stopped at the doorway, flashed a saucy smile at her boss then wiggled her way back down the corridor.

What I wouldn't give to be a saucy twenty-something again.

Nah. I was perfectly happy with my family and my lifestyle. Except for one pressing problem, which I hoped Rex and I could resolve today.

I sank into a comfortable and likely expensive leather chair and greeted the attorney. Dressed in a navy Armani suit, he could easily have posed for the cover of *Esquire*.

"Laurel, you look far better than you did Saturday night," Rex said. "How are you feeling?"

I shivered at the reminder of my winery nightmare, or possibly from the over-chilled office. "I'm fine. Thanks for hanging around to help search for me."

The attorney's Crest-white grin almost blinded me. "Maybe you should leave me to deal with Hank's case in the future. You don't want your children to lose their mother as well as their father."

If Rex thought his words would provide comfort to his client's ex-wife, he was way off the mark. I tried to control my trembling and replied. "My frightful experience might be worth it since the Sheriff's Department is taking another look at the case."

"They think Spencer's killer targeted you? You've been grilling people all over town. Maybe you've upset someone with your questions."

I frowned at him. The attorney was starting to tick me off.

"This week I've concentrated on annoying only one person—Spencer's murderer," I replied. "Given the circumstances, Tom suggested you contact the Deputy District Attorney and recommend reduced bail."

"That's not exactly how the legal process works, but if you want, I'll give Camille a call. Try not to get your hopes up for Hank's quick release though."

We stared at one another. I began to have second thoughts about hiring Rex to defend Hank. His reluctance seemed peculiar unless he calculated he would earn more in legal fees if he dragged the case out. That reminded me of his financial situation.

I didn't want to alienate the lawyer while he still represented my ex, so I eased into my questions.

"I've come across a litany of possible suspects," I said.

"Spencer wasn't the most popular guy in town." Rex crossed his legs and leaned back in his chair, assessing me warily.

"That's for sure. Did you know he took ownership of the Hangtown Hotel after he foreclosed on Scott Shelton?"

Rex nodded.

"I gather Spencer made large loans to several locals." I raised my eyebrows in Rex's direction, encouraging him to elaborate on his own financial transaction with the victim.

"Is that so?" He flicked a piece of nonexistent lint off the cuff of his perfectly pressed trousers.

"Yes." I waited for him to respond. The silence was so deep you could have heard an eyelash drop. A few of mine did since I kept blinking furiously wondering why my not-so-subtle questions didn't seem to be going anywhere.

The finest criminal defense attorney in town appeared far more adept at maintaining discretion than this amateur detective. After a few minutes of complete silence, I checked my watch and decided enough time had elapsed. I would ask Mother to continue her "networking," hoping she would learn more about Rex's financial issues. In the meantime, I needed to return to the bank and work on luring more customers into its deposit-hungry arms.

I reached for my purse and Rex stood.

"I'll try to get a bail reduction hearing for Hank," he said. "Don't worry. I have everything under control."

I shook his hand and walked to the door. I stopped to look back and caught Rex rummaging through his credenza. Everything might be under control from Rex's perspective, but I wondered if that was necessarily a good thing for me.

Or for Hank.

CHAPTER FORTY-FIVE

Surprisingly enough, Rex did have everything under control. Tuesday afternoon, he called to say the Deputy DA had agreed to a reduced bail hearing the following day. Because the detectives were looking at some new evidence, bail could be as low as $200,000. Too bad Mother hadn't landed on any buried treasure when she fell down the mine shaft. Mr. Bones was definitely not the kind of booty we needed.

Later that night, I sat on the sofa, my kitten perched on my lap, watching the local and state election results on television. So many Californians, including myself, vote by mail that it can take a while to tally the results. Pumpkin didn't appear to have a political preference, although every time either candidate appeared on the screen, she jumped off my lap to lick her butt. At this point, I almost didn't care who won. I just wanted a reprieve from the nonstop adversarial political commercials clogging the airwaves.

Our home phone rang and I leapt up. Pumpkin went flying, yowling in response. I apologized to my cat and jogged over to the phone.

"Did you see Chad Langdon is in the lead?" Mother asked. "After that incident at Mountain High Winery, my trust level in him has significantly diminished."

"I don't trust anyone running on a 'no-growth' platform who is a silent partner with a developer," I replied.

"With Spencer eliminated, I thought for sure Tricia would win. I guess Chad is popular enough to get a huge number of write-in votes, so there may not be a runoff in November."

"Did you call to discuss politics?"

"No, don't be silly. First, how are you feeling? Next, did you discover anything new about Mr. Bones? I need to list your grandmother's property while the market is hot. With interest rates climbing back up, real estate sales could come to a dead halt at any time."

"I'm fine and Jenna is reading through Harold's old journals, but it's not easy given his scrawling penmanship and the condition of the volumes. I purchased an interesting book from Abe that covers quite a bit of Placerville history during that period. I'll start reading tonight."

"Good, I appreciate it." She paused while I waited and watched Chad's votes tick higher on the TV screen.

"Do you think I'm wrong, forcing your grandmother to move to the retirement community? She's barely talking to me lately."

"No, I understand where you're coming from, especially after her fall the other day." I took the phone back to the sofa, patted my lap, and waited for Pumpkin to land in her favorite spot once again. She threw me one of her "I'll jump up when I feel like it" looks and trotted out of the room. "If I hadn't stopped and checked inside the shed the other night, who knows what could have happened to Gran?"

"I suppose." Mother sighed. "She's very effective at guilt-tripping."

A family trait Gran successfully passed along to my mother.

"I'll go ahead and list it tomorrow," she said. "With tourists arriving to watch the Wagon Train roll in this weekend, I might hold an open house on Sunday. People from the Bay Area love these old Victorians."

"Yeah," I agreed, "until they move in and discover what a money pit they are."

She chuckled and we hung up. I shifted slightly and reached for the pictorial history book I'd dumped on the coffee table. Reading about El Dorado County history couldn't be any duller than watching election results.

I scanned the Table of Contents and decided to begin with James Marshall's discovery of a few mineral flakes in Coloma on January 24, 1848. His off-quoted pronouncement—"Boys, by God I believe I have found a gold mine," changed California and the west forever, luring hundreds of thousands of people to the gold country.

Since my great-great-grandfather didn't arrive until ten years later, he missed the early days when all you had to do was bend over and pluck a gold nugget right out of the river. By the time Harold moved west, Placerville was prospering and rebuilding after a terrible fire almost destroyed the entire town.

Although I'd studied this stuff in school years ago, the discovery of Mr. Bones made the history of this area more personal. I learned that ten percent of Californians supported the Confederacy, which I found oddly fascinating. The book went into detail about the Bullion Bend robbery Gran had mentioned the other night.

The book also mentioned a copycat holdup barely a month after Bullion Bend. Three men not only robbed a stage a few miles outside of Placerville, but one of the desperadoes killed a wealthy merchant named Miles Mickelson who attempted to stop them. Sheriff's deputies later shot two of the men when they discovered them trying to rent fresh horses in town. The third man escaped and most likely took the gold and valuables with him.

Interesting story although it seemed highly unlikely the stolen gold was hidden in my grandmother's dusty shed.

But a girl could wish.

CHAPTER FORTY-SIX

On Wednesday afternoon, I toiled at my desk waiting to hear from Rex regarding Hank's bail hearing. My cell rang and I grabbed it from my purse.

"How's the ankle?" I asked my grandmother.

"Much better," she said. "I get by fine with a cane. Did you know your mother wants to show my house this weekend?"

"Gran, that place is too much work for you to maintain. It would be too big for *me* to keep up."

She remained silent. When she finally spoke, I could barely hear her. "I know, it's just hard after all these years…" Her voice faltered before she snapped back into my feisty grandmother. "But she better not take away my car."

Nope. Not this week. One battle at a time.

"Are you coming to the Wagon Train parade Saturday?" I asked, changing the subject. "I'm performing with Liz and the Sassy Saloon Gals."

"I'm not only watching the parade," she bragged. "I'm in it."

"What? You're not thinking of dancing with us, are you?"

"Hah. Not with this ankle. If I hadn't fallen, though, I might have kicked up my heels with you gals. I'm riding with the other former El Dorado Roses. They got carriages for us."

"Gran, that's terrific." Our family had been so proud of my grandmother when the committee selected her as the El Dorado

Rose a few years earlier, a distinction awarded to an elderly woman who devoted much of her time to the community.

"Yep. I could use your help, though, since my hands are kinda arthritic. I can't fasten the buttons on my dress. Can you fit that in your schedule?"

"Of course," I replied, already counting how many extra minutes it would take to fasten the thirty tiny buttons on the back of Gran's lilac satin dress.

We said farewell, and I'd barely shoved the phone in my purse when a familiar voice and an even more familiar man entered my office. Hank leaned over and planted a big kiss on my surprised lips before I could open said lips to say hello. Or in my case—huh?

"What are you doing here?" I asked, stunned by his appearance and the lip plant. Fletch stood by the door grinning and I turned to him. "And what are you doing here?"

"I gave Hank a lift home. They let him out with a $100,000 bail bond, so he was free to leave once someone paid the $10,000 fee in cash."

My brows sailed up past my bangs. "Who paid?"

"Abe did," Hank said, his grin an exact duplicate of Ben's, except his front teeth remained intact as opposed to my gap-toothed son. "I guess he and Rex were chatting about the case and my situation. Abe said his sales had picked up recently, and he didn't mind putting the money up. I promised I'd repay him as soon as Janet pays me for the work done on the hotel. Hopefully, she'll let me complete the job."

"Wow. Abe is so generous." Especially after Ben's crashing encounter last weekend. It was amazing how a small community stuck together when something tragic happened.

"Looks like you're good to go," Fletch said to Hank. They did a man slap thing that turned into one of those weird guy hugs where they swat each other's back. Fletch waved goodbye and Hank dropped in my visitor chair.

"I'd say you look great," I told him, "but you don't."

"If you ever need to diet, honey," Hank said then stopped when he caught my expression. "Which of course, you never would, the jail is the place to be. Their cook only knows four recipes."

"The kids will be thrilled you're out."

"I'd love to surprise them. Can we all have dinner tonight? I'll treat."

"I have Zumba class, but you're welcome to take the kids out."

"Darn. I hoped we could all be together." His eyes grew soft and misty. "Hunter told me what happened to you at the winery the other night. You almost died because of me."

"You met with Tom?"

"Yeah, he's not a bad guy. But I sure wish he wasn't stuck on you," Hank groused. "Tom came to the jail and grilled me for over an hour, but I think he finally believes me. There's only one catch."

"What's that?"

"With the exception of someone stuffing you in the grape crusher Saturday night, there's no specific evidence pointing to anyone but me."

Details, details—Jessica Fletcher wouldn't let a little thing like a lack of evidence stop her.

I sent Hank off to bond with our children while I worked on my suspect list. With Hank no longer in custody, the killer might try even harder to get rid of any obstacles.

Unfortunately, the only obstacles I could think of were Hank.

And me.

CHAPTER FORTY-SEVEN

The kids returned home Wednesday evening thrilled from a night reuniting with their father. Jenna's frail shoulders no longer looked like they carried the weight of the galactic empire. Ben wore an ear-to-ear smile, relieved to have his dad back in his life.

The man in question called me a few minutes before noon on Thursday.

"How's it going?" I asked Hank. "Is Janet letting you finish the renovation?"

"I hope so. She told me to check out the building and let her know how much it will cost to finish up. She wasn't involved with the project originally, so she's somewhat clueless about the whole thing."

"That seems fair. Is there a problem?"

He snorted. "Someone's been digging the place up."

It took less than five minutes for me to grab my purse and trot down to the Hangtown Hotel. Hank recommended I enter via the back door since the front door remained barricaded to keep vandals and looky-loos out of the building.

Metal scaffolding covered the exterior, but I wormed my way around it. Hank met me at the back door and held on to my elbow as we walked through the lower level. I trod carefully on the old wood planks covering half the floor. The remainder had been removed and the floor taken back to its original condition—dirt.

I glanced at the boards scattered everywhere. "How can you tell if anything's been touched? It's all a mess."

"Some of this is planned mess," Hank replied. "But some of it is not." He grabbed a fluorescent orange hard hat from a makeshift table and placed it on my head. I grimaced as I felt the hat graze my bump.

"You've had enough head injuries this week," Hank said. "Now look over there at the wall adjacent to Blake's bookstore. Be careful where you step."

I let Hank guide me, clinging to him for support. The last thing I needed in this week's busy schedule was to fall and break something.

"If you weren't familiar with this project, you might not notice someone's been playing in the dirt by the wall adjoining the two buildings," Hank explained, pointing to several spots. "Someone's dug fairly deep holes then tried to cover them back up."

I crouched down to examine the area more closely. "You're sure none of your men did this?"

He shook his head. "I only had two guys helping with the initial demolition. And neither of them had keys to this place."

"Maybe Janet arranged for someone to come in here?"

"Nope. I called her and she didn't know anything about it."

Hank scanned the room then moved past me to a window in the rear. He pushed on the warped wood sash, and it opened wide enough for someone to crawl through.

"Someone could have entered through the window," he said. I joined him and we stared down at the sawdust-covered dirt.

"If those aren't your footprints you could be right," I said.

"What do you think they were looking for?" Hank asked. "Did the murderer leave something behind he thought someone could recognize?"

"Maybe." I inspected the building, wondering why someone had been digging along the wall. "It's kind of odd they dug in so many places though. I suppose it could have been teenagers. You didn't run across any buried treasure when you started tearing things up, did you?"

He rubbed his newly-shaven chin, a big improvement over his former jailhouse appearance. "I wouldn't exactly call it treasure, but I found a couple of old coins. I think one of them might have been real gold, and an old pocket watch that had a cool picture on the front."

215

I was about to say "huh," when Hank showed me a photo of the watch depicting a miniature sailing scene on the front. "That's beautiful. What did you do with the stuff you found?"

"Spencer asked me to save anything I discovered that might have historical value. He mentioned something about donating them to the county museum. I remember the watch had someone's name in the inscription who Spencer recognized. I'm sure those things are either in his office or his house somewhere." I didn't respond so Hank waved a hand in front of my face. "Laurel, do you think those items are valuable?"

"Possibly," I replied, lost in thought.

"That old stuff's not worth killing for, is it?"

Now that could be the million-dollar question.

Hank and I looked around some more, but we didn't locate any new historical artifacts.

"You remember me telling you about that old skeleton my mother landed on when she fell down the mine shaft?" I asked him.

He snorted. "I would have liked to see Ms. Hoity Toity get her hands dirty for a change."

There was no love lost between my mother and Hank.

"Hey, my mother is mellowing," I said, although by definition that only meant she'd been downgraded from a Type A++ personality to a mere Type A. "I've been researching how that old corpse ended up in the bottom of my great-great-grandfather's mine."

"Sounds interesting—not," Hank said. "And what does that have to do with this building?"

"There were several stagecoach robberies in the early 1860s, one in particular that no one solved. What if a stranger rented a room in this hotel and hid stolen goods here? He could have concealed something under the floorboards. It's not like a crook could walk around town with an entire strongbox of gold on his person."

"True. But why would he leave it behind?"

"Because he'd been shot dead?" I answered.

"Okay, that bit of history is interesting." Hank looked around the demolished building with appraising eyes. "But I can't see it having anything to do with Spencer's death."

I started to reply when the back door opened and Doug Blake entered.

"I see you're back at work," he said to Hank, his eyes flashing angrily behind his glasses. "Are you going to raze my store without any notice?"

Doug looked ready to duke it out with my ex.

"Janet told me to get back to her on the costs to finish this job," Hank said. "I don't know what her plans are. I'm only the hired help. Say, have you seen or heard anyone working in here during my jail stay? Someone's been digging up the place."

Doug didn't say anything although his body seemed to wilt, and his expression grew fearful. He looked first at Hank and then at me. I leaned forward anxious to hear his answer.

"I gotta get back to my store," Doug said. "Don't bust through my wall without giving me notice first."

I reached out to stop him, but the bookstore owner eluded me and disappeared out the door without answering Hank's question. Or any of mine.

CHAPTER FORTY-EIGHT

"That seemed odd," Hank said. "Do you think he knows something?"

"I think he not only knows something, he might be the culprit," I said. "Doug has access to all sorts of history books. He probably knows about some of these old unsolved robberies. Plus he could easily sneak over here without anyone noticing. You didn't tell anyone about your finds, did you?"

A look of consternation crossed Hank's face. "Maybe."

"Who? That could be important."

"Well, I might have mentioned it the evening I got drunk at the Liar's Bench."

"The night Spencer was murdered? Who did you mention it to?"

Hank chewed on his lower lip. "Let's see, I know I mentioned it to Abe 'cause he gets old stuff in all the time, and I thought he might know how valuable those items would be. Doug was hanging by me for a while. And Lars was all over the bar that night buying drinks for everyone."

"So basically anyone in the bar that night," I stated.

Hank's Adam's apple bobbled as he swallowed hard. "What should we do?"

"I'll call Tom and tell him about your discovery. I'm not sure if Doug ever made it on the suspect list, but if not, it's about time.

I left Hank to his job and returned to my own. Stan sat in my solitary visitor chair.

"What's up?" I asked.

"You blew right past me with nary a hello," Stan said. "How does it feel to have Hank out of jail?"

"It's a huge relief, although he and I are both nervous since the murderer remains at large."

"Are you still dancing with Liz and the Sassy Saloon Gals on Saturday?"

I grimaced. "I don't know how I let her talk me into performing with the group. I'm almost more worried about making a fool of myself in front of the entire town than a killer stalking me."

"Well, this is your lucky day." Stan said. "You're going to have a bodyguard. Liz insisted."

"Tom?" I asked hopefully.

Stan pretended to pull a gun out of his pocket then blew on his index finger. "Yours truly. I'll dance with you gals and keep an eye out for bad guys. Make sure you're safe."

Hmm. Stan wouldn't be my first choice for bodyguard duty. But there was one thing he knew how to do and that was to entertain. He might even start a new tradition—the Wagon Train conga line.

I left a message for Tom regarding the unexplained digging Hank and I discovered at the hotel. I recommended he chat with the bookstore owner since Doug gave the impression he knew far more than what he shared, or rather what he refused to share with Hank and me.

Friday morning flew by as Mr. Boxer inundated my "in" basket. He'd come up with an urgent need for a flyer promoting this week's Wagon Train Special for deposits of five thousand dollars or more. I personally couldn't see how receiving a return of .02 percent on a savings account was significantly better than .01 percent, but what did I know? I was $4,900 short of opening an account myself.

The workload helped distract me from my domestic worries, if worrying about a killer gunning for me qualified as a domestic issue. After churning out a basketful of flyers, I decided to take a break. I grabbed my purse and headed toward the bakery. As I passed the Hangtown Hotel, I scooted under the scaffolding and peeked through the dusty windows. No sign of Hank anywhere.

Oddly, Blake's Books still bore the closed sign hanging in the window. The store remained dark with the exception of the dim lights Doug normally left on all night. I couldn't remember a time when Doug had closed the store during the week. Especially with the Wagon Train coming to town the next day.

My cell rang as I reached the bakery. Rather than annoy the pastry-loving clientele, I stood on the sidewalk to answer the call. My heart rate sped up when I saw Tom's name.

"Hi there" I said, breathing heavily, hoping I sounded more like a sexy starlet and less like a slightly pudgy not-quite-middle-aged out-of-breath mom.

"Are you at work?" he asked without a greeting.

"Well, hi to you, too," I replied.

"Sorry, this has been a hectic morning. Have you seen Hank today?"

"No. He's not at the hotel. Do you have his cell number?" When Tom replied in the negative, I rattled off the number. "Is there a break-through in Spencer's case?"

He paused for a few seconds. "Well, you'll hear about it eventually, so I may as well tell you."

"You caught the killer?"

"No," he said somberly. "But the killer may have struck again."

"What?" My shriek was probably loud enough to hear in South Lake Tahoe. They definitely heard me on Main Street since I noticed multiple heads turning in my direction. I scurried down the sidewalk until I reached the parking garage.

"Who died?" I asked.

"Doug Blake."

"Omigod," I frantically looked for a place to sit down and settled on a stair leading to the second story of the garage. "What happened?"

"I called him yesterday after you and I spoke, and we agreed to meet at his house at eight this morning. He thought it would be awkward to interview him at the store. I didn't mind stopping by his house if it made him more comfortable. Figured it would be less disruptive anyway.

"I arrived at eight sharp, rang the bell several times then banged on the door. I finally turned the knob and found the door unlocked. Doug lay on the sofa, and at first I thought he was still asleep."

"He died in his sleep?" I asked, saddened that a man in his early sixties would die so young, and alone.

"Possibly, although at this point, I think he might have had some assistance since he had a knot on the back of his head. Not unlike your injury from the winery. It might be nothing, he could have fallen, but we're examining everything in case someone smothered him. Several cushions were strewn on the floor."

"I can't believe he's gone. And if he was murdered—" Even though I'd considered Doug a viable suspect yesterday, this was terrible news. Tears ran down both cheeks as memories of Doug helping my kids select books over the years flashed through my mind. "But why are you looking for Hank?"

"Don't you think it's odd that as soon as Hank was released from jail, the killer may have struck again?"

CHAPTER FORTY-NINE

After that remark, Tom hung up. He had a crime scene to deal with, and I had, well, I didn't know what I had other than a sinking feeling. Tom thought Doug's death pointed to Hank again, while I felt the timing merely a coincidence. The killer must have been concerned Doug would reveal something critical to the police.

What had the bookseller seen that led to his untimely demise? Did Hank also possess some critical knowledge, even if he wasn't aware of it, which could be equally damaging to the murderer?

I left several messages for Hank, but he remained M.I.A. Where had that man gone? I not only had to worry about the killer coming after me but about my ex's safety, as well. At this point, I almost wished Tom would stuff Hank back in a cell so I could take Hank off my list.

I called Jenna at home and made sure she locked all the doors and windows. I hated to frighten the kids, but their safety came first. Then I called my mother to see if she and Bradford could stay with the children until I made it home. Mother was at Gran's house making a list of repair work that needed completion, but Bradford was available and more than willing to act as temporary babysitter/bodyguard.

By five-thirty, I was home from work. When I entered the kitchen, the scent of garlic and onions tickled my nostrils. And my curiosity. My stepfather stood in front of the stove, a loosely tied white eyelet apron barely covering his substantial girth. When I'd first met the man, I'd dubbed him Tall, Bald and Homely. Bradford hadn't grown any handsomer in the past nine months, but now he reminded me more of a lovable bulldog than a crotchety detective.

"Something smells heavenly," I said to our temporary chef. He smiled and waved a tomato-flecked ladle at me.

"Your mother enjoys my cooking, so I thought I'd try out one of my new recipes." He shot a glance at my pantry. "You're lacking a few ingredients, so I improvised."

"Improvise away." I plopped on a bar stool at the kitchen counter. "Did you hear what happened to Doug Blake?"

"Tom and I spoke a few minutes ago," Bradford replied, managing to talk and drain the spaghetti without losing any pasta down the sink, a feat I never could accomplish. "He'll stop by later. Have you heard from Hank?"

I shook my head, got off the stool and grabbed a goblet from my hanging rack. I poured a small amount of the David Girard Vineyards Rosé that Bradford must have brought with him. I sipped and sighed, wishing that my life could be as simple and rosy as the lovely liquid swirling in my glass.

"I don't have a clue where Hank is," I said. "I thought he would be working in the hotel today. I'm starting to get worried about him."

"Tom isn't a hundred percent certain Doug was murdered although he said the evidence points in that direction. He mentioned you thought Doug could be withholding information about Spencer's murder."

I walked to the stove and sneaked a taste of Bradford's sauce. Yummy. He swatted my hand, and I returned to my perch.

"I'm a detective and I can tell you're stalling," he said. "What did Doug tell you?"

"Hank discovered someone had been digging in the dirt floors of the hotel while he was in jail. Whoever it was covered it up but not well. Maybe they didn't expect Hank to be released so soon. He's the only person who would notice something like that. Doug stopped by, and we asked if he'd seen anyone sneaking around. At first, he seemed startled by our question. Then his expression changed, and I got the feeling he knew something. But he clammed up and returned to his store without revealing anything."

Bradford threw me one of his suspicious looks. "Did Hank notice Doug's response, too?"

"Yes," I said, already perceiving where he was going with this line of questioning. "But unless Hank unwittingly mentioned that Doug knew something important, he's completely innocent of anything to do with Doug's death."

Bradford grunted then spent the next couple of minutes ladling out plates piled high with heavenly smelling pasta. He pulled a ready-made salad from our refrigerator. I called the kids and in less than a minute, the four of us were sitting at the table. My stepfather and I switched the conversation to something more pleasant than the rash of homicides.

"What time are we going to the parade tomorrow, Mommy?" Ben asked.

With a fork full of spaghetti halfway to my mouth, I contemplated the answer. "Gran asked me to help dress her since she's riding in the parade, so we might have to leave early." I threw a beseeching look at Bradford who responded immediately. One of the perks of having an astute former detective in the family.

"Your mother and I can pick up the kids tomorrow," Bradford said. "Then you won't have to worry about them getting to the festivities on time." His answer also contained an implied reassurance that an adult would be looking out for them. Jenna was old enough to be on her own, but with a killer running around town, I preferred that a family member, especially one who knew self-defense, accompany both kids whenever they were out in public.

With that issue resolved, I relaxed until the doorbell rang. I peeked out the living room window to see if I recognized the car in the driveway. After ascertaining that an El Dorado County Sheriff's vehicle was parked in front of the house, I opened the door.

It seemed like a decade since Tom last held me in his arms. And I would have loved to spend the next decade in them. His lips were soft, then firm and demanding as he crushed me to his chest.

A loud "ahem" broke the mood and our embrace. We pulled apart and I glared at my stepfather. Tom continued to hold on to me, his arm wrapped around my waist.

"Nice outfit," he complimented Bradford, his lips tilted in a half-smile.

Bradford glanced down at the ruffled apron he'd forgotten to remove. "I'm exploring my feminine side," he chuckled.

"You can explore your feminine side anytime," I said to Bradford. "As long as you cook dinner for us again."

I turned to Tom and whispered in his ear, "And you can explore any side of me you want."

He squeezed me harder then dropped his arm when both kids joined us in the foyer. I told them we had official business to discuss and sent them upstairs to their rooms. The head of homicide, his former partner and I went into the living room to converse in private.

Tom sat at one end of my flowered sofa, and I cuddled next to him. Bradford squeezed into one of my wing chairs.

"Have you finished processing Doug's crime scene?" I asked Tom.

"Yeah, the techs brought everything back they considered relevant," he replied. "Including a couple of those bank flyers of yours that had been modified, similar to the one your boss found hanging on the bulletin board."

"Oh, so Doug was the culprit," I said. "That makes sense since he was upset with Spencer about his eviction. Did you find any other clues? Anything that might indicate he killed Spencer?"

"We realized something that's missing—Doug's cell phone."

"That is odd," I said. "Did you check the store?"

He nodded. "It's nowhere in sight. But we may have lucked out. We found a footprint in the flowerbed to the right of Doug's sidewalk. The soil was still moist from the drip irrigation, so it's definitely new, although it doesn't necessarily belong to the killer. Do you know if Hank owns a pair of Lucchese cowboy boots?"

"I'm no longer in charge of Hank's wardrobe, but they sound expensive."

"All I know is that Lucchese imprints a pattern on their soles which could be a break for us. It's urgent I speak with Hank," Tom said. "Are you sure you don't know where he is?"

I jumped out of my seat, not appreciating his implication that I was lying about Hank's whereabouts. "I don't have a clue. Honest, I'm not trying to protect him. In fact, I'm worried the killer may have harmed him. Can't you put out an APB or something on him?"

Robert harrumphed from his chair.

"Okay," I said. "You know what I mean."

"We've already sent Hank's license plate out, but no one has come across it yet."

I began to pace across my worn beige carpet. "You're wasting valuable time going after Hank. What about that long list of suspects you said you would follow up on?"

"Doug's death changed things."

The home phone rang, startling me, but I figured one of the kids could grab it. After a couple of minutes, Jenna brought the cordless phone to me.

"It's Dad," she said.

I snatched the phone from Jenna, so upset I almost pulled her thumb off. "Hank," I screeched into the receiver, "where are you?"

Hank's garbled response indicated he was on his cell. "I took off to go fishing." His next words disappeared amid static. All I heard was " ...came up with the..." and then the call dropped.

I hit redial several times but could not reconnect.

"See, Hank's fine," I said to Tom. "He went fishing."

"Heck of a time to go fishing, when we're still investigating Spencer's murder."

"After spending two weeks locked up, courtesy of your department, I can see why he'd want some fresh mountain air. He sounded like he'd figured something out, but then I lost him."

"If Hank calls back, tell him to return immediately. And you need to stay safe at home. No venturing out this weekend."

"I can't do that," I protested. "The kids and I never miss the Wagon Train parade. Plus, I'm dancing with the Sassy Saloon Gals."

"I haven't lived here long enough to know what the Wagon Train entails," Tom said. "Do many people attend?"

"It's one of the biggest events in this county," said Bradford. "Those folks leave Reno and drive their covered wagons, carriages and coaches along Highway 50 for eight days. At night, they stay at various campgrounds and host BBQ's for the public. Their arrival in Placerville is a big deal. The Hangtown Posse hosts shoot-outs and all kinds of entertainment. You don't want to miss it."

"I definitely don't want to miss an event that involves Main Street shoot-outs. I know the Sheriff's Office is utilizing extra personnel plus STARS."

"They're using celebrities?" How cool was that.

"Sheriff's Active Team of Retirees. I'm thinking of joining them myself." Bradford winked at me. "If your mother doesn't mind me donning a uniform again."

"I don't like the idea of Laurel being out there without any protection," Tom objected.

"It's okay. Liz drafted Stan to be the bodyguard for the troupe." I giggled when I saw Tom's expression.

"That's like sending the Keystone Cops after Jesse James," Tom snorted.

Maybe, but if nothing else, my bodyguard would be fashionably attired!

CHAPTER FIFTY

Worried about another sleepless night, I took a sleeping pill to ensure I wouldn't wake up looking like a hag. The pill worked so well I slept until ten a.m. making me one very late and not so sassy gal. I'd barely finished brushing my teeth when the doorbell rang. I overheard Jenna ushering my mother and Bradford into the house and flew down the stairs to greet them.

Mother, dressed in a comfortable-looking plaid camp shirt and blue capris, raised elegant eyebrows.

"Is that your idea of a dance hall costume?" She frowned at my attire, which consisted of an oversized sleep shirt and shorts.

I ran my fingers through my tousled hair. "I overslept. Thanks for taking the kids to the parade. I'm barely going to make it to Gran's house in time to button her up and drive her to the parade grounds."

She sniffed. "Your grandmother should stay home and rest."

"Oh, stop being such a poop. Remember how Gran loved being an El Dorado Rose and lording it over everyone. Don't rain on her parade."

Bradford snickered. My mother's blue eyes narrowed, but she let my uncomplimentary comment slide. I told Jenna to round up her brother. She ran up the stairs and a few minutes later, he joined us, dressed in an almost clean tee shirt and jeans, wearing a holster and holding his Star Wars light saber.

"I think you're mixing your weaponry," I said to Ben.

"Nah, uh. Remember that movie we saw, *Cowboys and Aliens*? I gotta be prepared for bad guys or space aliens riding in the Wagon Train."

You never know when a light saber may come in handy. I decided to let my mother and stepfather deal with Ben's arsenal, so I could get on with my shower and dressing in my own costume.

Once I donned my official Sassy Saloon Girls outfit, I realized there was no way I could tie the corset by myself. My grandmother and I would have to take turns fastening each other's costumes.

I arrived at Gran's house shortly before noon and didn't waste time knocking on the door. I turned the knob and let myself in.

"Gran," I yelled. "It's Laurel."

"It's about time. I'm in the bedroom."

I trotted down her hallway until I reached her bedroom, fortunately located on the bottom level. It would have been impossible for her to negotiate the stairs with her sore ankle. Gran lay on her multi-colored Wedding Ring patterned quilt, resting against a stack of pillows, already decked out in her lilac satin gown.

My heels skidded on the slick wood planks, and I grabbed on to her doorframe to steady myself. "Hey, you got dressed without any help."

She leaned forward and the back of her dress fell open. "Not quite," she said.

"That makes us even because I'm about to fall out of this stupid corset. I'm sure glad I wasn't born in the nineteenth century. Fashion was more work than fun."

My fingers proved far more nimble than Gran's arthritic digits. I finished buttoning her thirty odd pearl buttons and then turned around so she could tie me up.

"Suck it up, sweetheart," she said, "or I'm never gonna get these laces tied. Have you gained some weight this past week?"

With all my stress eating the last few days, I'd been afraid to step on my scale. While Gran complained that fastening my laces was worse than roping a heifer, I sucked in to the max. I would barely deliver her to the starting point at the allotted time.

We were tottering down the sidewalk, dressed in our nineteenth-century finery, when Gran suddenly noticed something amiss. She pointed to the back yard. "That nice young deputy left the shed door open. Do we have time to close it?"

I gazed down at my remaining pair of fishnet stockings. "No, we don't. Your backyard is a full-service destruction zone. I'll take care of it when I drive you home after the parade ends." Gran climbed into the passenger seat, grumbling the entire time. I helped her buckle the seat belt, strapped myself in then backed out of her driveway.

I shifted into drive and had my car tooling down Bedford Street when my own brain shifted into gear. "What nice young man? Did Tom stop by to see you?"

She shook her head so vehemently I worried both her bonnet and her wig would flip off. Today, Gran wore Queen Elizabeth II gray curls, suitable for El Dorado Rose royalty.

"Not that hunky fella you keep pushing away. That other dude. The history buff."

"Oh, you mean Deputy Fletcher. What did he want?"

"He came by this morning, asked if you finished with Harold's journals. He thought they would be helpful solving our case."

"Jenna's reading them, but it's slow going. That's sweet of Fletch to be so concerned about proving your grandfather's innocence."

"He's an eager beaver. That's for sure. He was real disappointed I didn't have the journals. Told me he'd check out the shed again and maybe the area up by the mine shaft in case he can find anything else helpful. I guess he didn't shut the door all the way."

"Wow. They should have used Fletch to solve Spencer's murder. He's quite the detective, isn't he?" I reached the stoplight and waited, counting the seconds until it changed to green. My cell rang and as usual, my Bluetooth was nowhere in sight. I recognized Hank's ringtone, but no way would I chance a cell phone ticket today of all days. I instructed Gran to pick up the phone and to hit the green button.

"Helloo, who's there?" she trilled. She listened to the caller then turned to me. "Kind of hard to hear, but I think it's your husband."

"Ex-husband," I said automatically. I pointed to the speaker button at the top of the phone. "Hit that button for me."

She punched it and Hank's voice filled the car. "Laurel, where are you?"

"Better question, where are you?" I asked.

"I'm in Pollock Pines," he said. "Listen, I think I figured out the killer."

"What?" Gran screamed. She lifted her thin arms in the air and in one lithe move flung my cell out her passenger side window. The hot-pink encased iPhone soared through the air. At its current speed, it would hit Hangtown Creek in five seconds or less.

"Oops."

CHAPTER FIFTY-ONE

I stifled the urge to scream at my grandmother that we were literally up the proverbial creek. Losing the phone was a pain in the butt, but the situation could be remedied at a store later today. Everyone I knew would be hanging out on Main Street, so worst case, I could resort to an old-fashioned method of communication—face to face conversation.

The more serious question was who did Hank identify as the killer and was he currently in jeopardy?

I took a few deep breaths to calm down. "Hank said he was in Pollock Pines, so he should be in Placerville in less than ten minutes."

"You did hear him mention the K word, didn't ya?"

I nodded while simultaneously flicking my right turn signal and easing down the exit ramp to Broadway.

"Just because Hank thinks he knows who the killer is doesn't mean he's right. I have a list of viable suspects and see how far I've gotten."

"But the killer has struck twice now. They must be concerned you're getting close."

I secretly agreed with her, but I didn't want to worry her more than necessary. For now, my priority was to safely deliver Gran to her buggy and then get my own chassis down to Main Street. I turned into a parking lot filled with covered wagons, horses, cowboys, and all things western. A few classic black carriages festooned with ribbons clustered together.

I jumped out of the front seat and zipped around the car to assist my grandmother. Her authentic ivory button-top boots made walking in Manolo Blahnik stilettos look like an Easy Spirit walk in the park by comparison.

"Damn boots," Gran muttered. "Didn't women have bunions back in those days? It's a good thing I can sit on my butt during this parade 'cause I can barely stand up straight." She demonstrated her point by listing to the right and almost knocking me down.

I straightened her up and held on to her elbow as we went to join the other Roses. The three elderly women, decked out in jewel tones of satin, velvet and lace, used dainty hankies to blot the rivulets of perspiration running down their powdered cheeks. It wasn't easy wearing authentic nineteenth-century attire in the summer months. For the first time, I felt grateful my costume veered toward the slutty side of gold rush fashion.

The women welcomed Gran with air kisses and hellos. The carriages and covered wagons scattered around the parking lot looked to be somewhat chaotic, but I assumed someone was in charge of the convoy. A familiar face in an unfamiliar suit popped into sight.

"Fletch, my word, aren't you a sight for sore eyes?" I giggled at my weak attempt to emulate Miss Kitty. Or maybe I was doing Scarlett O'Hara.

Gran rolled her eyes at my idiocy. "Looking sharp, young man, although you look kind of like a dude in that getup." She pointed to his gray felt bowler, black frock coat and red brocade vest. His boots were standard cowboy issue though.

"Oh, Gran, I think Fletch looks quite the dandy—very Butch Cassidy and the Sundance Kid."

Gran eyed the deputy. "You do remind me of a young Robert Redford. I had such a crush on that man. I wonder if he's single. When you get home, can you gobble him and find out, Laurel?"

"Google, not gobble. Sure thing, Gran. I'll get right on that since I have NOTHING else to do with my time. No killer to catch or anything."

"You must be happy about Hank's release," Fletch said. "No more sleuthing to do."

"I won't be happy until the real murderer is behind bars. Tom is re-examining the case, so maybe you'll get to work with the homicide division."

Fletch shook his bowler-topped head. "Nope. Too late for that. I gave notice yesterday. I'm moving to Florida to spend time with my mother. She's been ailing, and I feel I should make her my priority."

"Aren't you a good son?" Gran beamed at Fletch then sent me a dark look. "Your mother could take lessons from this young man."

"Mother is only doing what she thinks is best for you."

"Maybe it's time she did what *I think* is best for me," Gran retorted. "Hey, let's send her down to Florida to help out Fletch with his mother."

"I'm sure she would enjoy the company." Fletch winked at me. He escorted Gran to an elegant carriage pulled by a beautiful black mare appropriately named Black Beauty. "May I have the honor of driving you down Main Street, Mrs. Sprinkle?"

"Sure can," she responded with a slight curtsey and swirl of her lavender skirt. I watched Fletch assist Gran onto the hard leather seat. He reached into his pants pocket and removed an old-fashioned pocket watch. The shiny object drew Black Beauty's attention, and she nudged his arm. The timepiece flew in the air and landed at my feet. I bent over to retrieve it before one of the horse's slender, white-stocking legs crushed it to pieces. The watch sprang open, and I glanced at the engraving on the left side before snapping it shut. As I returned it to Fletch, I glimpsed the lovely pictorial design on the front.

"What a unique timepiece," I said to him. "I noticed the inscription to Miles Mickelson. Was he a relative of yours?"

Fletch stared at me, his face reddening and replied, "Sure" before he shoved the watch back into his pocket. "Ready to join the others?" he asked Gran.

"Could you take a photo of us first?" I asked Fletch. "I lost my phone so we'll have to use yours." I shot a look at my grandmother who fiddled with her parasol, choosing to ignore my comment.

Fletch pulled his cell from an inside suit pocket while I climbed in the buggy next to Gran. Fletch politely snapped a couple of photos. He started to put his phone away when she interrupted. "Laurel, take a picture of me with this fancy fellow."

Fletch looked ready to protest then thought better of it. He reluctantly handed the phone to me and we switched places.

I snapped a couple of photos of the two of them then scrolled back to see how they came out. Gran would shoot me with her own

rifle if I screwed up. My eyes jumped to some earlier photos that
bore a remarkable resemblance to the interior of the Hangtown
Hotel. I recognized several shots taken along the wall adjoining the
hotel and the bookstore.

How odd. I looked at Fletch. "Why did you take photos inside
the Hangtown Hotel?"

He reached down, snatched his iPhone from my grasp and
shoved it in his suit pocket. Then he flicked the reins and the carriage
rocketed away. Gran bounced backward against the seat but quickly
recovered. She waved her hand with the panache of Queen Elizabeth
herself.

Gran's carriage was about thirty yards away when I remembered
the other question I'd wanted to ask Fletch, whether he'd found
anything interesting in the shed this morning. His tenacity
investigating our cold case continued to amaze me, especially now
that he no longer worked at the Sheriff's Department.

I climbed into the Prius and headed for town. The parade
required the closure of Main Street for much of the day, so while
I searched for a parking space, I also searched for answers to the
questions buzzing through my brain regarding Fletch's photos taken
inside the old hotel. I finally squeezed the car into a spot on Spring
Street, a half-mile from the Bell Tower where I had agreed to meet
Liz and the rest of the Sassy Saloon Gals.

After hoofing it from my car to Main Street, my face felt like
it matched the color of my satin skirt. A restaurant offered a fifty-
cent sarsaparilla special. I gratefully slugged it down while I jostled
through the crowds on the sidewalk. I located the women in the
distance, easy to spot in our matching smutty not-so-finery.

The Hangtown Posse, a group of volunteers who evidently
never outgrew playing Cowboys and Indians, were also easy to
locate since most of them were lying in the middle of the street, the
result of one of their impromptu shoot-outs. The scent of discharged
guns combined with the aroma of popcorn from the Candy Strike
Emporium made me smile.

Gosh, I love this town!

I braced myself against a storefront as a throng of sticky-
fingered kids passed by. The back of my head bumped against the
metal historical marker placed on the building. I turned around to
read the inscription and discovered that the building housing the

Antique Arcade was originally known as the Mickelson building, the same name inscribed on Fletch's watch.

In smaller font, a brief notation indicated Miles Mickelson died tragically in 1864. Suddenly I knew why that name resonated with me. I'd read about the merchant in the history book I'd purchased. Miles Mickelson was the unlucky person killed in that unsolved stagecoach hold-up. The robbery where the gold and other valuables had never been found.

Or had they?

CHAPTER FIFTY-TWO

What a strange coincidence Fletch possessed a watch belonging to poor Miles Mickelson. I supposed the watch could have been passed down through several generations of his family. But Fletch had never mentioned the connection before. If my forebears had a building named after them, you could be darn sure my friends would all know about it.

A prickly sensation filled my stomach. And I didn't think the sarsaparilla created it.

Fletch might have purchased the pocket watch from an antique store. But from my brief glimpse of the unique timepiece, it looked identical to the one Hank had shown me on his iPhone, the watch he'd discovered in the hotel and then turned over to Darius Spencer.

Did Hank tell Fletch about the historical items he'd discovered in the hotel? And did that information have anything to do with Fletch's continued interest in solving our backyard mystery despite his recent resignation?

As Alice in Wonderland would say, things were becoming curiouser and curiouser.

I wasn't about to point my finger at Fletch and yell "*J'accuse*" the next time I saw him. I wasn't the star of *Les Miserables* and I was definitely no Inspector Javert. But this was definitely worth mentioning to Tom.

Especially since Fletch planned to leave Placerville—forever.

Was that one coincidence too many?

Of all the times to have lost my cell. I zigged and zagged around tourists and locals. One of my zigs almost caused my corset to zag, not an approved maneuver for any place other than the bedroom.

I was passing by Antiques Galore when an idea came to me. I threw open the door and raced into the store looking for Abe, whom I found chatting with a middle-aged couple. I reached his side and interrupted him mid-sentence.

"I'm sorry, Abe, but I have to know who sold you that antique jewelry set in the front window."

Abe's expression indicated his displeasure. "I can't give you that information, Laurel."

"It may be a matter of life and death," I said. "Just nod if I'm right."

I proceeded to whisper my suspect's name in his ear. I was both relieved and saddened when he nodded. I apologized to the couple and flew out the door. A minute later, I joined Liz and Stan who stood in front of the Bell Tower. Stan was dressed to kill in his hot pink satin shirt, matching bandanna and a jumbo white Stetson.

"Liz," I said panting, "I," huff, huff, "need your" puff, puff, "phone."

"And where exactly would I hide a phone in this outfit?" she replied.

Shoot. She was right. The skintight tops didn't allow cell storage space.

"Mary at Placerville News let us store our purses in her back room," Liz said. "You need to get a move on it. We perform a short dance then we're supposed to round up some more guys to throw in jail."

"You've been deputized?"

"No, silly, we stick them in the fake one over there." She pointed to a large makeshift jail just down the street. "The 'prisoners' are supposed to raise bail money from their friends in order to get out. All the proceeds go to the Kids Club Nonprofit."

"I think someone in the parade needs to be thrown into the real jail, but I'm not sure if I have enough proof yet. Have you seen Tom around?"

"Suzette deemed Tom cute enough to bring in a nice chunk of change, so she threw him in there a few minutes ago. I think he's hoping you'll bail him out."

"Geez, they better take plastic. Be right back," I yelled over my shoulder as I headed to the fake jail.

Several of Placerville's leading citizens were currently vacationing behind bars, calling out to friends and family to help rescue them. I eyed the cutest felon in the bunch dressed in a white polo shirt and shorts. Everything Tom wore molded to his body in all the right places, but still...

"Did they arrest you for violating the dress code?" I asked him. "This is Wagon Train Day, not tee time at the country club."

"My girlfriend forgot to mention that to me." He accompanied his comment with a heart-ratcheting grin. "I like *your* dress code though."

My pulse rate skyrocketed before my brain overrode the automatic stimulus of Tom's comment on my overactive hormones.

"I know who the killer is," I said, just as the crowd began hooting and hollering as the Wagon Train rolled into town. Chad Langdon and Janet Spencer waved from a splendid buggy near the front of the parade.

"I'm sorry," Tom replied, his attention diverted by the spectacle. "What did you say?"

"The murderer. I figured it out." I fumbled with my wallet trying to find enough cash to spring Tom. "I think."

He sighed. "And you know this how?"

His question tripped me up. The evidence, which he might consider somewhat circumstantial, was on the person of the man driving my grandmother's carriage.

As the four buggies containing the former El Dorado Roses came into view, I glared at Gran's driver.

Fletch tipped his bowler in my direction then smirked.

Okay, that did it. I had to do something. Unfortunately, the only thing I could think of was to point at Fletch and scream, "*J'accuse!*"

CHAPTER FIFTY-THREE

"Who the heck is Jock Cues?" yelled Tom from behind bars.

Men! Our next date would include a late night showing of *Les Misérables* so he could bone up on the French translation of, "I accuse you!"

One of the horses up ahead suddenly balked, and the parade halted.

I ran over to Gran's buggy. "You need to get down from there," I said to her, flicking my head in Fletch's direction.

"Laurel, what in tarnation has gotten into you? You got a crick in your neck or somethin? Stop bothering us and go back to your hussies."

"We need to move forward." Fletch's voice cracked with fear. "Get out of our way."

He lifted his booted foot and kicked at me. I jumped back but managed to catch sight of the Lucchese imprint on his sole. That combined with the guilty look on his face only added to my suspicions.

Which Fletch confirmed when he pulled a small gun from an ankle holster. He pointed it first at me then at my grandmother.

"That gun almost looks real," she said, not quite catching on.

"It definitely is, Mrs. Sprinkle," Fletch said, "and it comes with real bullets. Now tell your granddaughter to move away from the carriage so no one gets hurt."

Gran's faded blue eyes grew as large as the teacups decorating the front window of Placerville Hardware. She threw me a frantic look.

I climbed on the first step of the carriage hoping to extricate my grandmother from the horse-drawn vehicle. Fletch shoved me, and I fell to the ground in a puddle of satin and crinolines.

"Hey, Mom, look, a fight!" Some children called out from the crowd.

"Don't you go hurting my granddaughter," yelled Gran. She stood and clouted Fletch with her violet parasol. The unexpected attack from his passenger caused his gun to go off. The bullet hit the pavement less than a foot from where I'd been thrown. Asphalt chips assaulted my face and seared my bosom.

Now that really ticked me off!

Black Beauty reared then galloped toward Stagecoach Alley. The police had blocked the narrow street with a sawhorse to keep cars from inadvertently driving onto the parade route. Fletch brought the horse under control, but instead of rejoining the parade, he sped around the temporary barrier.

Fletch had hijacked Gran!

Liz and Stan each grabbed one of my arms and pulled me to my feet.

"Where's that fellow going with your grandmother?" Liz pointed at the carriage now almost at the corner. It would soon be out of sight.

"I don't know, but someone has to stop him." I flagged down a stagecoach driven by one of my former suspects.

"Will you help me catch a killer?" I yelled up to Scott Shelton. With a lift of his left eyebrow, he reached down and attempted to haul me up next to him.

Okay. This looks a lot easier in the movies.

Between Liz and Stan both shoving me, and Scott yanking me up, I finally landed next to the driver.

I pointed toward the escaping killer and his involuntary hostage. "Follow that buggy!"

CHAPTER FIFTY-FOUR

Scott yelled something to his horses that increased their pace from a slow walk to a trot. He turned to me and with nary a twitch said, "May I ask who it is we're chasing?"

"Jim Fletcher, a former deputy. I think he killed both Darius Spencer and Doug Blake."

"You have proof?" Scott asked.

What was it with men and their need for proof? I didn't have time to explain everything I'd discovered. Fletch kidnapped my granny. I chose to appeal to his protective male nature.

"He shot at me," I said.

Scott looked at me in alarm and yelled at his team. I mouthed thanks, grateful for his help. As the horses trotted faster, I bounced up, down and sideways. We hit a pothole, and I almost flew off the coach. I grabbed hold of a bar located to the side of the uncomfortable cracked-leather seat and held on for my life.

Up ahead, Fletch paused at the Center Street intersection. He had two choices—either turn left and run into the rest of the Wagon Train on Main Street, which I imagined must be in a complete state of confusion by now, or turn right and merge onto Highway 50. Even with banners proclaiming Wagon Train Days and the reduced speed limit of forty m.p.h. through town, most travelers wouldn't expect to find a stagecoach chasing after a horse-drawn carriage on a four-lane highway.

Fletch made his decision and turned right onto the highway. Scott skillfully held on to the reins as he attempted to catch up with

Fletch, but the bulky stagecoach was no match for a speedy surrey. A couple of cars passed us in the left lane. Passengers rolled down their windows to view our progress.

I had no idea how Fletch planned to escape, and I had a feeling neither did he. My primary concern was to reach my grandmother before she suffered an accident or a heart attack. Tears blurred my vision as we raced past the clapboard and brick buildings that backed up to the creek on our right. Up ahead, the light at the Bedford Street intersection abruptly switched from green to red.

Good. Fletch would have no choice but to wait for the light to change again. After driving less than a block, my lower back and my butt hurt. And my twenty-first-century butt possessed far more cushioning than the posteriors of those early settlers.

We were slowly gaining on Fletch, who twisted around in his seat to check our progress. He must have decided that waiting was not an option. He flicked the reins and expertly wheeled the buggy around in a U-turn, reversing direction.

Scott attempted to follow in Fletch's buggy tracks. The unwieldy stagecoach tilted to the left then it rocked to the right as we also attempted the U-turn. I clung to the bar with a death grip, my stomach and chest heaving. I'd better not heave myself out of my bustier, although at this point, a wardrobe malfunction seemed the least of my worries.

Scott finally steadied our vehicle, and we began gaining on the carriage. Fletch glanced back at us. He bent down, pulled out his gun and aimed it directly at me.

I ducked.

Scott wasn't so lucky. The bullet hit him in his left forearm. He cried out, dropped the reins and fell against me. I grabbed on to his good arm, worried he would fly out of the stagecoach and land on someone's windshield.

With no one driving our vehicle, the horses sped up, free to do whatever the heck horses do when no one is in charge. I bent down, scrambled to grab the reins and yelled, "Whoa."

The two lively bay horses snorted in unison, completely unimpressed by my piloting skills. Scott's face matched the ruffled white shirt he wore; his jacket sleeve was covered with blood.

"Are you okay?" I shouted at Scott. "Should I head for the hospital?" I tried to sound upbeat, not disclosing that the horses were kind of in charge right now.

He waved his right hand in a forward movement and accompanied the motion with a guttural curse, "Go get that asshole who shot me."

CHAPTER FIFTY-FIVE

I screamed at my horses to move it, hoping to narrow the gap between our horse-driven vehicles. Those must have been the magic words because they sped up, and we were soon closing in on Fletch. If only the traffic would disappear.

Cars veered to the left and right, leaving Fletch sufficient room to maneuver his buggy to the side of the road. He slowed it almost to a stop. Then in one athletic move, he jumped off and ran up the steep Coloma Street off ramp.

With no one holding on to the reins, Black Beauty went wild, and the buggy rocketed down the highway. From a distance, I could see the frightened horse swerve back and forth, her white stocking feet making me dizzy. At one point, Gran stuck her head around the back of the buggy. Although I couldn't see her lips move, I guessed they were crying, "Help!"

My first priority was rescuing Gran, but I was also worried about Scott's condition. Not to mention the killer was on the move. Suddenly, an unlikely hero burst on to the scene.

A chestnut quarter horse ridden by an unusual looking cowboy galloped down Center Street. The cowboy wore a San Francisco Giants black and orange baseball cap and a plaid shirt I'd ironed on many an occasion.

"Hank," I cried out. His horse bolted over a red Mini Cooper heading east, knocking off the antenna before it successfully landed in the inside lane of the westbound highway.

A huge Dodge pickup truck narrowly missed ramming Hank and his horse, possibly not noticing the fleet-footed animal that could apparently leap over small cars, that was now passing on his left. The driver gave Hank a one-finger salute then pulled off to the side of the highway. Good move, because our stagecoach was inches from ramming the Ram's tailgate.

The roar of a motorcycle startled me. I pulled up on the leather reins and much to my surprise, the horses responded. I guided the team to the side of the road hoping a CHP motorcycle would come to my rescue.

I looked to the left and right before I craned my neck to peer ahead. Nope, no bikes in front of me. I peeked over my shoulder at a motorcycle-free road. That's when I switched my gaze to the only direction left—UP.

A shiny red Harley streaked across the pedestrian walkway that crossed over the freeway, joining the shops of downtown Placerville to the historic residential district on Coloma Street. The biker must be chasing Fletch. If he timed it correctly, he could reach the killer in seconds, depending on the dirty deputy's speed and stamina. I hoped the pursuer—whoever he might be, knew Fletch was armed and getting more trigger-happy by the minute.

I took a moment to check on my rancher. "Hanging in there, Scott?" I asked. He merely groaned. I couldn't tell if it was due to my insensitive question or his wound. Blood continued to pool on his jacket and drip onto his pants.

Meanwhile Gran's carriage careened down the highway. I could see her holding on to her lilac bonnet with one hand as she bounced from side to side. Black Beauty swerved around a police car attempting to halt traffic and aimed for the Kentucky Fried Chicken.

The horse must not have been in a batter-fried mood today. Seconds later, it switched directions and galloped across both lanes heading directly for the enormous hill bordering the right lane of the westbound highway. Gran's buggy was seconds away from crashing into a slab of solid rock.

I watched in horror, too far away to do anything.

Hank and his chestnut mount galloped down the pavement, only a few feet behind the runaway horse. My jaw dropped in shock as my ex-husband caught up with the crazed animal. Somehow, he managed to grab the loose reins and halt Gran's carriage mere inches from the unforgiving mountain of rock.

My eight-legged team and I had finally come to a mutual agreement that I was the boss of them. As I approached the buggy, I could see Black Beauty and the chestnut horse nuzzling one another, while Hank comforted my grandmother who seemed none the worse after her terrifying ride.

Knowing Gran, she'd undoubtedly relished every minute of it.

I reined in my horses, and they drew to a stop, surprising the heck out of me. An ambulance pulled next to my stagecoach, and the paramedics quickly loaded Scott for the short trip to Marshall Hospital.

A Hangtown Posse member offered to take my place driving the stagecoach, and I gratefully relinquished my reins to his more capable hands. I slid off my perch and followed one of the EMTs over to Gran's carriage. He offered to take her to the hospital, but she declined, saying she wasn't missing out on any action.

I joined Hank who stood to the side of my grandmother's carriage.

"Amazing horsemanship," I said to my former husband. "I didn't know you could ride and jump like that."

He blinked and his face paled under his sunburn. "Neither did I. Never jumped a horse before."

Gran put her hand over her heart. "Mercy me. You got guts, I'll say that for you." She leaned down and whispered in my ear. "Not too bright, is he, dear, but very gutsy."

"That motorcycle rider took a chance going after Fletch," I said to Hank. "Did you recognize him?"

"Couldn't you tell?" he said, "that was Tom. I never pictured him for a biker type. He was wearing casual clothes when we ran into each other earlier. Do you know if he carried a weapon on him?"

Oh, crap. I couldn't decide if Tom was being a hero or an idiot going after an armed former deputy when he himself was without a weapon.

A shot rang out and my heart stopped.

CHAPTER FIFTY-SIX

I've never been to Pamplona for their annual running of the bulls, but the pandemonium in Placerville that afternoon probably came in a close second. El Dorado county police cars zipped up Spring Street and down Coloma Street in search of their quarry. California Highway Patrol officers drove their familiar black and whites up various side streets searching for the presumed killer.

If I'd had any doubts about my theory, Fletch's crazed escape and his Grannapping added proof to the evidence file by the minute.

I was tempted to leap onto the horse Hank had borrowed and search for Tom myself, but I decided the law enforcement officials didn't need any two-legged saloon gals or four-legged animals clogging up the roadway.

Bradford arrived, slightly out of breath, to check on Gran and me. He told us Mother wanted to come to our rescue, but he'd convinced her that watching her grandchildren was her highest and best use today. I borrowed his cell and spoke with Mother and the kids assuring them Gran, Hank and I were all fine.

I wasn't exactly fine since I still didn't know Tom's circumstances. Who fired that one lone shot? Was anyone hit?

I glanced up at the pedestrian bridge looming over the highway that Tom had roared across only minutes earlier. I squinted when I spotted someone's dark hair through the mesh panel above the short solid wall of the bridge. It looked like a child with a pumpkin-sized head or an adult crawling back to town.

The head disappeared then bobbed back up as the bridge merged onto the open third floor of the parking garage. Although he'd discarded the frock coat, red brocade vest and bowler hat, that long-legged man was either Fletch or his identical twin. He stopped in the stairwell between the first and second levels and peered at the crowds circulating below, confirming my suspicions when he paused to rub his left shoulder exactly where Gran had thwacked him with her parasol.

The former deputy eased down the stairwell then donned a pair of sunglasses. Fletch's car must still be parked over on Broadway where the Wagon Train participants met up this afternoon. He couldn't escape without it or some other type of transportation.

"There he goes," I said to my stepfather, rapping his bare arm for emphasis.

"What the—" Bradford rubbed his forearm.

I pointed to the deputy now headed into the parking garage. "I think that's Fletch sneaking back into town."

"That SOB. I trained him myself." Bradford pushed Hank aside and heaved his bulk onto the saddle of the chestnut horse. The horse whinnied, complaining about the new rider whose weight exceeded Hank's by at least seventy pounds.

Bradford leaned over and mouthed something to Gran. She winked then handed her lilac parasol to her son-in-law. He grabbed the ruffled umbrella and galloped down the street as if he were personally leading the charge of the Bumbershoot Brigade.

Drivers of cars haphazardly parked to the side of the highway leaned out car windows and snapped photos and videos of the chase. Instagram might soon receive credit for whittling America's Most Wanted list down by one.

My immediate goal was to locate Tom. Two of the squad cars that had stopped to assist with traffic control peeled after Bradford. Seconds later, a motorcycle flew across the pedestrian bridge heading for the parking garage, the sun's rays turning it into a roaring fiery-red dragon.

If Tom rode the motorcycle, I prayed he possessed enough skill to manage the sharp curves of the narrow ramps leading down to the ground floor. My grandmother grabbed my clammy hand and squeezed it tight.

The sound of brakes squealing and the crash of metal meeting metal echoed from the Center Street parking structure.

I dropped Gran's hand as if it were a hot potato and raced toward the garage.

CHAPTER FIFTY-SEVEN

Uniformed officers and cowboys in full western regalia sprinted past me, unencumbered by high heels and low-cut costumes. I slowed my pace as I neared the structure, almost afraid to discover who or what had crashed.

I let out a huge sigh of relief when I discovered one squad car had collided with another. Two tan-shirted officers argued, causing me to wonder if they would ticket each other.

Bradford and Tom were nowhere in sight, but I spied a ring of cowboys standing by the Bell Tower. With so many officers milling about, I didn't feel apprehensive about my own safety, only concerned about the well-being of the men in my life.

I scooted closer to the Hangtown Posse. The local cowboys graciously let me ease through. No need to stomp on anyone's boot—something I was prepared to do if necessary.

The bright red Harley rested on its side next to the Bell Tower. The chestnut horse Bradford had borrowed from Hank seemed to have handled its second mission of the day with aplomb. My stepfather gripped the shaft of the umbrella, prepared to attack or defend using any means necessary—even a pastel parasol, which I noticed dripped blood on the pavement.

Tom shoved a handcuffed former Deputy Fletcher down the stairs of the Bell Tower. A nasty head wound bled down Fletch's right cheek. Two deputies latched on to Fletch, read him his rights and escorted him in the direction of the garage.

I threw myself at Tom, knocking both of us to the ground in front of the Hangtown Posse, the mayor, my family, and a few thousand onlookers. He sat up, shaking with laughter, while I wondered why the one time we ended up lying next to each other, we had to have an audience.

"Are you okay?" I asked.

He rubbed the back of his head where he'd smacked into the pavement. "I felt fine until ten seconds ago. I didn't realize you were a linebacker in training. What about you?"

I glanced down at my saloon girl outfit, fearful of a potential fashion disaster, but none of my assets were celebrating in public. I let Tom haul me to my feet where he gave me a proper kiss.

The crowd hooted, hollered, and clapped as we strolled, arm in arm, over to Bradford and his equine pet.

"So who caught Fletch?" I asked the two men.

"Robert bashed the back of his head with that unorthodox weapon." Tom smiled and pointed at the ruffled parasol. "When Fletch stumbled, I took him down. I didn't have my handcuffs with me, but your Hangtown Posse came prepared."

Tom nodded to the men clothed in frontier wear who circled us. They shook Tom's hand and mine then wandered off in search of more action. I imagined their playacting shoot-outs wouldn't seem nearly as exciting now that they'd participated in a real chase.

Within seconds, Mother, the kids, Liz, Stan and Brian joined us in a frenzy of group hugs. The Mayor and Tom conversed for a few minutes before Tom joined our noisy group.

Holding tight to my children, I tried to answer their questions. All any of them knew was that Deputy Fletcher had buggy-nabbed Gran, and that Hank, Tom, and a myriad of police officials had gone after him. Not to mention Scott and me, leading the chase. I hoped the rancher's gunshot wound didn't end up being too serious.

"I'm confused, Mommy," Ben said, clinging to my hand. "Where did you disappear to?"

"I think we're all somewhat bewildered," Mother remarked. "Laurel, you can enlighten us. Although, first, let me chastise my husband for terrifying the life out of me." Mother marched over to Bradford's side. Having sat through a million lectures from my mother, I could imagine the tirade he had in store.

The chestnut horse breathed a horse-sized sigh of relief when the supersized cowpoke climbed down. Bradford tied it to a pole and joined us.

"I don't know where that horse came from, but hopefully Hank can track down its owner," Bradford said, resting his arm on my mother's shoulder. He looked over at me. "Now, Laurel, tell me exactly how you came to your conclusion about Fletch. Why on earth did he kill Spencer?"

"And tell it quick," Tom said. "I need to get back to headquarters and interview the guy before he lawyers up. All I know is that former Deputy Fletcher shot at Laurel, although it could have been accidental, and he jumped off a moving carriage leaving your grandmother in danger. The fact he tried to run from the law doesn't help his case, but I need more than that to charge him with murder."

"He shot at me twice," I said, my face reddening in anger. "But wounded Scott Shelton instead. Thank goodness you found that motorcycle and went after him."

"No one takes a potshot at the woman I…" Tom's voice trailed off as the carriage carrying Hank and Gran, clip-clopped up the street, halting when it reached us. Hank jumped out, tied up Black Beauty then assisted my grandmother. Mother rushed to Gran's side while Hank threw his arms around me.

"Help," I mouthed to Stan. He grabbed Hank's arm and pulled him away.

"So you did get my message about Fletch," Hank said to me.

"What are you talking about?" I asked.

"When I called you from Pollock Pines I said the killer might be Fletch."

"Your call disappeared when my cell…" I glared at my grandmother who was looking at everyone but her granddaughter, "when I lost my phone. Anyway I didn't catch that."

"Next time you determine the identity of a killer," interrupted Tom, "how about calling the cops?"

Hank's eyes practically bulged out of their sockets. "Like you would believe anything I tell you?"

Hank had a point, but I didn't want the two men to come to fisticuffs, or worse, have Hank join his former football teammate in a cell.

"Why did you decide Fletch murdered Spencer?" I asked him.

"That night in the bar, before the hanging, I was in a real foul mood. The guys kept ragging on me about that argument Spencer and I had the night before. After Fletch bought me a couple of drinks, I dished about those old valuables I'd found during the renovation. I knew Fletch was all into local history, so I asked what they could be worth. I thought maybe that cheapskate Spencer could sell a few things and finally pay what he owed me."

"How did Fletch respond?" Tom asked.

"Said he'd research it for me, but honestly I'd drunk so much that night I didn't even think about it again until Laurel and I noticed someone had been digging inside the hotel. Not until I went fishing to clear my head did I remember my conversation with Fletch."

"That's not exactly staggering evidence," Tom growled at Hank. "I hope you've got more proof than that."

"I do." I beamed at Tom. "I borrowed Fletch's iPhone earlier to take some photos of Gran and him. When I checked to see how they came out, I noticed he'd taken interior shots of the hotel, close-ups of the section along the wall where Hank had found a few valuables. They were taken while the crime scene tape was up."

Tom frowned. "I'm not sure what that proves. Maybe Fletch was trying to play detective. Not that he was supposed to go into the crime scene since he's not on the homicide squad."

"In addition to that, Fletch has been researching the history relating to the body in the mine shaft," I said. "I think he learned about that old stagecoach robbery that took place back in 1864. When Miles Mickelson was killed."

"Was that Mickelson the one the Mickelson Building was named after?" asked Mother. She turned an appraising eye on the building, as if estimating its current as well as historical value.

Good grief. The woman had a one-track mind. If the deputies hadn't carted Fletch off to jail, she'd be shoving a listing agreement and pen in his handcuffed hands.

I continued citing my evidence to Tom. "The horse guiding the buggy bumped Fletch's arm causing him to drop an old-fashioned pocket watch that looked exactly like a watch Hank found in the hotel. Plus when I picked it up, I noticed the inscription with Miles Mickelson's name on it. When I asked Fletch if he was a relative he responded 'sure.'"

"Sure?" Tom shoved his hand through his already unruly hair. "Please tell me that's not your only evidence. Maybe the men were related to one another."

"And maybe he stole the watch and a trove of other valuables from the Hangtown Hotel where they were buried long ago. Abe told me he recently purchased some valuable jewelry from Fletch."

Tom stared at his notebook. He didn't look as convinced as I was.

"Don't you think it's strange Fletch up and quit out of the blue?" I asked him.

"It could be a coincidence," Tom said. "He said his mother needed him in Florida."

"One more thing," I said. "Check out his boot heel. I think it may be a match to the print you found at Doug's house."

"It's a start. And between shooting at Laurel and wounding that Shelton guy, Fletch committed enough felonies around here to give me grounds for a search warrant."

"Plus, he about terrified me to death," Gran added, "when he threatened to kill me."

CHAPTER FIFTY-EIGHT

After Tom took off to complete his official duties, Gran beckoned me to her side.

"That dude didn't really threaten to kill me," she admitted. "But he did threaten to throw me out of the buggy after I walloped him."

"Close enough," I reassured her. "Once they search his house, I'm positive they'll find more items he stole from the hotel. Along with proof he killed both men."

"Do you think Spencer caught Fletch digging around in the building?" Hank asked.

"If I had to guess," Bradford said, back in detective mode, "the most plausible explanation is that Spencer arrived early for his appointment with Hank and caught Fletch messing around. Fletch clobbered him with that piece of wood they found with Spencer's blood on it. Once Fletch realized he'd killed Spencer, he had the foresight to make a spectacle of the victim, knowing the man had made an enemy or two along the way."

"Fletch is a smart man and he almost got away with it," I interjected.

"Do you think he killed Doug, too?" Hank asked.

"I guess that's up to Tom to figure out," I said, slightly distracted by the figure hurrying past our group clustered next to the Bell Tower. I put my hand out to stop him. "Hi, Rex. Did you hear they arrested Deputy Fletcher? We think he killed Spencer. "

He smiled at me and at his former client. "Don't forget a man is innocent until proven guilty. I'm heading to the jail right now to make sure my new client remembers that."

I stared at Rex, wondering why I'd ever thought the attorney was good-looking. His white-toothed smile looked more rapacious than the shark in *Jaws*. Thank goodness, Hank and I didn't have to rely on him anymore. Now it was Fletch's turn.

Imagine having two paying clients for the price of one murder. Talk about highway robbery!

Mother and Bradford offered to drive my children home, and Hank said he'd give Gran and me a lift back to my car. It seemed a lifetime ago that I'd watched her drive off with Fletch. I doubted any of us would forget this Wagon Train parade.

Once we arrived at my car, Gran thanked Hank for rescuing her. "Anytime, Gran," he replied. "You know I think the world of you."

I started to choke up then almost choked when Gran spoke.

"I'm looking forward to having you as a roommate, Hank," she said. My contacts almost bounced out of my eyes and onto the pavement. Hank smothered a grin, and Gran tittered at my expression.

"Hank and I had a nice chat after he saved my life. I told him your mother wanted me out of the house because it's too difficult to keep it up at my age. Hank said his landlord gave him notice while he was in jail, and he needed to find a new place."

"I can fix everything in the house that needs repairing," Hank said to me. "It's perfect. Don't you agree?

What could I do but congratulate the new odd couple?

The Hangtown version.

CHAPTER FIFTY-NINE

Sunday I almost welcomed the opportunity to catch up on the chores I'd deferred for three weeks. Fletch's arrest would keep Tom occupied as he assembled evidence for his case. After our crazed Saturday, I looked forward to a quiet day.

Halfway through my vacuuming, Jenna called my name. She flew down the stairs, her fingers holding a place in one of the old diaries.

"What's wrong?" I turned off the vacuum, alarmed at her expression.

"Nothing," she said, her face flushed. "I found something in Harold's diary that answers some of our questions about Mr. Bones."

"That's terrific, sweetie. Although now that Gran is rooming with your father and refuses to sell the house, it's not as critical. But it would be nice to put Mr. Bones and his identity to rest."

Her eyes gleamed. "I'm beginning to understand why you enjoy detecting so much. I think I figured out the killer."

"You realize the only reason I've become involved in these cases is because someone I know and love has been accused of murder."

"Yeah, sure. But after doing all of this research, I'm rethinking my career path. I'm not sure I want to be an astronaut after all."

I glanced at the leather-backed diary in her hand. "So this project has inspired you to become a historian?"

She shook her head so adamantly her auburn tendrils smacked me across the face.

"Don't be silly. I want to be a detective."

CHAPTER SIXTY

Over the next few days, after the Wagon Train dust settled, I gave thought to my upcoming birthday. Something about the impending big four-O, the fact that you may have reached the midpoint of your existence, makes you pause to consider what you've accomplished in your life and what goals and dreams remain.

I had much to contemplate, but for now, I was grateful my family and friends were all healthy and safe. Also thankful that no new crow's feet had appeared, nor had any mysterious hairs sprouted from my chin. Although it dawned on me if my vision began to diminish, how would I even know?

I informed my friends and family that I did not want a big celebration replete with black balloons, dead roses, and mugs covered with corny sayings. Gran offered to host a small dinner party at her house with only our family in attendance.

The best gift of all would be if Tom could stop by for at least part of the evening. He'd been working 24/7 on the case. Fletch remained in jail, charged not only with Spencer and Doug Blake's murder, but also with shooting Scott Shelton, kidnapping Gran, and one very reckless and disorderly ride through town.

Stan surprised me with a small celebration at work, which perked up my flagging fortieth birthday spirits. Oddly enough, the majority of my coworkers' wrapped gifts held dark chocolate. How did they guess? The bank president even dropped off a present for me as his thanks for Hangtown Bank winning first place in the decorating contest.

While I'd never thought about asking for a personalized gold pan, it was definitely a unique gift.

Mother and Bradford agreed to pick up my kids, saving me from backtracking home to get them, so I arrived at Gran's house before the rest of the family. I pushed on the front door but it didn't budge. My grandmother's new roomie must have implemented a new lockup policy. I rang the bell and seconds later, Hank greeted me from the doorway.

"Happy birthday, sweetheart." He grabbed my hand and yanked me into the foyer. I evaded his birthday peck, mumbled a hello and headed for the kitchen.

"Hiya, toots," Gran yelled at me, her hands swathed in red hot pads the size of catchers' mitts. "Your honey and I are cooking your birthday dinner."

"My 'honey' hasn't arrived yet," I growled at her. Savory aromas drifting from the oven turned my frown into a grin. "Something sure smells good."

Hank followed me into the kitchen and proceeded to toss what looked like a Caesar salad. Another hit with me.

I picked up a lid, bent over the bubbling pot and sniffed.

"Stop that." Gran swatted my hand with a puffy mitt. "It's a surprise."

"Fine." I backed away and assessed the domestic scene in front of me. "You two seem to be getting along."

Hank beamed. "Gran is great. She cooks for me and keeps me busy fixing stuff."

My grandmother is a recovering member of compulsives anonymous. When something doesn't work right, she just keeps punching it until she completely breaks it.

They were a match made in Home Depot heaven.

A few minutes later, Mother and Bradford waltzed into the kitchen, followed by my kids, their arms laden with foil-wrapped boxes and shiny gift bags. Now this was the way to celebrate a birthday!

Tom arrived shortly after with a dozen roses, a bottle of wine, a box of truffles, and a very welcome kiss.

The man did know me!

We attempted to keep the recent murder from intruding on our celebration, but it remained unspoken for less time than it took for all of us to sit down at Gran's mahogany dining room table.

Hank brought the subject up first. Considering his short-term imprisonment, he was the most vested in the answer.

"Did you locate any more historical stuff at Fletch's house?" Hank asked Tom.

Tom eyed his forkful of beef stroganoff with longing. He sighed and put down his fork.

"Fletch had boxed everything up for his move," Tom replied. "We also found some antique jewelry and gold coins in a suitcase."

"Did you find proof of him killing Doug?" I asked. "Like the missing cell phone?"

"I can't really share that information with you," he said, although his head moved up and down while he spoke.

That was super secret detective code for yes.

"I heard they're charging Fletch with voluntary manslaughter for Spencer but murder for Doug Blake," Gran stated.

We all stared at her.

"Hey, I got my sources."

Mother shook her head while Bradford snorted.

"I feel sorry for that young man," Gran continued. "I'm sure natural curiosity got him digging in the hotel to begin with. Spencer must have surprised him and Fletch just popped him one. Then discovered he'd killed him." She leaned in Tom's direction. "How am I doing so far, Detective?"

"Better than those Sacramento detectives we hired." Tom threw a glance in Hank's direction. "No hard feelings, I hope."

Hank glared at Tom but remained silent.

This seemed like the perfect opportunity to discuss Jenna's findings.

"Honey," I said to my daughter. "Why don't you tell them about your discovery in Harold's journal?"

My criminologist-in-training put her fork down, but before she could address the group, Mother spoke up. "So is that skeleton George Clarkson? And if so, why is Harold's watch down there with him?"

Jenna shrugged. "I can't say for certain it's George Clarkson, but there's a strong possibility. Let me explain about the watch, which started the entire chain of events. One night, Harold was playing cards in the Gold Nugget Saloon on Main Street. According to his journal, he'd been losing all night and was almost out of money.

When he drew four of a kind, which he considered a sure thing, he threw his watch into the pot."

"There is no sure thing in poker," Bradford stated.

My mathematical daughter is no slouch at Texas Hold 'em. "Nope," Jenna agreed, "especially when one of the players cheats. At least, that's what Harold claimed."

"What does that have to do with the stagecoach robbery?" Tom asked. "We still don't have the DNA results back, so I hope you'll solve my cold case for me without it. That will free up some time to spend with my favorite person."

The smile I sent Tom glowed brighter than the chandelier shining above our table.

My teenage detective continued her lecture. "A month after the poker game, George and his wife, Anna, invited Harold over for dinner. When he arrived, he discovered they had company—a male cousin of Anna's had dropped by. Walter, the cousin, was the poker player who won Harold's watch. According to his diary, Harold accused Walter of cheating. Then he stormed out of their house, jumped on his horse and headed for home."

"Can't blame the man," said Gran.

"The next morning, Anna arrived at Harold's house, sobbing. She confided that when George learned about Walter cheating, he made him hand over the watch so George could return it to Harold. He also ordered Walter to leave. That's when Walter revealed he'd robbed the stagecoach resulting in Miles Mickelson's killing. Because the sheriff was looking for him and his companions, he needed to hide out at their house for a few days."

"Wow, this could be the plot for an old-fashioned western." Hank mimed holding a movie camera. Ben pretended to shoot his father with an imaginary six-shooter. Everyone else ignored the boys and kept their eyes on Jenna.

"After Walter's confession, George grabbed his hat and coat and said he was riding to town to inform the sheriff. The two men supposedly argued while they walked away. Ten minutes later Anna heard a distant gunshot."

"So Walter shot George and shoved him down the mine shaft?" asked Bradford.

"I guess we won't know for sure until the DNA results come back," said Jenna. "Harold rode to Placerville to speak with the sheriff. He wrote that he later learned two robbers were shot dead, but neither George Clarkson nor Walter were heard from again."

"But that means..." I said.

"The gold is still missing," said Mother. I imagined her agile brain calculating a strongbox full of gold at today's prices.

"The sheriff later discovered Walter spent one night at the Hangtown Hotel although he left before dawn," Jenna added. "As far as I can tell, that was the end of him and the treasure until Dad began the remodel."

We all turned our heads to stare at Hank.

He glanced around the table. "Guess I better buy a shovel."

CHAPTER SIXTY-ONE

A few days after my birthday celebration, Hank asked me out to lunch as a thank you for helping with his case. Despite his hairline receding another inch in the last few weeks, Hank had regained his tan and seemed to have recovered from his brief stay in the county lock-up.

"So how are you and Gran getting along?" I asked, before nibbling on a piece of spinach from my healthy salad entrée, an attempt to make up for my stress-induced chocolate frenzy of the last couple of weeks.

"Your grandmother is a hoot," Hank replied. "She's asked me to chauffeur her to some of her club meetings, and I'm happy to accommodate her. Then she introduces me to her friends as her new 'boy toy.'"

I gagged on the spinach and reached for my iced tea. That was so Gran. I hoped I'd be half that feisty in another five decades.

"I'm glad the DNA results came in proving Mr. Bones is related to the Clarkson family," I said.

"Your Gran's sure happy she's not the granddaughter of a murderer. Although don't be surprised if she starts digging up her backyard looking for that Wells Fargo loot."

I might need to hide Gran's shovels the next time I stop by her house. "Speaking of hidden loot, when will you be able to complete the renovation?"

"The historical society finished going through the place yesterday. They found a few more coins and a couple of lockets, but no missing strongbox. I can go back to work tomorrow."

"I guess we'll never know which of the bandits had the strongbox and where they buried it. Is there any chance Fletch dug it up?"

Hank shook his head. "Nope, I visited him in jail, and he said he never located it." I must have looked surprised about Hank's visit because he elaborated. "I went there because I wanted to ream him for letting me take the blame for killing Spencer. He told me he never thought the police would end up arresting me. After we talked awhile, I actually felt kind of sorry for the guy."

"Well, I don't. The man was responsible for me almost being pulverized into grape juice."

"Fletch said he didn't mean you any harm. He only meant to scare you away from the investigation. After you two chatted at your grandmother's house the day before, he worried you might be getting close to figuring it out. He knew you were as tenacious as a bulldog and wouldn't give up until you proved I didn't kill Spencer. Fletch hoped to divert suspicion onto Chad Langdon, at least until he could get out of town."

"Bulldog?" I growled at Hank. What was with the men in this town? Didn't any of them picture me as a sexy detective? "So what's his current status?"

"Fletch's preliminary hearing is set for next week. His list of crimes is longer than your Gran's 'to do' list for me."

My appetite evaporated as I thought of the poor victims. "How does a man go from serving the law to breaking it?"

Hank shrugged. "Fletch wouldn't discuss any details about Doug, but he admitted Spencer surprised him while he was digging in the hotel. He panicked and grabbed the first thing he found which was that piece of lumber. He couldn't believe he killed Spencer with one blow. I guess when he looked out the window to see if anyone on Main Street heard anything, he got the idea to string Spencer up from that old dummy."

Hank reached across the table and grabbed my hand. "You saved me, Laurel. I don't know how I can ever repay you."

I tried to think of a polite way to tell my ex-husband that butting out of my love life would be a nice start, but he beat me to it.

"I realize you and Hunter have something going, and that it's definitely over between us." Hank stared at the partially eaten hamburger on his plate. When he looked up, his eyes were misty. "And I need to get on with my own life. I just want to thank you for being there for me when I needed you."

"Hank, you know I'll always care about you." My eyes began to water, so I switched subjects. "That was a heck of a horseback rescue you did for Gran."

Hank grinned and dipped his head. "All in a day's work, Ma'am. I think she's getting a kick out of her notoriety."

One of the videos posted on the internet had turned Gran into an Octogenarian YouTube sensation. Next thing we knew she'd have her own Vlog.

"You weren't any slouch yourself driving that stagecoach," Hank said to me. "You could be the next Charley Parkhurst."

My ex was full of compliments today, I thought. Now he'd just compared me to a one-eyed female stagecoach driver who everyone thought was a man.

"How's Scott Shelton doing?" Hank asked me.

"Much better. I returned some horse tack I borrowed from Vicky Parsons, his next door neighbor, so I stopped at his house to thank him. He said despite getting shot, the chase was the highlight of the Wagon Train for him this year."

"Since he was one of your primary suspects, weren't you worried about going off with him on the stagecoach?"

"Scott made it on my list, but, despite having motive, I never could picture him killing Spencer. I since found out how he got the money to buy back his six shooters. The man not only raises horses, he likes to gamble on them. Abe told me Scott won a Pick Six at Golden Gate Fields that netted him eight thousand dollars."

I looked out the restaurant window and spied Janet Spencer on the arm of the new District Six Supervisor, Chad Langdon. I pointed them out to Hank.

"Is it easier working for Janet than Spencer?" I asked.

He chuckled. "She's a nice woman. Not to speak poorly of the dead, but I think she's much happier these days. And she pays on time, so I've been able to make weekly installments to reimburse Abe for having enough faith in me to pay the $10,000 fee for my bond."

I smiled thinking of the kind merchant who'd come to Hank's financial rescue. Abe had been appalled to discover Fletch had sold him stolen merchandise. Not to mention he'd killed two people.

"I'm still curious about that deed I saw granting Chad's ownership to Spencer," I said, "but I guess that's between Janet and Chad at this point. Did she ever find out who made those threatening phone calls?"

"The calls were made by Phil McKinley, your neighborhood builder and bully," replied Hank. "Janet was still concerned, so Chad did a little investigating. He is not happy with his former partner."

I lifted my brows at Hank. "Former?"

"Yup, Chad's severed all ties with that partnership. I think the man has the potential to become a great asset to our county."

"He's definitely one smart politician," I said. "He felt so bad about my near-death experience at his winery that he dropped off a case of their reserve chardonnay for me. Now that's a way to win my vote."

CHAPTER SIXTY-TWO

The following evening Hank and Gran arranged to take the kids up to Lake Tahoe for an overnight visit. The door had barely squeaked shut behind them when I called Tom and invited him over for dinner. It had been weeks since we'd spent an evening alone together.

The criminal community appeared to be vacationing, so Tom arranged for Kristy to stay with his parents. After dinner, we nestled on my patio glider, rocking side by side under a starlit sky.

Tom had surprised me by arriving with a guitar case and the intent to serenade me under the stars. I was looking forward to it.

At least I hoped I was.

I leaned back into the cushion as he plunked out a few chords and tuned his new instrument.

"I didn't realize you played the guitar," I said, curious why he'd never shared his musical talent with me.

"I played through college, but when I joined the force, I never seemed to have the time. I finally gave my Gibson to a friend over twenty years ago."

"Where did this one come from?"

Tom shook his head and a swatch of dark hair fell over his eye, giving him a rakish rock star look. "Believe it or not, I was on my way to the Hangtown Hotel to check on something when I walked by Main Street Music. The guitar sat center stage in the window display. It seemed to reach out and touch me."

I could relate to that sensation although when it came to being touched, I would take Tom over the guitar.

He strummed a few notes then stopped.

"It's been a difficult month," he said.

"Challenging," I replied, "on so many levels."

"Adversity can sometimes strengthen a relationship." Tom's comment as well as his dark eyes seemed to be searching for some type of reassurance from me.

I rested my hand on his thigh while I searched for the correct response. "I know how frustrating this has been for you, but I think Hank's situation brought him and me closer together." I stopped as I sensed Tom withdrawing from me. "Not closer romantically because that is and has been over for a very long time. But we'll remain as a divorced couple who will be able to parent well together. I sincerely hope that is something you can live with. Because it's important to me to have you in my life."

He slid a few inches closer. Instead of answering my question, he began to serenade me in a strong baritone. Tom was right. His singing combined with the guitar's melodious notes delivered musical magic.

Tom ended his rendition of Toby Keith's "You Shouldn't Kiss Me Like This" and followed it with a heart-pulsating, fireworks-blazing kiss.

"You're amazing," I said breathlessly. "Do you have any more secret hobbies you'd like to share with me?"

He threw me a sexy half-smile. "Maybe."

"Am I one of your hobbies?" I asked flirtatiously.

The light from the full moon made Tom's dark eyes glitter. He rose from the glider and carefully placed the guitar back in its case. Then he crouched down on one knee in front of me.

"You could be a hobby," he said, reaching for my palm, his expression as serious as I'd ever seen it. "Or you could be the woman I spend the rest of my life with. The decision is yours because as far as I'm concerned, I'm dying to be your..."

My mouth opened wide, dumbstruck for once in my life. He leaned over, his soft lips barely brushing mine, before he completed his sentence.

"Dude."

THE END

GRANDMA'S AWESOME CHOCOLATE TOFFEE CHIP COOKIES

2 cups flour
1/2 tsp. baking soda
1/4 tsp. salt
3/4 cup quick oats
3/4 cup dark brown sugar
3/4 cup white sugar
2 large eggs
2 tsp. vanilla
1 cup salted butter
1+ cup chocolate chips (any flavor you choose)
1/2 cup toffee bits or to taste
1/2 cup coconut (optional)

Bake 350 10- 12 min or until browned - transfer to rack to cool

ACKNOWLEDGEMENTS

Many thanks and hugs to the awesome friends who willingly read my early painful drafts: Cathy and Carl Allyn, Jonathan Corbett, Karen Charlton, Lisa Dane, Bonnie Holbrook, and Jana Rossi. As always, my critique group was there to answer my countless emails: Kathy Asay, Pat Foulk, Rae James, and Terri Judd. Four of my favorite authors, Heather Haven, Liz Jasper, Linda Lovely and Mary Beth Magee chimed in with wonderful suggestions. Thanks to the staff at David Girard Vineyards. What a great place to do research! And thanks to my creative friend, Darlene Neeley, who loves to help me plot.

A special thanks to the legal, medical and professional experts, who let me bombard them with questions: Kimberly Gin, Sacramento County Coroner, Lt. Tim Becker, El Dorado County Sheriff's Office and Ron Dosh, Esq. I'd like to acknowledge the wonderful volunteers at the El Dorado County Historical Museum who were a huge help.

The support and encouragement I receive from my fellow Sisters in Crime and the authors who belong to Sacramento Valley Rose, California Writer's Club and NCPA helps to keep me motivated when my spirits flag.

Thanks to my editors, Baird Nuckolls and Kathy Asay, and my cover artist, Karen Phillips, who is as amazing as she is patient. I had so much fun tabulating the votes for the cover contest. Thank you, Christine Rippey, for your romantic song suggestion. It was perfect.

I am so grateful to everyone in the Placerville community who helped with my research and who continue to support my writing endeavors. The Wagon Train Association just celebrated sixty-five years on the trail. What an awesome group of people. Keep those wagons rolling!

A special thanks to those fans from around the world whose emails make this journey so much fun. It's not always easy to wake up in the morning and create an imaginary world. Your smiles and words of encouragement make it the best job ever!

ABOUT THE AUTHOR

Cindy Sample is a former mortgage banking CEO who decided plotting murder was more entertaining than plodding through paperwork. She retired to follow her lifelong dream of becoming a mystery author.

Her experiences with online dating sites fueled the concept for *Dying for a Date*, the first in her national bestselling Laurel McKay mysteries. The sequel, *Dying for a Dance*, a finalist for the 2012 LEFTY award for best humorous mystery, is based on her adventures in the glamorous world of ballroom dancing. Cindy thought her protagonist, Laurel McKay, needed a vacation in Hawaii, which resulted in *Dying for a Daiquiri*, a finalist for both the 2014 LEFTY Award and the 2014 Silver Falchion Award. Never has research been so much fun.

Now hold on to your hats for a wild ride as Laurel returns to Placerville in *Dying for a Dude*. The West will never be the same.

Cindy is past president of the Sacramento chapter of Sisters in Crime. She has served on the boards of the Sacramento Opera and YWCA. She is a member of Mystery Writers of America and Romance Writers of America. Cindy has two wonderful adult children who live too far away. She loves chatting with readers so feel free to contact her on any forum. Sign up for her newsletter to find out about upcoming events and contests.

Check out www.cindysamplebooks.com for contests and other events.

Connect with Cindy on Facebook and Twitter
http://facebook.com/cindysampleauthor
http://twitter.com/cindysample1
Email Cindy at cindy@cindysamplebooks.com